THE RETURN OF THE MOHICANS

By

James Edmund Adams

~

The Return of the Mohicans

Copyright © Year 2022
All Rights Reserved.

No part of this eBook/Book can be transmitted or reproduced in any form, including print, electronic, photocopying, scanning, mechanical, or recording, without prior written permission from the author.

This is a work of fiction. Unless otherwise indicated, all the names, characters, businesses, places, events, and incidents in this book are either the product of the author's imagination or used in a fictitious manner. Any resemblance to actual persons, living or dead, or actual events is purely coincidental.

The author and publisher shall have neither liability nor responsibility to any person or entity with respect to any loss or damage caused or alleged to be caused directly or indirectly by this eBook/ Book.

Library of Congress Control Number: 2022905266
ISBN: 978-0-9897940-3-9

Dedication

To Alicia, my wife.

You are my heart. Your belief, patience, and inspiration never wavered through the many years this book was in the making.

To our Native American brothers and sisters. I see you. Many of us see you. And many of us still cry with you.

About the Author

James Edmund Adams was born in Darby, Pennsylvania. As a child, he loved visiting libraries and fell in love early with adventure, fantasy, supernatural, and science fiction, reading Mark Twain, Ray Bradbury, Isaac Asimov, J.R.R. Tolkien, Stephen King, and many others. He also enjoyed competitive swimming and music.

He attended three colleges, graduating with a degree in Nursing, where he worked for many years in emergency, psychiatry, and addictions (to name a few). He held many positions as a Registered Nurse, including staff and management. He assisted thousands of patients in physical or mental crises during those years. The experience has been transformative.

Raised in a faith-based home, James later spent several decades deeply immersed in reading and researching comparative religions. He has also studied shamanism and has gained the ability to travel into hidden realms and communicate with spirits. Everything that exists is alive and has a spirit. Connecting to the web of life has provided him insight and communion with the elements and forces that affect us all, providing harmony and balance.

He and his family have lived in several rural areas near Indian reservations. They attended numerous powwows and other Native American events, developing a passion and interest in their spirituality, culture, and challenges. Their suffering and disadvantage haunt him.

James has been married for over 30 years to Dr. Alicia Adams, a Nurse Practitioner and retired USAF Lt. Col. He and his large family have lived in Pennsylvania, Virginia, Texas, Utah,

Nevada, and California. He values the wisdom gained through enriched family life and always looks forward to the next fun family adventure or gathering. He has also looked forward to retirement as a time when he could begin another life passion – writing.

Table of Contents

Prologue

Legend says that many portals in the world let you travel to 'The Great Myst,' a place where souls reside, that become for many people the Ark of Salvation to have faith in; to believe that there will come a day people will be brought to justice.

One of the gateways is deep in the forest of the Adirondack Mountains, where you can still hear pale waves of the river, which once was a source of sus0tenance for the locals. The Native called the playa *"Cherokee Achak Algonquin,"* and they have received the tribunal message, as it was written in their scriptures, from their ancestors that have been watching over them for five hundred years from the spirit world. They have seen the oppression and severe difficulties that many of their people have faced every day as the treaties have been broken by the US government, which prefers the natives to be "out of sight, out of mind."

Since the arrival of the early settlers in the 1500s, either because of the outbreak of a vicious disease or because of persecution, they have been forced to move from their historic lands.

When the French and Indian war broke out in 1754 against the British, the Indians were pressed and manipulated by both sides into service. Yet, when the British won the war and gained the territory from North America to the Mississippi River, the Indians were left with betrayal as they were forced out of their settlements and given only limited areas to settle into. Of course, the unity they had between them broke miserably, and they have survived the bounty hunters and outright slaughter. At the same time, they were still considered subhuman by the government and called "the merciless Indian savages."

Since then, the strongest warriors amongst them, including Uncas, thought to be the last son of Chingachgook, have been martyred, serving their people for their rights and bringing forward what the truth is; they knew that there would be vast army recruitment. An army made from the Spirit World led by four warriors and recruits from the living.

As written in the scriptures, these warriors have the heart, soul, and mind of the righteous. They will be firm in their belief in truth and justice and have strength, courage, and great powers. They will also speak with frankness and will not be afraid of the consequences that come along. They will be leaders and warriors and be known as compassionate humanitarians. These warriors will be given the powers that no person on Earth has ever witnessed; better yet, the warriors will only unlock their true potential and learn to maintain control during the trial of recruitment. So, their true capability is something that they are yet unaware of.

The Ark of Salvation for the Native has revealed to their people about the five hidden stones that depict their stars and powers. The preparation has begun, the letters to their people have been sent out, and the time for the cataclysm has finally arrived.

These warriors descended from the most committed American Indian families, including Chingachgook, the last of the Mohicans whose long-lost son, Cayuga, who was presumed dead, suddenly returned to him after learning of his brother Uncas' death.

The Natives are more joyous than ever, as they hear their leader reappearing, and the mist in the forest speaks to Cayuga Chingachgook, now the last of the Mohicans who went into occultation, the true descendent of the paramount chief, the person who raised Hawkeye.

Cayuga tells them that not only will he recruit, with the succor of his ancestors, but they have given him the ability to reincarnate from amongst them the strongest of warriors, who were at the path to bring justice.

The last of the Mohicans has brought with him the true scriptures. So, he asks the people to spread the news about the three portals. One of which has been opened, through which he came. The first mystery unfolds as the passage to the Myst has come up front, in the full moon.

The second will be opened when the four warriors are recruited, and it will be their task to understand what powers it holds. For now, it remains a secret to us. The only thing we know about it is that it will reach its full potential at an eclipse, and their birthstones shall be placed in consonance to the passage being unlocked in front of them that very day.

They will lead each coterie, assigned to the place of distress, and shall, as fated, lead the way to egalitarianism.

But just as much there is good in the world that will endeavor to shall spread it beyond the horizon, the stronger an opponent they will have to fight against.

Cayuga tells his people that Blaine Keir, the wicked son of Magua who is named the Dark Lord due to his lineage, actions, and intentions, will soon get released from the frontier, and because we shall still be recruiting at that time, we shall never be able to stop that.

However, his attempt to find the third portal, where all the darkness and all evil entities are inhabited, can be stopped, as Cayuga knows the way to the Forest of Limbo and has set forth two enormous thunderbird totems to protect and mark the entrance. The Dark Lord plans to destroy them and open the gates forever so that the entities in the nine circles of Hell from the core of the world can join him to make him stronger than ever.

"The Four-Leaf Clover," the medallion recruit will have to figure out the pattern, the mannerism of his attack as "The Whisperer," and stop the loop of calamity.

They will not only have to stop them. Better yet, they will also fight his army and trap him in the core of Hell forever. And the curse would not lift until they do so.

The tribe celebrates the end of the occultation with dinner presented to Cayuga on a windy night with a full moon and a beautiful campfire. As they learn about the recruitment, the medallion recruits, and the Dark Lord, a young man named Dakota Kanienkehaka makes a rather eerie entrance.

Dakota looks at his leader, Cayuga, with an astonished look on his face, as he says that he felt as though the skies were talking to him to ascertain about Cayuga's reappearance.

"I feel like I have seen you before, somewhere. Is it true?" Dakota continues.

With a soft smile on his face, Cayuga replies to the ensemble crowd, "My people, many of you may have seen me before. I was there when you needed me. My ancestors informed me about the calamity, and I was sent to various junctures to help one way or another in different shapes and forms. But now I am here for as long as I live. And tyranny will reach its culminating destination."

Chapter # 1:
The Old Nurse

"Are you serious? You've got to be kidding me!" the triage nurse shouted. "Dr. Whitefeather, I've got a lot of sick patients here in the ER Waiting Room. You're the one who is throwing up. Seriously!"

Jeromy Whitefeather Ph.D. was well-known in the local community. As a professor of Native American Studies at the University of Wyoming in Laramie, he had become a bit of a local youngest celebrity and legend for his profession in Wyoming and South Dakota - including with his tribe at the Pine Ridge Indian Reservation. If anyone in the local non-Indian community wanted to know something about the local tribes or Native American history, he was the go-to guy. He was sought out by community leaders and educators across several states for his knowledge of the history and suffering of Native Americans across the land. He had been a guest speaker at numerous universities over the years. He was also thought to be blessed by the spirits. However, today he was green, pale, and feeling very un-legend-like.

Jeromy was also fairly tall at 6' 2", but he only weighed 150 pounds. Some would say he was gaunt or frail-looking. His thick, black-rimmed glasses frequently slid down his rather straight nose, and they constantly needed to be pushed back up. Although he enjoyed hiking and rock climbing, he had the appearance of someone weak and not very athletic. And then there were the allergies, fears, and phobias. Altogether, he did not strike the pose of what one thinks about when they picture a strong Native American man.

The old, voluptuous nurse was wise and worn from years of working in the emergency room on the reservation or "Rez.".

Her feet were flat and painful, and she only made it through her shifts due to wearing a double support hose. She wore lines across her face from years of facing emergencies and stress. Patience was neither her interest nor her virtue, and she wasn't having any of Jeromy's queasy stomach crap today.

She quickly rolled out from behind her triage desk, extending her somewhat corpulent arm and pointing her short stubby index finger while she continued her lecture.

"For crying out loud!" She scolded him.

She then helped a wobbly-kneed Jeromy find a seat.

"I'm sorry, Carrie," Jeromy said as he adjusted his fogging spectacles and then slid his slender frame onto one of the waiting room's metal folding chairs. He was noticeably pale, and cold sweat had broken out across his forehead.

"You know how I get. I just can't stand all the smells and blood and stuff here. I mean... look around!"

He started pointing to some of the patients and families sitting in the waiting room. Some held basins to throw up in. Others were holding pressure on minor wounds or dealing with other injuries or illnesses. In the chair next to him sat an elderly native man with a heavy, dirty, homemade dressing on his left foot that was oozing through some kind of green liquid. To Jeromy, the odor was almost suffocating. He looked at the old nurse to see some acknowledgment of the environment and situation. Some thread of pity. But he immediately saw she wasn't having any of it today. No sympathy there. If looks were weapons, he was about to be eviscerated with a well-worn, blunt verbal knife.

"Look, Carrie... I just came by to bring Issabelle her lunch. That's all. Can I just leave it with you, please?"

The old nurse slowly straightened one of her tightly folded arms and pointed to the only place on her desk that wasn't piled up with patient charts and neatly stacked urine specimen containers.

"There," she said. "Just let it sit there, sit back down before you faint, and I'll get you a cool washcloth. Doctor Whitefeather, for the life of me, I don't know how our Nurse Manager can be your twin. I mean.. really!"

She replied with a frown on her face.

Jeromy had broken out into a sweat, and the heavy glasses had, once again, slid down his nose. He pushed them back up and dabbed his forehead with the sleeve of his blue jeans jacket. At least he didn't need to remain any longer among the odors and oozes. He looked genuinely relieved.

He took a few slow, deep breaths and was about to head towards the desk when an urgent announcement was broadcast overhead:

"Code Blue, Emergency Department."

"Code Blue, Emergency Department."

"Code Blue, Emergency Department."

The stout drill sergeant of a triage nurse sprang into action upon hearing the announcement.

First, she ordered Jeromy to stay put. "Stay in your seat!" She snapped.

Second, she lumbered across the waiting room and to the patient treatment area behind the desk.

"Oh my God!" Thought Jeromy. *"Surely this isn't happening right now!"*

He knew what a code blue was from his sister's stories and didn't want to be anywhere near it. He was about to blow off Carrie's order and try for the exit when two paramedics crashed through the automatic doors with a patient on a stretcher. A third paramedic was straddled, sitting on top of a blood-covered patient to whom he was giving CPR on the rolling stretcher.

"ONE One-Thousand, TWO One-Thousand, THREE One-Thousand!" He called out as he compressed the patient's chest.

They stopped briefly when the IV bag sitting on top of the patient fell onto the floor… less than 15 feet from Jeromy.

"Move, move, move!" Shouted the lead paramedic. "We are losing him!"

That was the last thing that Jeromy remembered. Everything after that was fuzzy… and then black.

Some 15 minutes later, Jeromy opened his eyes and realized that his head hurt. It was throbbing and felt wrong somehow. Reaching up to the right side of his head where something felt strange, his hand was grabbed, and he wrestled himself awake.

Jeromy's sister, Issabelle, stood over him, staring down and smiling. She had caught his hand before he ripped out the IV she had inserted, a regular and routine task for Issabelle. As the Nurse Manager at the hospital's Emergency Department, she was also responsible for floating to other Indian Health Services clinics on the Rez. Today she was at her home location in the ER.

"Steady, chief. Easy, boy." She said.

Jeromy began to open his eyes. There was an overhead exam light that was blinding bright, so he squinted, and it took him several seconds before he could open them enough to see.

"Little Feather…" He called his sister, doubting it was her, "Is that you?" He weakly asked.

"Yes. It's me. How do you feel?" She responded.

Jeromy couldn't see clearly but could now tell the blurry figure next to him was his twin sister. He squinted to get a clearer view and focused by looking into her welcoming, brown eyes. They were more like warm, milk-chocolate pools surrounded by marshmallows…

"Jeromy… wake up!" She pushed verbally.

Jeromy blinked hard a few times.

"Wow," he replied. "Have I told you how much of a pain you are?"

"Yes," she replied, still smiling. "You have told me nearly every day for decades. But I asked you how you are feeling?"

"My head is killing me. What happened?" Jeromy could not remember anything.

Issabelle reached over to a side table, picked up Jeromy's glasses, and handed them to him. "Here, put these on so you can see straight."

And then she laughed. She wasn't trying to be insensitive, but she was very familiar with Jeromy's queasy stomach and sensitivities, which had become all too familiar.

"What?" Jeromy managed to speak while his head continued to clear. "What happened?" He was further confused by Issabelle's laugh.

"You came to bring me lunch, and you had an incident. You fainted and hit your head a little," She tried to say it soberly while keeping a straight face, "So, we picked you up, put you on a stretcher, and carried you back into an exam room. You cost us a lot of paperwork, Jer."

Jeromy suddenly remembered the scene before he fainted, his eyes opened, and he felt morbidly ashamed.

"Oh, Jesus! Izzy," he replied softly. "Oh my God. I am such an embarrassment. I am so sorry."

Issabelle just stared back at him with her loving eyes and warm, understanding smile.

Jeromy was still drowsy when Issabelle's voice caught him from falling asleep.

"Jeromy! Are you fully awake?"

Jeromy pulled himself out of the fog, blinked hard a few more times, and focused on his response.

"Yes. I'm awake. Sorry about that."

"Listen, Mouse, take it easy. Give yourself a break. It's ok. When you were created, you got in line twice for brains and must have missed the line for the indomitable spirit. That's all."

Jeromy looked up at his sister after she used the old pet name for him and replied. "Not helping, Issabelle. Not helping. Besides, when my time comes, I'm going to have a little chat with the Great Spirit about kicking me out of that line!"

…and then they both laughed.

"What I want to know is," he continued… "Between the two of us, how did you get all the courage and the good looks too?"

Issabelle snickered before gently placing her hands on the IV to pull it out.

"Easy now, boy, you don't want to strain anything. Ok?"

Jeromy looked as far away from the procedure as he could. He started getting anxious again, but Issabelle was finished in a flash. As quickly as he looked away, the IV was out, and she was applying a bandage while the old nurse stood next to her and stared.

"Done and done." She said.

"Wow, Little Feather. I sometimes forget just how good you are at this stuff."

"Well, I'm good at this and a lot of other stuff, too. It was always easy to beat you at anything," She replied.

"Tell you what…" she continued. "Why don't you first sit up and then get up and let's see how steady you are on your feet?"

Jeromy obeyed and slowly sat up, but something was weighing on his mind other than his still nauseous stomach.

"Wait, what are you doing here? Is today your regular day in the ER? And why didn't you tell me that you're coming?"

He was about to start getting woozy again but thought that talking helped.

"Good Lord, Jeromy! I was visiting other reservation health settings in the area last week. Now, I am here this week, and you know that. Snap out of it! Besides, there is something important that I need to talk to you about."

Sitting up on his elbows and gently shaking his head, Jeromy looked at her with a frown and furrowed brows, a questioning look that needed a reply.

"What's up, Little Feather?"

Issabelle stared at the old nurse who took the hint, gave Jeromy another evil-eye look, and then waddled away. Issabelle leaned in closer and lowered her voice so she would not be overheard, "Did you get the letter of recruitment?"

"I only received an email from an old friend a day before yesterday, but all it had was a cryptic mess that read '*Whitefeather, you are needed.*' What does that mean? Have I been recruited?" He replied.

Jeromy sat completely upright, "Izzy, I had a vision yesterday! I fell sick after that; I felt weak in my knees."

Jeromy grabbed her arm tightly, subconsciously, while telling her. "I heard a voice! It felt as if the skies were talking to me."

Issabelle decided to change the subject so that she could talk once they reached home. This was a very secretive discussion, and Jeromy was not being quiet about it especially recovering from his tap on the noggin. She carefully removed the damp washcloth from his forehead, tossed his jacket at him, and asked, "Do you want to get lunch?"

"Didn't you get your lunch on the way here this morning?" Jeromy replied as he caught the jacket and threw it at a chair near him.

"Ahh… no. You brought me lunch, but you landed on it when you fell out of the chair and hit your head. It was squashed flat. And then someone decided to bring it to the desk in the back, but instead, they sat it on a table holding urine specimens. I took one look at the flat, oozy bag surrounded by patient pee and decided to take a pass. I guess you brought it for both of us. Too bad, eh?!"

Jeromy looked at Issabelle and then replied. "The ooze may just be the banana frappes. Not pee?"

"Ewwww," replied Issabelle.

Then they both broke out in laughter.

"Let's get you on your feet and out of here, Chief." Offered Izzy.

"Sounds good to me." Said Jeromy. "Do you want me to get you another lunch?"

"Ah, no. That's okay. I think we both should head to your place so I can watch you and we can make something together. How about beetroot and beef in spinach, like Grandma taught us? Besides, that should be safe!"

And they began chuckling again.

Jeromy got to his feet, hugged Issabelle and started making his way out of the treatment area.

"Maybe I can get out of here without running back into Carrie." He hoped.

He made sure he kept his eyes straight ahead, laser-focused on the way to the waiting room. However, Carrie stood there with both arms folded when he arrived, looking like she was ready to peel him like a grape.

He thought he would try to apologize for causing a problem, but the look she gave him made him think wiser of it. One look from Carrie cleared that thought away very quickly. He definitely wasn't going there.

And the smells of the waiting room reminded him that he really needed to leave.

"Bye, Carrie." He said as he started walking briskly away. He turned briefly to see the old nurse trying her best to hold back a big smile as he approached the exit. She instantly covered her mouth with her hand. Their eyes met briefly, and she quickly gave him another forced scowl to take with him on his way. When he was out of sight, she burst out laughing.

"You, flirt! Seriously?!" said Issabelle.

"It's called being a ladies' man. When are you going to stop being jealous, Izzy?" The way home was a typical sibling conversation.

"The moment you realize I am not interested in dating women, you loser!"

On the way to his old '99 red Jeep Wrangler, Jeromy repeatedly stopped to steady himself and stop the world from spinning around him, but he wasn't so miserable that he didn't feel embarrassed.

"This is ridiculous," he thought. *"I turned 36 this year, and I can't believe that I still get this way. God, I'm a mess. Some Indian I am!"*

Thinking he needed a little more time to clear his head, he decided to take a few minutes and sit on one of the benches along the walkway between the ER and the parking lot. He turned his face toward the sun, and a cold, gentle breeze swept across him. It was quite refreshing, and it helped him to think. How did he get this way? Why wasn't he stronger like most of his native brothers? What could he do to get past his sensitivities?

Issabelle lightly tapped his arm, "Hey, you're my favorite brother. You know that, right!"

"I just need to get a damn grip. And stop reading my mind, Izzy!" He muttered and rolled his eyes.

"Listen, I know you are meant for something great. You'll know that soon enough?" She was hinting at the letter for recruitment.

Jeromy took a few slow, deep breaths. He focused and chose to quiet his thoughts. But the one constant thing that came to his mind was whether or not he was actually being recruited; it meant everything to him.

After a few more minutes in the cool air, both his mind and stomach were doing much better, so he stood up and continued walking across the parking lot.

After reaching his Jeep, he pulled out his keys and waited for Issabelle to catch up. He looked out at the vast, cloudless blue sky and its striking contrast to the dry, rolling plains stretched out before him. It was another absolutely bright and beautiful day on the Rez. Too bad the Rez itself was so run down neglected by the government.

Taking a deep breath, he muttered: "That big sky stuff in Montana is nothing compared to Wyoming and South Dakota." He thought it was too bad that the nice weather wasn't going to last, and tonight was the last night before he may have to travel tomorrow.

Feeling much better, he opened the driver's door, but Issabelle jumped into the driving seat.

"I'm driving. You may come in from that side! Thank you very much!" she cautioned him.

He looked at her in disbelief but chose to go with the flow because he was in no mood to argue. He did not want to feel any stress or sickness again.

On the drive home, they had a lot to catch up on, so they did talk about their family and how they were always teased because they were the youngest. But Issabelle pivoted the conversation in another direction.

"Hey, how is Chumani?" she asks with a sarcastic nuance.

Jeromy replied with a frown on his face, "Things didn't work out. Come on! You figured that!"

Issabelle gave him an I-told-you-so look, glad that Jeromy had gotten away from that girl. She was no good for him.

As they reached his front porch, Jeromy and Issabelle got out of the jeep and saw a fire burning on the welcome carpet… The house was on fire! They ran immediately towards it to catch sight of something else burning. It was the mailbox, and an enveloped document had fallen out of it and had caught fire, too.

"Jeromy, that's the recruitment letter! Quick! Wait! I'll get water!" Issabelle clamored in distress.

She ran towards the car to fetch the water bottle and turned back to witness something she had never thought of. Jeromy grabbed the burning letter in his hand, and the fire did not spread to his arms. Instead, the orange-red flicker turned to light blue. It was as if the Spirits were protecting him or trying to send him a message.

Issabelle threw water on his hand while he was trying to open the envelope. "Jerry! What is wrong with you?!" She yelled with wide open, scared eyes.

"What's wrong with me? What's wrong with you?!" He replied in a shrieking voice as the letter turned to ashes as Issabelle attempted to put the fire out. "Wait, do you think that someone did this on purpose to keep me from being recruited?"

"No!"

"Then…" Both of them discern to observe the letter turning back to its true form from the ashes.

"Wow… Holy smokes! You're right! There are spells flying left and right on this thing. Someone really does not want you to be recruited, Jeromy."

Chapter # 2:
Tracks to the Past

The letter confirmed he had been recruited, and there was no time to waste. He had less than 10 hours before he was to get on a train.

Jeromy and Issabelle sat by the old wood stove following dinner and after they were done with his packing.

They did not change anything after their grandmother passed away.

"This place looks exactly the same, Jerry," Issabelle says to him as she takes their plates back to the kitchen. "Dude, I can't believe you managed to keep the woodstove clean. Did you get this polished?"

"I did it by myself!" He said proudly.

"God! I miss her!"

"Yeah! I miss her too. You know there was a point when I did not want to believe in anything she told us, once."

"Like what?" She asked curiously.

"Like how our people are suffering at the hands of the government. Like how we are lucky even to be alive because they are literally clearing us out." He sighed.

"And now? Now you believe it?" She asked again.

"Well, I was just a kid then. Now I teach about our Indian histories. And, as adults, you and I have seen so many Natives cry, suffer and die, Izzy. We have seen them lose their homes. And... worst of all, I have seen our own mother suffer for simply being an Indian...."

"What?" Issabelle was shocked. She knew nothing of the sort about their mother. "What did they do to mother?"

"She was constantly discriminated against. She was harassed and whatnot. One time, she was pulled out of our car while I sat in the passenger seat... yeah, well, never mind. I never told you because she asked me not to." He looked away, and Issabelle understood that there was no point in talking about this right now.

"It is true, though... The Indians are suffering in the US like it is not their home...." She added and then decided it was time to change the topic. The very mention of the US government was enough to cast a depressive environment.

Jeromy finally made an effort to move from his favorite sofa while attempting to flaunt about keeping his sister's room in Bristol fashion. "You know..."

"Oh my God! Wow! My old room looks immaculate!" Issabelle announced as she crossed the hall.

"I just stood up to show that to you, Izzy!"

"Is this where Chumani came every time you guys had a fight?" Issabelle smirks but immediately regrets after saying that. "I'm sorry, I didn't......."

"No, that's okay! And yeah, actually." Jeromy said as he got a flashback of him apologizing to Chumani, but she shut the door on his face while going into Izzy's room.

"I'm sorry it didn't work out."

"It's been a couple of months now. Besides, she's already dating someone else.

"What? Who?" A shocked Issabelle replied.

"Charlie Spotted Horse."

"Charlie? Really? Of well, it is her loss. Let's change the subject."

Issabelle was unsure what to say other than hold his hand in reassurance.

"You know, Izzy, we both work so much for our jobs, and we travel a lot too. It's nice to sit and catch up. We need to do it more often."

"Ahhh, don't get mushy, Jerry!"

After a long pause, Jeromy sighed and continued, "We better get going! It's getting really late."

"Right! Go get the keys, and I'll…."

"Hey, Izzy! Which army do you think I'm from?"

"You're definitely an Inadi, you dumb," she shrugged and continued, "…but don't worry, brother smartass! You'll find out soon enough. Now come on! You are off to change the world. Right?"

Jeromy grabbed his bag, and while Issabelle grabbed a few things from her old bedroom, Jeromy asked:

"Can you keep the jeep over at your place?"

"Sure. Can Sofia drive it if she keeps it on the Rez?"

"Sofia? Who is Sofia?"

"A friend."

"Just a friend? I thought you weren't into other women?"

"I'm not, you dumb! Really? Jesus Jer… don't tell me you are turning into another one of 'THOSE GUYS'?" she replied using finger quotes.

They both just stared at each other, smiled, and jinxed a reply in unison:

"Sorry."

"The twin thing!" Issabelle continues. "And this is how I will know if you are in trouble. So, take care of yourself, brother."

"I'll do my best."

Issabelle pulls up to the train station at 4 o'clock in the morning as the letter instructed. The station and its dimly lit lounge looked like a set of a horror movie with an eerie silence. And there was a thick mist around the silhouettes of the dried trees at some distance. The yellow lights that lined the paths flickered in a few spots. The wooden platform showed wear from thousands of footprints.

On the tracks sat what looked like a midnight black, old west locomotive with only two passenger cars and a caboose. Steam was whooshing out from the sides of the old iron horse. Smoke puffed and blasted out from its smokestack.

Jeromy hugged his sister.

Issabelle tried to hide a single tear streaming down her cheek, said nothing more, and simply turned and left.

Jeromy saw that only four people were waiting in the lounge, so he decided to settle inside the train instead of waiting there.

As he crosses the platform, he sees an old Indian holding and swinging a lantern-like light near the front of the locomotive near where the cowcatcher could have possibly been. Mist, steam, and smoke made it difficult for him to see details clearly. The branches of the weak twigs of the tree adjacent to the train were only a few inches above the roof of Jeromy's train car.

When he takes his first step to get inside, the wind starts to blow, causing the branches to scratch away at the roof. Jeromy already felt as if someone was looking at him from the tree. He hears a whisper from the wind.

Jeromy... this is for you....

There was definitely a divine presence there, and it was not scary anymore. He stepped back as he was sure that there was something important he may be missing out on. A small-for-an-ant tornado-like wind comes from the tree, and the blowing wind carries a new letter. Jeromy looked around and saw that the other people waiting over in the lounge seemed indifferent. Maybe they had not noticed. The wind had handed over the letter to Jeromy before swirling away and disappearing in thin air.

Someone was guiding him, looking out for him. The previous letter that he had received at his house that had almost burned had stated nothing except a few good points:

A. Jeromy was selected to be tested in the recruitment journey, and,

B. He was supposed to arrive at his destination by boarding this strange train at this particular station.

Jeromy immediately put the letter in the side pocket of the bag he was carrying after hearing a man coming from the lounge with a porter. He had a fast-walking pace and a loud baritone voice that, if it were to echo, a person would not be able to distinguish between the starting pitch or the one being carried forward.

As Jeromy moved forward to his place on the train, he felt as if this man was following him. The night was strange enough, and Jeromy was not sure if this could turn into a crime scene right there. He turned back, concerned about this man but then yelped when the man said,

"Hi! I'm Akwiraron!"

Jeromy hesitated for a second but then realized that this was not a man trying to mug him but probably just a passenger.

"Hey! Jeromy Whitefeather!" he replies with rather an agitation.

Akwiraron Okwaho was from a tribe of warriors in Mobridge, and he certainly made the cut. He was a tall man, of about the same height as that of Jeromy, wheat-ish brown skin tone, and hazel light brown eyes.

As the two men walked onto the train and got seated together, Jeromy came down to the immediate assumption of the man, not only to be confident but rather over-confident. But something rather unlikely happened. His assumption turns out to be terribly wrong when Akwiraron endeavors the chat.

"I suppose we would be traveling together." Akwiraron delays to continue, "I am from Kirktown… Umm, where are you from?"

"Right here in South Dakota. Pine Ridge Reservation! My grandmother raised my twin sister and me." With the subsidiary details added to the conversation, which Jeromy cared to heed, Akwiraron felt more comfortable opening up and resumed. But Jeromy continued anyway.

"Wait… Kirktown, you mean Mobridge? You must be a trained swordsman? Are you from the Okwaho family?" Jeromy smiled, glad to have met him.

"Yup."

"All aboard!" a man's voice calls from outside.

A bell begins clanging.

Jeromy was wide-eyed.

At this instance, Jeromy did not know whether he wanted to know Akwiraron better or he was trying to prove himself right this time. And this thought was running through his head while they were having tea, garlic bread, and macaron cake that had been set out for them in the booth of their car.

It was all surreal.

Akwiraron smiles softly and replies, "Yes, you are right! But I'm not quite sure at this point whether or not I'm good at it." After a break off to have another bite of his garlic bread, Akwiraron tells Jeromy how eager he was to be the best and the troop leader.

The train slowly pulled out of the station with a lumbering *chuga, chuga, chuga* sound.

Jeromy thought that he was not quite as ambitious as Akwiraron, and he had gotten his fingers crossed even to have been one of the recruits. As of this moment, Jeromy was only trying out his luck.

The other two passengers waiting in the lounge had also boarded the train, and Jeromy saw the station remaining behind as the train sped up.

There was something weird about the train.

The chuga sound never stopped speeding up. Before long, it was no longer discernable and had simply become a steady hum. As Jeromy and Akwiraron looked out of the train's windows, they soon saw nothing but a whitish blue light.

"How fast is this old train moving?" Remarked Akwiraron.

Strangely enough, Jeromy felt somewhat changed. As if the world around him was suddenly new, or as if there was some magical energy in the train.

In less than 20 minutes from the start of their train ride, an overhead voice called out: "Navajo Nation Station."

"What!" Jeromy cried out. "We just left South Dakota. We just went 900 miles?"

"Man!" Replied Akwiraron. "We must have been flyin'!"

The bluish-white light outside the train quickly gave way to a dry, discernable landscape, and then the train came to a quick but smooth stop without inertia.

"Hey, Navajo Nation Station. I believe this may be the second to last stop, and we'll be here for a while. Do you want to get off and have lunch at a cafe nearby? They don't cost much and also serve generously?" Akwiraron suggested, interrupting Jeromy's train of thoughts.

Jeromy could not help but think to himself, *"Ahhh... is this his confidence, or is he just blunt? Wait! Am I judging him, or am I just confused? Ugh... do I even trust this guy?"*

There was too much going on in his mind to answer immediately. What happened to his letter was still a great mystery, and although Jeromy is not usually like this, he felt threatened by pretty much everyone at the time.

"I mean... it's your choice," Akwiraron shrugged and smiled as he was going towards the door, not having received any response from Jeromy.

"Yes, I'll join you in...." Jeromy stood up and walked towards him.

The half-open door slammed against the corner of the cabin wall. Jeromy and Akwiraron both got panic-stricken.

"I'm sorry! I thought the door was closed, so I lost grip. You can't exactly blame me. It's a sliding door!" Akwiraron defended himself.

Another man appeared during this scene and looked at the two men standing shocked beside the train's door.

"You've been assigned this cabin?" Jeromy asked.

Erik put his camo mobility bag on the top-most bed as he saw that it was the only one that was empty. Erik 'TaWit' Tier was dressed in survival clothes. He then turned towards Jeromy and offered to shake his hand, "Hi! I'm Erik Tier!"

"You're from the TaWit tribe?! I believe you're quite familiar with witchcraft and wilderness totems," Akwiraron responded with excitement.

"Half Navajo, half Filipino. I suppose you're an Okwaho!" he turned to answer him, looking at him closely and observing his attire.

"Wait!" Jeromy interrupted. "Can you guys read minds or something as well?" Jeromy was genuinely confused about how they could tell each other's tribes like that.

"No! It's a gut thing, Erik replies. "You know how we Indians are with our instincts and all! And by looking at you," He said, looking at Akwiraron, "I can also tell that you will be recruited in Kekuwatan."

Erik then turns back towards Jeromy, "But I'm not quite sure about him...."

"Neither am I! My grandmother was a part of Gedhe Samun." Jeromy responded.

"Right!"

After all three of them acknowledge the awkward silence, Erik continued, "Okay, so it was really nice meeting you. I am going to head out for lunch. I am starving!"

"Let's go to the café at…." Akwiraron looks at his phone and continued, "Imperial Hotel?"

"Yes! Absolutely! They serve generously!"

Nervousness and thoughts of insecurity that were taking root in Jeromy's mind eased a bit with Erik's presence. For some reason, it provided him with a bit of relief.

The three men walked out of the train at the stop and found the café nearby. Erik boldly ordered three steakburgers and three banana milkshakes. He only cared to ask if Jeromy and Akwiraron would want to have the burgers with cheese or not, to which Jeromy immediately replied, "Without! Without! I don't think I can have that much anyways. We just ate a snack!"

Jeromy definitely did not want to feel sick on such an important journey, so the cheese was not a good idea.

Akwiraron noticed immediately that the waitress was checking Jeromy out while serving, and after she left, he whispered to him, "Dude, I think Claire here likes you."

"Wow! How?" Erik added, excited about a little fun before they get started on their mission.

"Umm… Why?! Is it because I'm underweight?!" Obviously, Jeromy's insecurities were apparent from his response.

Both look at him with an astounded expression.

"Guys! Breathe! I'm just kidding! And I actually don't know; it's equally as weird for me as it is for you two," Jeromy covered up.

Akwiraron changed the subject immediately afterward and asked Erik, "Why don't you tell us a little about yourself? Your parents?"

And the same time, Erik says, "Guys, did you hear about the second letter?"

The thought of this mystery lying hidden in Jeromy's bag came to his mind, and he felt anxious. In order to distract himself, he tried to get involved in this conversation.

"What second letter?"

"Wait! You don't know about it?" Erik was shocked but continued, "Well, my mother was a doctor, and she was from the same coterie as Jeromy's grandmother. She was a spiritual healer for our people. My father was in the military and died during his last deployment."

"Oh, I'm really sorry, I...."

"No, that's okay! Let's get back to the real topic at hand."

"Umm, okay! Yeah! How come you don't know about the letter, Jeromy?" asked Akwiraron.

"People say there are silver lining letters that have been handed out by Cayuga himself."

Erik continued, "They say that the portal through which he came has some sort of unexplainable energy. And these letters have something to do with the portal."

"I mean, we basically were brought up knowing all of these things. Didn't your parents tell you all of these things?" said Akwiraron.

"My parents died in an accident when my twin sister and I were nine years old. We were raised by our grandmother, and I was bullied a lot as a child. She would tell me all of these things to console me, but I was forbidden to use my energy in this world, so I did not believe in many things when I was younger. I'm still not sure what I believe in or not. What I do know is that all of my family members died to save our people, and that did not make us weak but rather stronger. That's why I'm here."

"I didn't mean to…."

"I think we have a long way to go… It's better not only to get to know each other but also to let it out." Erik disrupted Akwiraron's apology and continued as he looked towards Jeromy, "You have faith, Jeromy, and that means that you are already well-aware, and that will make you stronger than most people."

Surprised at the encouragement these men were giving him, Jeromy thought to himself, *"This is twice in a row, in the same day, that I have misjudged people."*

The three returned to the train, and the door automatically shut behind them. They turned around swiftly at the unexpected closing of the doors and realized that the train's door was now locked. Erik tried sliding it to open but … nothing.

Panic took over them within seconds, and then, the train felt as if it was elevated or flying. For some weird reason, they could feel the gravity loosening under their feet, and Jeromy was worried that he might feel sick. Thankfully, the feeling of 'flying' like one does in an airplane eventually subsided, and Jeromy did not get sick at all. Instead, the recruits looked around and witnessed a letter floating in mid-air of their cabin as they switched the light on. Jeromy made an effort to get a hold of it, but the surrounding glowing ball of light around the letter apparently was a protective cover. An electric shock stopped him from a second attempt. Akwiraron tried to get it, but Erik stopped him and stepped forward instead. After Erik got the same reaction, the letter started burning.

Akwiraron runs to find a fire extinguisher in the train but then stops midway near the door when he hears his name being called...

Akwiraron...

He turned around, amazed, and saw a nebulous image standing there. The flames brightened more before a blinding flash took over the train's cabin, and the men felt the train's rough turbulence under their feet.

What's happening?!

All of them grabbed the nearest seats or handles to balance themselves, and then, the light dimmed, and the letter landed in Akwiraron's hand.

They were all stunned by this turn of events. It was indeed a fantastical journey for them, and something had definitely changed. They all felt as if they had gone through a portal or something of the kind.

After they were able to recollect themselves, they looked at each other, and in their silence, they all understood that the recruitment had begun.

"Is this the second letter?" Erik asked.

"I suppose!" Akwiraron was in shock, "Did you guys see something?"

"No, but I sense a presence. The same when I got the second letter..." Erik confirmed.

"Wait! You did, too?!" asked Jeromy.

"What do you mean you did, too? You received the second letter?" Erik asked.

"Wait! I'm so confused right now." Said Akwiraron.

As Erik took his second letter out, Jeromy and Akwiraron did the same.

When Jeromy took the letter out of his bag's side pocket, he asked, "Guys… do you think this to be a coincidence?"

These were the recruits, and now they knew. But where was their destination? They had all sat in this train, knowing that they were being taken to their destination, but since the blinding flash of light had stunned them, the train had not stopped once. The windows also showed only a bright light blue light.

"Guys, I don't know about anything else, but one thing is for sure. We have been chosen…." Erik pointed out.

Jeromy was not sure either, or he was not confident enough to say anything, but his instinct told him that they were not in the country that they had boarded the train from. His mind constantly told him that they were in another time and another place.

When the train finally came to a stop, the view outside the train's windows became visible again. Akwiraron peeked from one of the windows and gasped. "Did we just travel through time?!..."

Chapter # 3:
Hawkeye

Jeromy, Erik, and Akwiraron arrived at the east side of the Hudson River. Dozens of people were already there. Upon their arrival, they got to know that the people were from many tribes and were here for recruitment. They would be traveling by foot towards a small village outside of Albany, New York, where Cayuga was now.

Jeromy noticed that one of many walking with them appeared white, and he Struck up a conversation.

"Hello, my name is Jeromy Whitefeather. Forgive me, but I noticed that you do not look Native American." He looked at him questioningly.

The tall man had long, black hair and was indeed white; however, he was dressed like the others. He also carried a very long rifle covered in a leather wrap.

"My given name is Natty Bumppo – but my friends call me Hawkeye."

Another man who seemed to be Mohawk jumped into the conversation. "He is La Longue Carabine – Long Rifle. You don't want to be downrange from this one."

The two men laughed, and then Hawkeye continued.

"The Mohican tribe raised me, and I am a scout mostly. Right now, I am trying to get everyone to the village without attracting attention, so we need to keep our voices down and be on the lookout for both French and English alike. We don't have any business with them and don't need any run-ins."

Jeromy noticed the wisdom in his statement and replied, "Agreed. Thank you… but just one more question: Can you tell me what year this is?

Hawkeye smiled, knowing that they were from another time by the way Jeromy and the newcomers were dressed.

"It is the year 1760, Jeromy."

"Thank you, Hawkeye. Thanks for leading us. Nice meeting you."

Hawkeye led the group to the small villa that seemed to be some sort of a headquarter for information. When they took their first step towards the porch, all the wind chimes started to ring like a storm was about to hit. But, when they turned to see, the territory behind them was not even windy, and people were busy talking about Cayuga.

"Look! Your pocket is shining!" Akwiraron pointed towards Jeromy's bag's side pocket.

Jeromy looked and saw a little light emerging from his pocket. "Yeah, you're right. It's the envelope…."

"Guys, look! The place is empty. I don't understand…."

Erik looked towards the lounge and felt as if people had disappeared; it was like someone blew a candle, and the fire went out. There were crowds of people around here when the men had arrived, but now, there was no one there except these three.

"Okay! I'm glad you said that out loud. I felt…"

Jeromy completed Akwiraron's statement, "…like you were hallucinating?"

While they still inspected the villa, Jeromy asked them, "Then why didn't you guys turn around?"

A voice from the middle of the camps wailed loudly, "Where did everyone go? Hello? Is anybody here?" A female voice echoed.

Jeromy, Akwiraron, and Erik ran towards the source of the voice. A group of three people was standing outside a nearby tent. The voice was that of Anna Otsi'ta.

Jeromy's throat dried out as he took a look at her. Anna had deep black, thick hair tied up in a high pony with a sleek straight texture. A few strands hung from near her forehead. Her fair skin tone was complemented by her big almond-shaped eyes of dark black color with long thick eyelashes.

Anna was wearing a half-sleeved black t-shirt tucked into her skinny black jeans along with a heeled pair of boots that complemented her height of 5' 7" beautifully.

She was standing there with her friends, Denisse and Alice. Denisse was a short-heighted girl with long, mahogany hair, running straight from the scalp but curling loosely at the ends. She was wearing a sleeveless off-white shirt with blue ripped Capri jeans, and a dark green stole loosely wrapped around her neck.

"Who are you, people? I don't understand… what's going on? I thought I saw a lot of people here," said Alice, confused like the others as she stood rigid with a set of bow and arrow in her hand, ready to shoot. Alice had medium-length brown hair with bangs that were French braided. Jeromy couldn't help but notice that all the others were younger than him… maybe about five to ten years younger, which only added to his lack of self-confidence about his recruitment.

Akwiraron had an immediate admiration of her look, which was put together with baggy camo trousers with four zipped pockets and a plain black tight shirt, making her athletic figure quite prominent.

Akwiraron had to try hard to avoid staring at Alice.

"So… where did everyone go?" asked Erik.

"Why don't we all calm down? I feel like this is a test," said Jeromy.

"Yes! And I think the next level to this test has a secret that lies within that small cottage where you three were standing a while ago. We came from there, too," said Anna.

All of them walked towards the villa. The creek of the door was loud and directional that only Jeromy could sense. So, he quickly asked among the murmuring, "Shhh… do you guys hear that?"

"What?!" Erik asked.

"The door is over here, but the creek sound wasn't… it was like a map directed towards that corner under that small chandelier in the corner."

As everyone approached that area, they saw the light coming from the side table adjacent to that area.

"I believe the direction is a little tilted, Mister," Anna added and then suddenly noticed a chest lying open in a corner that appeared to be full of weapons.

"Well, you know what they say about being alone in strange places? We better be prepped against trouble!" Denisse suggested as she walked towards the chest and picked out a dagger for herself. The others followed without hesitation, and each of them picked a weapon that suited them.

Then, they all heard a light whooshing sound.

"Hey, there's a letter floating right here on this table next to this candle," Anna noticed.

"Wait!" yelped Denisse, "What if you get a shock? Remember when I touched your letter…."

"Good Lord! You guys… really…." Alice grabs the letter and tries to read it. "I don't understand! Is this even a language?"

Anna took that letter from her hand and tried to read the envelope.

It said D | | *D* | \ |

"I think these are Chakchuwana codes. I can't seem to recall exactly, though…."

"May I?" asked Jeromy, and Anna slid it into his hands. By this time, everyone in the room could feel the sense of attraction between the two.

"You're right! It says *burn*! The code translates into 'burn'!"

Jeromy went towards the candle and started to light it up from the corner. The candle blew out, and the letter didn't feel like itself anymore. In the darkness, Jeromy's hand started to glow. Everyone noticed that and started to point it out.

"Jeromy… umm…" Erik paused, lost for words.

"Dude, your hand is glowing!" yelled Akwiraron.

"There's something inscribed on his hand," Anna grabbed his hand and opened it wide for everyone to read the glowing words.

Welcome to the next round...

The glowing words continued on Anna's wrist.

Each one of you has a task that is better when...

"Quick! Give me your hand, Denisse!" Anna said as the words were about to reach the end of her sleeve.

"Is someone keeping track of what the scroll is saying?" Denisse asked as the letter continued on her arm.

"My turn..."

By this time, everyone was reading it out loud.

...in pairs. Choose wisely.

Denisse grabbed Erik's hand as it continued...

Go to the... arch playa of Berrima... hollow caves of Lovesley...

Erik was about to hold Jeromy's hand when he and Anna screamed, "No!"

"Okay! Akwiraron, give me your hand!"

The last half of the letter continued...

Hold at the mist near the forest of limbo...

When everyone started to plan a scheme inside of their heads of who should go where exactly, Akwiraron's arm began to glow again and said, as Akwiraron reads it out loud for everyone:

The blood moon south to the River of Cayuga…

When the letter had been read, the five recruits looked around and saw nothing but darkness. The candle went off, too.

They heard footsteps nearby, and a female voice near them whispered, "Kǫ."

It was Alexa, and she was here like the rest of them. Anna smiled at her – they knew each other from their earlier meeting on a train, and they had known each other for a while before they saw each other here. She said the same thing, and a flick of fire flowed over their heads like candles as they walked. This was a spell that they had learned from their ancestors.

"Okay! So, let's sit back and discuss who is going to which place," Anna suggested. "I think Denisse and I should go to the River of Cayuga," she added.

"But I think… umm…" answered Jeromy.

"I'm certain that I should go... Why? Did you think I'm an Inadi?" She asked sarcastically.

"You are quite well-aware!" With a smirk on his face, he continued, "But no, I don't think you're an Inadi. You're a Roh Jahat!"

She looked at Jeromy with an astonished expression and respect. Pulling a strand of her hair at the back of her ear, she continued, "Umm…." Clearing her throat, she said, "Ahem, sorry, yeah! So, what are you suggesting?" while she turned her face towards Denisse, reminding herself of how important it was for her.

Jeromy's expression immediately changed to answer that, "I think this is a tricky stage. It can't be that easy."

Erik could tell where this was going and added, "Yes! Yes! You should go with Akwiraron, or... umm...."

"Alexa," She said her name out loud, "And may I ask why exactly?"

Jeromy stood up and answered this, "The cave may have tribesmen to fight with, not only a magical barrier. And let's face it: if we're recruited and if the mission has started, it is not only a battle of minds but a battle to be won with soul and physical strength, too."

"What else, Jeromy? I believe this stage we're at right now is all yours," Erik put his hand on Jeromy's shoulder in support of his knowledge.

"Okay, guys, stand up!" Jeromy said with excitement in his pace, "We...."

"...Are leaving towards the river? What if the medallion recruitment is for the test of time as well?"

Anna interrupted with a question that seemed valid to all of them.

Alexa and Anna immediately picked their stuff up to leave.

"Let's go, girl!" Alexa said with a smirk on her face, straddling her arrow case on her shoulder.

"Oh, Lord! Wait! Why didn't I think of that?" Akiwraron got frustrated, "Jeromy! Come on! Where am I supposed to go?"

Jeromy was somewhat conflicted at that instance because one thing stood in the way of making the right decision. He thought of leading a team at the first stage and how the 'four-leaf clover' of Cayuga was a big deal for Jeromy. He wondered if any one of them was going to be recruited into the medallion.

Akwiraron snapped his fingers in front of Jeromy's face, "Dude!"

Erik and Akwiraron were hunched towards the floor as if before a long run, desperately waiting for his response.

"I am certain that I have to go to the playa," Erik declared.

"I really feel like I'm missing something out… Let's go back to the side table where we found the scroll." Jeromy explained.

Everyone started to pace up towards the corner, but Akwiraron used his lightning bolt speed, "What?"

Jeromy picked up the candle in his hand. Akwiraron wondered out loud: "Are you sure we're not just going to split into pairs as written in the scroll that we found earlier in this place?"

"Not just yet. This isn't a test of memory, Akwiraron! The events would not literally repeat themselves. This is the test of knowledge."

"Found it!" Denisse put her right hand up in front of Akwiraron's face.

"What? The candle?!"

"Absolutely," Denisse gave it to Akwiraron. "No, wait… something is going on with this candle… it's changing… now it looks clear and, it looks like there is… an hourglass inside?!"

"Turn it over in the opposite direction," Jeromy suggested like he knew what was going on.

"Okay!" Denisse replied. She looked at Erik, "Erik! Right?!"

Erik nodded his head, "Yes!"

"Akwiraron, please do the honors.

"Look, guys! The wick is coming out from the opposite end."

"Erik, now!" Akwiraron yelped.

"Nizhónígo ch'aanidíínaał," Erik held out the palm of his hand and repeated a spell that he had learned long ago. There were some elemental spells that these recruits knew from their families and tribes before this journey began.

The wick slowly moved out of the wax. After it fell off, a small hourglass popped out and into Erik's hand, which he immediately put on the table, and the wick started to float in mid-air for a few seconds and then expanded and opened up like a scroll and said:

Among you are the chosen ones, and this is where your potentials are tested.

The hourglass slowly vanished.

"Holy Spirits!" remarked Alice.

This small villa that the seven recruits were standing in was the school where they would be trained. This was where they would be tested, and this was where Cayuga would shortlist the four recruits among them that will go forward on the mission as his Four Leaf Clover.

"So… what is this place? Where are we right now?" Erik asked as he was clueless.

All the others were clueless, too, but they all had their own imaginations and ideas about what their being there could mean.

"I believe we are in another time. That train we got off of? I think it took us through a portal," Akwiraron voiced his suspicions.

"I believe so, too," Alice agreed with him. "When we came here, I met a native woman in her 20s who said that she thought this was somewhere in the 1750s."

"1760, to be precise." Added Erik, who had learned that from Jeromy.

"Uh, yes… okay. But I didn't know that time travel was even possible before this." Jeromy stated, who was still coming to the realization that they were indeed in the past and not just in the past, but centuries behind from their present lives.

The recruits were now sitting on the rugged stairs in the villa's lonely lounge when they saw a sharp white circle emerge in the air in front of them. It expanded into a portal as a tall divine-looking man walked out of it.

"Time travel will be one of the first things you will learn here. This is the family, the tribe, the kin, the house that will prepare you for all your tests and trials ahead. This is your house until you are either selected or sent back home."

The group looked at the man in amazement, wondering if he was even human. "Who-Who are you?" Alexa asked sheepishly.

"Cayuga," He responded with a warm smile before disappearing along with his glowing portal again.

"Cayuga? Chief Cayuga?! This is Chief Cayuga! Oh, my God!" Anna squealed as if she had just met a celebrity. Of course, all the recruits there knew at least a little about Chief Cayuga, and they all knew that seeing him there talk to them was an honor in itself.

Chapter # 4:
Training at the Olta

The seven recruits were surprised when they came out of the villa's corner room. They saw the once empty building swarmed with dozens of people of different ages ranging from 15 to over 50. They looked around in wonder as the murmur of a crowd surrounded them, and they were still taking the change of the environment when they heard an older woman's voice from their right.

"Did Cayuga send you here?"

They turned to see a woman wearing a feathery headband dressed in traditional Native American attire, suspiciously looking at them.

Erik responded, "Y- yes. Chief Cayuga directed us here… Uh… what is this place? Where are we?"

The deeply-set wrinkles around the older woman's mouth curved as she smiled. "Welcome to the Olta. Among you will be the best of ours. Among you will be the Indian heroes."

The recruits felt proud of themselves for being there. This villa would be their training center, and the woman led them towards a staircase through the crowd of people going left and right from different rooms to different places.

As the seven recruits looked around, they saw dozens and dozens of people milling about. They appeared as young as 15 and as old as 60 or 70.

Spirit Magic was happening all around them. Denisse noticed a man in his early 30s sitting at the edge of an indoor garden wall. He was wearing a black hoodie that complemented his pale skin. She realized that his hands were glowing with a dim blue light emerging from them as if he was performing a spell. She had brief eye contact with him and then immediately looked away before it got awkward. From his attire and age, she presumed he was under training there, too. All the students appeared to be wearing tan-colored buckskins.

The seven recruits followed the older woman's footsteps as she walked them to the first floor. The hallway suddenly lit up with what appeared to be lanterns lined on both sides of the walls surrounding them as if leading them towards a point.

Every move the recruits made was inspiring them. They could feel that they would grow to become tremendously skilled in this place. As they walked a little further, they could see no more people around them, and the older woman stopped in her way and turned to face them.

"As you all know, Cayuga has recruited you and put you under training here. From this evening, your training begins. You will be made into warriors prepared to fight the darkness that could potentially surround this world."

The recruits listened to her with inspiration. She seemed so gentle and fragile, yet there was something very empowering about her – they could feel that she had great strength and could easily take them down if she wanted to.

The old woman walked towards a little wooden box that stood on a small table in the hallway's corner, a few steps from where the recruits stood. She first removes a sage bundle from the box and then a few scrolls after shuffling through them. She put all the scrolls back into the box except for one that she set on the table.

"First, we will start with a blessing to cleanse ourselves and the area from unwanted spirits."

She held the sage bundle inches from her pursed lips and quietly whispered, "Ko."

The whitish-green leaves first produced some smoke and then caught fire. She allowed it to burn a bit while the recruits formed themselves into a circle and held out their hands, palm facing up, ready to receive the blessing and cleansing. Then, she blew out the flame, but smoke continued to billow from the sage into the air.

The seven bowed their heads slightly and closed their eyes. As she carried the smoking bundle around the circle, she stopped briefly in front of each person as they each reached their hands forward into the smoke and pulled the purifying medicine up toward their heads. One by one, they gently waved the smoke toward their faces and into their hair as they all had been taught.

As the woman finished, she took her free hand and held it several inches over the smoking sage bundle. She slowly closed her hand into a fist without touching the bundle, and the burning and smoke immediately stopped. She placed the sage bundle back into the box.

Next, she unfolded the scroll and looked at all seven recruits to check that she had the correct ones.

"You have all been chosen because you have demonstrated great abilities. However, each of you will be stronger in certain areas, and you need to be aware of your greatest strengths, including your element of power. Who, among you, is Jeromy?" She questioned with a raised eyebrow.

Jeromy adjusted his glasses and stepped forward, "Uhm.. Me. I – I'm Jeromy." He was stammering a little due to nervousness.

"And Denisse?" The old woman inquired.

Denisse stepped forward, too.

"You two – Jeromy and Denisse... you two belong to Telik Inadi, don't you?" She confirmed.

"Yes, we do." They looked at each other and said, almost in unison.

"Stand to this side," She gestured to her right with her free arm. "Your element of power is Air. It represents intelligence, and Cayuga has assigned you under this training course."

Jeromy smiled. It felt like he was chosen for great good, and he could already feel powerful knowing that he would be bestowed with the best knowledge in this particular arena. He looked at Denisse, who could not hide her lips curving into a smile either.

The other recruits looked at each other, excited, curious, and nervous at the same time. This felt good – the ability to be trained and reach their fullest potentials.

"Akwiraron and Alexa?" The old woman demanded.

The two named recruits immediately stepped forward. "Yes, ma'am."

"Ma'am?" The old woman looked up from the scroll with a raised eyebrow that indicated that she did not really like this title. "If you must call me anything, call me *Na'nitini*."

"Yes, ma'am – I mean… Na'nitini." Akwiraron corrected himself.

The woman eyed him from head to toe, then announced, "You both are from the Kekuwatan tribe, so your powerful element is Earth. It represents physical strength so that you will be trained accordingly. Step to a side here."

As per her gesture, Akwiraron and Alexa obeyed and stood beside Denisse and Jeromy. Denisse and Alexa intermingled their fingers as they held each other's hands. They were both nervous like the rest of them, but they were glad that at least they had true friends in one another to calm them down.

"You must be Erik?" The woman presumed as he was the only man left in the group to be assigned a course.

"Yes, Na'nitini," Erik nodded and stepped forward.

"Good. Erik and Alice, you both belong to the Alas Gedhe Samun tribe, and you will be trained to use water as your powerful element. Awareness of the wilderness will be your specialty once you are trained under this course. Stand aside."

She gestured to her left, and Erik and Alice stood opposite Jeromy, Denisse, Alexa, and Akwiraron. Now, only Anna was left standing in the middle to be assigned an element.

"Are you a Roh Jahat, Anna?" The older woman looked at Anna differently. She had a kinder gaze towards her as if she respected the girl already.

"You have great strength, Anna. With your tribe being Roh Jahat, your element of power is fire, but even besides that, I see great strength in you to combat evil not just within you but even in external entities in the physical realm. You can travel through wormholes as angels do. Stand to this side."

She gestured her to stand with Erik and Alice.

Anna felt powerful already, like she was ready to take on the world, but of course, she needed the right training to execute her strength. For some reason, Jeromy felt good hearing about Anna's potential. He saw her as the strong woman she was but curiously, he felt proud of her when the Na'nitini praised her.

Now that the seven recruits were all assigned their elements of power, the older woman explained the training structure to them.

"You will all live here in this villa as long as you are under training. There are some lessons that you all will study together along with some other recruits. Those are the common sessions. Each day, after your common sessions, you will all divide and go to your assigned grounds to receive the training for your separate elements."

The recruits listened to her closely as she went on.

"Today, you can roam the villa and its surroundings to familiarize yourself with the area, but tomorrow, as soon as the Sun rises, you must all assemble in the lounge. Do not be late. Time is the first essence of discipline in the Olta."

With that, the woman turned and walked away into the darkness of the hallway.

"So… that was interesting…." Alice said out loud to break the silence that had engulfed the group. Of course, they were all still in amazement at how their lives were suddenly changing. Coming from ordinary lives with no association to magical or fantastical elements other than their families belonging to the Native tribes, this was all very new and exciting for the recruits.

"Yeah…" Jeromy agreed. "This is like a school of spirit magic and strength, isn't it?"

Jeromy's question was answered by an unfamiliar male voice, "Not just a school. It is a preparation for the battlegrounds that you will be fighting in."

They looked to see who it was, and Denisse realized that it was the same man she had seen downstairs. The one with the black hoodie robe, pale skin, and glowing hands.

"And you are…?" Alexa inquired.

"You can call me Dakota. I am a student, but I also help with training the recruits." He explained dryly.

The recruits all looked at each other as if asking for each other's approval to trust this man. When none of them felt intimidated by him, they allowed him to continue to advise them of what to do and what not to do around here.

"I would suggest that you do a quick tour of the villa so that you don't have trouble finding your training grounds tomorrow. Then, you can all go to your element's rooms."

Dakota walked the group past several full-sized statues and exhibits dedicated to famous Chiefs across tribes and time. Then he turned and led them down the main hallway to show them where they would each live during their training. He explained to them that there were four separate native quarters off of the master hall corridor. Each of these suites was divided between the four Spirit Elements. So, all Inadis would join together in the same suite, while the Kekuwatan tribe's recruits go in another, and so on.

"Well, it's going to be fun meeting other recruits, no?" Alexa sounded excited.

"Uh... fun for *you*. I mean, you have Akwiraron staying with you. I know no one in my elemental room...." Anna frowned. "What am I going to do all alone?"

"So... you have a problem with sleeping alone?" Jeromy teased her, and she snapped her offended gaze at him, which clearly said that he must not mess with her right now.

"Uh, I meant... you won't be alone. You never know; there could be others, or you might run into someone you know from your tribe in there...." He tried to cover up, and Anna just rolled her eyes at him.

"Yeah... I hope so." She said as they walked around the villa.

It had a very antique structure. There were pillars of sand that stood tall and strong at every corner. The floors were sandy, too, as opposed to the cemented floors that most of these recruits were used to walking on in their lives back home. Obviously, the whole trip back in time, and that, too, ages back, was a bizarre experience for each one of them.

After a lot of moving around and being amazed by all the gifted students and the unique infrastructure of this villa called the Olta, the recruits were led by the pale-skinned, black-robed man into the kitchen.

"This is where the Olta's people prepare our meals. Some regular villagers are employed here for cooking and other tasks – not all of them are Natives, but they are well aware of the strength that we, as recruits, need during training."

The recruits listened to him closely as he went on, while Erik and Akwiraron looked at each other, suppressing their smiles as they both felt hungry upon the very mention of food.

"It is almost time for dinner, so we can all gather there," he said, pointing at a circular table made of stone that sat in the corner of the lounge.

The recruits seated themselves at the table, and a young woman emerged from the kitchen with a pile of metal plates in her hands. She spread the plates around at the table in front of everyone and then called out to someone in the kitchen to "Bring in the food, Gam!"

An old man followed her order and brought a big bowl of boiled chicken with gravy and bread on the side. The recruits were hungry and did not wait for an invitation to start serving themselves. Their dinner ended with a herbal tea being served to them at the table. Whatever it was, it all tasted great to the seven recruits who had been on one hell of a journey through time and place.

"I'm off to rest now. You all should rest, too." The mystery man who had been touring the place with them suggested.

"Wait," Denisse said, "Dakota…." She said his name carefully as if confirming that was his name. "Thanks for showing us around. Will we see you tomorrow?" She asked, smiling.

"Sure." He said dryly before getting up and vanishing as he turned by the corner of a wall in the lounge.

"Okay, I'm glad we have good food here. Like, I was *very* concerned about what we're going to be fed with!" Erik laughed.

"Meh… I didn't like the gravy too much… Had too little salt for my taste…." Alice complained, to which the recruits all snickered.

Denisse began laughing.

"It's called *healthy* food, Alice, and it's supposed to have lesser salt! Do you want to be bloated and tired all the time?!" Denisse announced.

The group walked back to the staircase leading to the hallway on the first floor to find their rooms as they were instructed. In the hallway, they met another recruit who directed them towards their tribes' rooms.

"Okay, so we'll see you guys at breakfast then?" Jeromy asked everyone but looked at Anna.

"Yeah, sure," Anna said, dreading to go alone into her room while everyone else went in pairs.

Anna walked into the Roh Jahats' room and saw tens of beds lined up against the walls. The room was not too spacious, but it was not too crowded either. There were several boys and girls of various ages there who were sleeping. Some were talking to each other, while some older ones were just sitting on their beds revising their days' lessons.

Anna walked in hesitantly, shutting the door behind her. She took a few steps in, hesitated, and then continued walking toward an empty bed that had new buckskin uniforms neatly folded on it along with a label that read *Anna*. As she walked towards it to take her place on it, a voice from the bed beside hers stopped her.

"New here?" Another man, younger than her, was sitting up on his bed.

"Y- Yeah. Is this bed taken?" She asked, not sure if she should take this place.

"No. You can take it." He said, smiling warmly and then moving to lay back on his bed.

"Hey…" Anna said as she sat on the bed, trying to get comfortable. "What time do you get up in the morning? I don't want to be late for the training on my first day…."

"Don't worry. There is going to be a loud siren here that will wake us all up on time." He responded before dosing off to sleep.

Anna nodded, relieved that the room was actually not bad. She lay on her mattress and thought about the day's events unfolding in front of her eyes. It had been a crazy day, indeed, and she fell asleep thinking of how tomorrow was going to be.

* * *

A loud siren wailed through the Olta when morning arrived, waking everyone up. All the recruits got up from their beds, dressed in their Olta buckskin uniforms, and got ready to begin the day. Anna woke up to see the room for the first time – it had been dark last night when she had come here, so she could not see much other than the beds.

She could now actually begin to believe that they were indeed in ancient times as she looked around. There was not much that these recruits had seen since the train journey but watching outside the window of this room in broad daylight showed her largely empty grounds, sandy winds, and little huts made of stone or other sandy materials.

"Wow…" She whispered. "This is real…." She turned around to see that almost everyone was now heading out from the door she had entered the room from last night.

Let's go, then. She told herself after getting ready and picking up her bag that she carried around.

As she walked downstairs towards the lounge adjacent to the kitchen, she saw Akwiraron and Alexa already seated at one of the round tables and joined them.

"Hey," she said, looking around at the other recruits with who she was not familiar. There must be approximately a hundred more of them.

"Hey, did you sleep okay?" Alexa asked.

"Yeah. I had a pretty good sleep, actually. Probably because of how tired we all were yesterday," She expressed. "Where's Jeromy and the others?"

"They should be here soon now. Theirs was the last door in the hallway, and from what I heard, the doors open in a sequence, so…" Akwiraron explained.

The girls nodded in understanding, and just as breakfast had started to be served, Jeromy, Denisse, Erik, and Alice walked into the lounge along with several others.

"There you are!" Anna waved at Jeromy to call them over to the table.

After all the seven recruits were done with breakfast, their first training class began. Following the others, the seven recruits gathered in the training lounge as directed by the old woman the previous day.

A Native American man dressed in traditional attire walked to the front of the crowd of recruits.

"Yá'át'ééh!" He greeted the recruits in the Native language. "We have some new people among us today, and we will learn to first identify ourselves as the Natives." He introduced.

The seven recruits looked at each other, excited to see what they would learn in this session. This was all very different from their daily lives, very bizarre.

"I was told that Chief Cayuga's Four-Leaf Medallion recruits had arrived here. Are they among us at this moment?" The man announced, asking for a response.

Jeromy looked at the other six recruits he had arrived with and stepped forward with his hand raised. "Uh… it is us." He gestured, and Anna, Erik, Akwiraron, Denise, Alexa, and Alice all stepped forward, too.

"Ah… there are seven of you. Which of you are you the four chosen ones?" The Native man smiled, moving swiftly towards them to have a closer look. He looked at them from head to toe before continuing.

All seven stood silently, for they weren't sure who the final four would be.

The man simply nodded.

"I am Ahiga, your spiritual mentor for as long as I live and for as long as you need me, even when you leave the Olta." The man faced all the gathered recruits.

"*Mitakuye oyasin*. We are all one. We are all connected. May our spirits guide us through this mission that we have begun. May we live - and live victoriously."

Jeromy smiled broadly as he recognized his native Lakota language.

The recruits were then directed to be seated on the ground as Ahiga began telling them the stories of some of the bravest warriors among the Indians.

"Since the arrival of the Europeans, we have fought and struggled greatly, but no more. No more will we allow the darkness of the enemies' hearts to burden our spirits...."

The lecture went on for about three hours, and all the recruits listened attentively with a growing feeling of enthusiasm to fight the injustice and a passion for being their people's heroes.

"Maybe one day, someone will be telling stories about us. We'll be heroes, won't we?" Akwiraron was already feeling emotional like most of the other recruits. The stories being told by Ahiga featured a lot of details about the pain and injustice that the Indians were going through and had been going through for ages now.

"Dear recruits," Ahiga said after he had ended one of the most recent stories about a Native hero who died fighting the government for his village's people's rights. "We have talked about different people from different events, but do you realize the one element that remained constant with all these stories?"

He looked at the recruits to see if anyone wanted to answer, but he was not expecting one. Then, he went on, "Time. It is time that connects all these events. Our lives are like timelines, too, but above all, the most important establishment that I want to make about time is that today, right here, right now...." He paused to provoke some dramatic curiosity to keep his listeners interested.

"Right now, all of you, each one of you, are here from ages ahead. You *traveled* in time to be here – and by defying time itself, you have completed one part of your mission's milestones. It is all due to Chief Cayuga for gathering you all here from different times, here in the 18th century."

There were a lot of gasps and *oohs* from the crowd of recruits who had just realized how far they had traveled back in time through the train journey that brought them here. Ahiga smiled at the surprise of his students.

"Don't you worry. Once you achieve your goals, once the mission is accomplished, you will be sent back to your present times," He comforted them.

"But..." one of the recruits said, "Won't our families and friends realize that we are missing?"

Ahiga chuckled. "No... No, they won't. Cayuga has used his strongest spirit magic spells to stop time in your present ages, so when you return to your present times, you will find everything mostly as it was when you had left it."

The recruits were amused. They were all looking at each other in amazement, and as the day went on, Ahiga told them of the many sacrifices made in the history of Native Americans.

Then, they were all sent for lunch before the next section of the mentoring that day.

"It's very strange that time has frozen, and we are present in the past…." Anna wondered out loud at the lunch table.

"It is… But we are here for a huge purpose, and it would be truly an honor to be able to do something for our people." Erik stated as Akwiraron nodded, chewing a piece of bread rolled around some mashed potatoes and chicken.

"That's right. But what exactly is the plan here? I know that we are on a mission to overturn the US government or at least make them realize that they cannot continue their injustice towards the Natives, but how exactly are we going to do that?" Jeromy asked, and the other six recruits fell silent with their trains of thoughts, too.

After the recruits had had lunch, they were all summoned back into their training ground. Ahiga was already present there, along with another aged woman who was presumably another mentor at the Olta.

"Welcome back, recruits. Now, each day that you are here, this is going to be your routine. You will all gather here for spiritual mentoring after breakfast every morning, and after lunch, Orenda here will teach you spirit magic spells that will make you stronger on your journey ahead." Ahiga concluded the session and left the recruits to Orenda, a 47-year-old woman with red hair, dressed in a multicolored robe that reached down to her ankles and showed her slightly swollen feet.

"It is a pleasure seeing you all here," Orenda greeted the recruits with a warm smile. The recruits suddenly remembered that this was perhaps the same woman who had led them to the hallway earlier.

"I believe I have already personally met the four chosen ones," She smiled knowingly at the group as they looked at each other and then smiled back at her.

"So, you have already been lectured enough by Ahiga. I will not talk anymore but proceed with the practical implementation of the first basic spell that you must all know."

The recruits were all excited to learn spirit magic, and they felt proud to be chosen as the warriors among the Indians… for the Indians. Orenda blew off all the lanterns in the ground, thus turning the training ground dark. Then, Orenda whispered, "Ko!" and a small ball of fire lit up the place. The ball of fire was levitating in the air slightly above Orenda's open palm.

"And that's how we can make fire. Now, this can be used in several situations: Both, as a weapon, as well as to light your way in dark caves or other paths." She explained.

Anna and Alexa looked at each other and smiled. They already knew this spell – they had learned this one earlier in their lives and had even used it when they had found the scroll earlier with the other recruits.

"Ko," Anna whispered effortlessly under her breath and created another ball of fire in her palm. Orenda looked impressed.

"I can see you are a powerful Roh Jahat, Anna."

Then one after another, the other recruits started saying the fire spell, too, creating little balls of fire in their palms.

"Now, now, be careful, everyone. Don't let the fire spill anywhere, or it could burn someone near you," Orenda warned the tens of recruits, creating fireballs.

"My hand feels hot! Is it burning me?!" One of the other female recruits said out loud in panic as she frantically moved her hand, and the recruits around her quickly moved away from her, worried that she might spill the fire on them.

"It's supposed to burn a little, Bertha. Calm down."

Orenda said with a tinge of amusement in her tone. It was evident that she loved her job – she enjoyed teaching the recruits these amazing magical abilities and then watching them first be amused, then inspired, then scared, and then master it. For her, it was like watching flowers sprout.

The training ground was brightly lit by now by all the fireballs in the recruits' palms when Orenda proceeded with the lesson, "Now that you know how to create fire, one must also know how to put it off. Does anyone here know how to…"

She was cut off by Alexa raising a hand. "I do!"

Orenda raised one of her eyebrows and gestured her free hand in a 'go ahead' motion.

Alexa slowly closed her palm over the fire and turned it into a fist as if crushing the fire in her hand. Then, she dusted off her hands proudly to show that it was done.

"Very good," Orenda commented and then looked at the other recruits as if expecting them to do the same. One by one, the other recruits crushed the balls of fire in their fists, too. And the room was dark again except for the ball of fire still lit in Orenda's palm.

"Now, I know all of you will experience slight burning or itching in your palms when you do this spell, but every spell has a price. Magic, especially spirit magic, is not easy – it exhausts your spirit, your soul, depending on what spell you cast."

Orenda explained to the recruits how this was not to be taken as a play but rather a resourceful weapon that had to be used very wisely and smartly.

"Only when needed," She repeated, "Only when you must."

"However," She said, "You will need to practically do all these magical spells that I am teaching you over the course of your training here, so be mentally prepared to sleep exhausted at night." She warned before going on.

The recruits felt powerful by now. They all thought that if a spell as basic as the fire spell could make them feel so spiritually empowered and strong, the whole training course would be extremely beneficial for their physical and spiritual growth.

"Now, what I am going to show you is how you can use this same fire spell as a weapon in an encounter with any human, demon, or legendary creature. But," she paused with an emphasis on her last word, "No one – I repeat, no one will follow what I am doing right now. Today, you will only observe how I am bending the fire to attack, but none of you should create any more fireballs or cast this spell unless I instruct you to. It is not safe when you are not in control of your powers. Not yet. Not safe for you, not safe for anyone around you."

The recruits all gathered around Orenda, keeping a little distance, and she started to show the recruits several ways of using the fireball as a weapon. First, she demonstrated how the fireball could be thrown at someone, and that was done with a simple change in the hand gesture that looked like she was pushing the ball away in the direction she wanted to throw it. Then, there were several variations of similar attacks that were all done by different hand gestures.

The recruits were all amazed by how much just one simple fire spell could do. It was, indeed, a very useful power. The class went on until dinner, before which Orenda concluded the session with the announcement that the recruits are all required to keep today's lessons in their memories as they will be exercising these spells in tomorrow's training session after lunch.

"Tomorrow, the fireballs will be in your hands to use as weapons. Proceed to dinner and have a good night's sleep. Tomorrow's session will be a tough one for you all." With that, Orenda left the grounds, and the recruits went for dinner.

"Hey," Alexa whispered to Anna. "Do you think we should try out any of those attack tactics?"

Anna looked at her eyes wide in surprise, "No!" She hissed. "We should live by the rules that our mentors set for us. We're not trained yet; we could harm someone!"

Alexa rolled her eyes at her, "Ah, you're such a teacher's pet…." She groaned.

Anna did not mind that. She was a fun-loving person but was also very responsible, mature, and disciplined. She thought what the consequences of her actions would be before she proceeded with any actions.

At dinner, the seven recruits had identified their regular table now. All groups among the recruits had unofficially marked their tables in the kitchen by simply sitting there regularly. It became an implied understanding of who sits at which table so there were no conflicts or unnecessary dramas.

The next day, they followed the same routine but learned newer things. During Ahiga's session in the morning, he told them what spirits truly are.

"The Great Spirit… the supreme force that governs everything that is living, dead, or inanimate. It is the spirit that looks after us when we are lost or troubled." He continued to discuss the numerous spiritual implementations and beliefs of the Native Americans, including the importance of spirit guardians in their lives.

"The Sun, the water, the Earth, the nature… everything looks out for us, protects us, sees us for who we are," He stated. The session soon turned into a discussion of how different tribes believe in similar yet slightly different concepts of the spirit.

"There is a spirit in all things. Above all, there is a spirit in us that does not vary in concept with any geographical boundaries or tribal connections. We are divine, and the purer our spirit is, the more divine our existence is. With bravery, fortitude, wisdom, and generosity, our spirits our fed…."

The way Ahiga talked to the recruits proved that he was, indeed, a true mentor. He motivated them, piqued their passion for fighting for their people, and encouraged them to find themselves.

Several days followed, and the recruits were being trained well both in terms of spirit magic and spiritual alignment. Orenda had taught them the telepathy spell by now, and the recruits enjoyed it the most. During these sessions, especially the ones involving telepathy, the seven recruits grew much closer to each other. They often communicated without words, which strengthened their connection on another level.

On the last three nights, they were moved into their own bedroom that had been set up for them. There were eight beds, and they took up seven of them.

Among other spirit magic spells, throughout their training at the Olta, the recruits learned how to teleport from one place to another, cast a protection dome spell, turn invisible to visible, and vice versa. They also learned other such skills that could help them win the war against the injustice of the US government. The medallion recruits would be the chosen ones to lead the warriors into the revolt against the US government and take over the White House. That was their goal, their sacred mission to liberate their people.

But, much earlier before they could even think about doing that, they had to fight the one entity encouraging all the violence against the Indians; the evil one thirsty for the blood of the Natives in the name of revenge, and the one influencing several governors and rulers as his brainwashed puppets to hurt the Natives.

"Do you think we can do that? Are we that powerful?" Anna once wondered aloud as they were all in their beds trying to sleep.

"I believe we can… Otherwise, we would not have been chosen by Chief Cayuga for this journey," Jeromy responded with great motivation.

He could not help but think to himself with his eyes closed how his life had changed dramatically, and more importantly, how he had transformed into this new, strong, motivated person.

"I used to be such a loser… Before I came here. Before I was chosen, I was just a college professor who would get sick at the sight of blood… and now…." Jeromy was talking dreamily, as if he could feel his old life gradually seeping out of him, away from him.

"And now, you're a warrior," his train of thoughts was interrupted by Anna's voice. He opened his eyes and looked to his side to see Anna in her bed, smiling at him.

The Olta had brought the seven recruits closer to each other. They had found friends and family in one another and were now indeed warriors who would not fear sacrificing even their lives for one another anymore.

It was their last day at the Olta now.

Ahiga returned to visit with the seven and asked to speak with Alexa, Denisse, and Alice.

"Your courage and spirit cannot be questioned, and your abilities will be very valuable." He began. "However, you three are the youngest, and we have concerns that you are not yet physically strong enough to become warriors… not yet at least. However, we have not made a final decision. The trial will begin. Continue working hard. We will be watching."

And then he walked over to join Orenda, who stood there waiting to say goodbye.

Alexa, Denise, and Alice shared their concerns quietly; however, they were at least happy that they could continue with their fellow recruits.

It was time to leave the Olta and begin the journey. The rest of the dozens of students were not yet ready for graduation trials and would stay back at the Olta and undergo further training. But now, it was time for the seven to leave for their trial destinations.

"Stay together, and stay loyal to each other," Orenda told them just as they were getting ready to leave.

"Remember, the spiritual powers bestowed unto you through our teachings must never be used for personal gain or evil intent. The purer your spirit is, the stronger your spirit magic abilities will be," Orenda warned them, knowing that it is easy for power to get to young people's heads.

"We have been chosen for a sacred mission, Orenda. We will never misuse our powers," Jeromy confirmed, speaking for his group.

"Good. Here is the scroll that you had found earlier. Chief Cayuga had indicated that it would guide your trial assignments once you leave the Olta," Orenda handed Jeromy a golden scroll, the one that they had found when they had just arrived at the Olta.

As soon as Jeromy unrolled the scroll to read it, it started to glow slightly again, and the words appeared on it:

"And the path of the playa is clear for you. Take the hourglass with you."

"The hourglass?" Anna looked confused. The recruits looked at Ahiga for clarification on the matter, and he nodded and reached into his satchel to take out a small hourglass. He looked at it for some time as if saying goodbye and then handed it over to Jeromy.

"Keep it well and safe, Jeromy Whitefeather." He added.

Jeromy looked briefly at the hourglass and noted what looked like four tiny tea leaves mixed with the sands. He nodded before putting the hourglass in his waist bag.

"Let the trials begin." Announced Orenda, and then he and Ahiga left the recruits to themselves after bidding farewell and wishing them luck. The recruits were now deciding on their pathway. They had to go to the Arch Playa of Berrime, the Hollow Caves of Lovesley, and the River of Cayuga and hold. They would not enter the Forest of Limbo yet.

After discussing who should go where, the seven recruits came up with a plan.

"Erik and I are going to the playa. Is that good with everyone?" said Jeromy.

"Wait! Look! The words vanished, and it's repeating something," added Denisse, referring to the scroll in Jeromy's hand, and she continued to read it out loud.

Take the scroll as a light in the dark beyond the mist in the shallow place.

Denisse then took the scroll in her hands, "Okay, let's go, Akwiraron!"

"No... sorry. I suppose I'm not as smart as you and Jeromy, but even I can tell that this clearly implies that your firepower wouldn't be enough there. Anna is needed." Akwiraron looked at Denisse questioningly.

"You're right...." Jeromy and Denisse jinxed, so she looked at him with a raised eyebrow.

"I guess it's time to light the way," replied Anna. "Den, you aren't strong in my realm; stick to yours, and Alexa... you come with me. Arch Playa of Berrime, here we come!"

Anna and Alexa started rushing towards the door.

"Now, what are you waiting for, Erik?" Jeromy asked.

It was at this point that Jeromy realized that his lifelong strength to read people was actually his power to read minds, literally.

He could hear Erik talking to himself, *"Ahhhh should I perform the teleportation spell? I think I can't do it! Dad..."*

And so, Jeromy subconsciously told him, *"You know that you're strong enough, Erik."*

Erik could not only sense Jeromy's power, but he felt a transfer of energy. Jeromy then grabbed his wrist, "Now, Erik."

"Celik Praraha!"

A mist that was moving as fast as a cyclone started circulating them from their feet till their heads, and then the two women warriors left the cottage behind as they vanished in thin air.

Chapter # 5:
Four Leaves in the Hourglass

Running deep towards the south of the River of Cayuga, Anna and Alexa felt a force pulling them to stand straight so firmly as if someone was trying to grab their feet from the ground beneath them.

"Did you feel that?!" Alexa exclaimed as she tied her hair, with a relief that the feeling left as quickly as it came. "Wait! Look! Your hand is glowing."

"I feel like this is someone from our…" then she started reading off of her hand.

Anna, we found a scroll. We haven't split yet.

"I suppose this is Jeromy," Alexa suggested with a smirk on her face as the message continued on the other hand.

We're supposed to meet by the thunderbirds at the entrance of the Forest of Limbo all together.

"I'm not quite sure at this instance," Anna replied with her sight fixed towards the message being inscribed on her hand in the interim. "It may be Denisse!"

"Probably! Only those two brains are capable of performing the interim inscription spell," Alexa agreed.

"How did you figure that out about Denisse?"

"Shhh… did you hear that?"

"No! What?!" Anna looked around in the opposite direction and said, "I think we should pick up the pace."

"Ummm… Anna, I think we should start running," Alexa said with an uneasy tone that Anna didn't expect from her.

"What happened?" Anna looked in her direction and, shocked, saw a few large crocodiles crawling towards them. The crocodiles had purplish scaly skin like that of a snake, and they slithered along the wet sands like nothing the girls had ever seen before.

"Crap! I have never seen this big of a crocodile." Anna said as they walked in a backward direction, freaking out. Apparently, their test had started.

"These aren't crocodiles!"

"Umm… What are they, then?!" Alexa asked in a panic.

"…They're cromendylus! Don't you see that?" Anna whispered to Alexa. "I think these are troops of another group. We may find more in the forest."

"Cromendylus? Never heard of that, but whatever it is, does not look good," Alexa stated in a rush of words as the two girls sped up their steps, trying to get away from the creatures following them.

"Yup, I saw them in the Olta during one of my classes! Now, run!" Anna exclaimed.

"Do you know the reverting spell?" Alexa replied, "I'll make sure that they don't follow us to the thunderbird totems."

"I don't understand! I can't do this without an Inadi!"

"What?! Have we made the right split, Anna?"

"Yes! Wait! Let me think!"

Within less than a few seconds, she ordered, "Quick! Give me your arrows!"

As soon as Anna started to perform the spell on the evil troops to revert them from Cromendylus to humans, they started running towards them by reverting half of their body back to men themselves.

"Hawa lantern ijo"

Anna blew it onto Alexa's arrows, and they started to float in the air with a green glow around them.

Alexa grabbed four of the seven green levitating arrows altogether, and as they jumped to attack them,

Anna gave voice to her energy, *"Crema Praha,"* and a protective dome appeared around them, and Alexa started to levitate in midair, shooting the arrows aimed right at the top of their heads.

"Bullseye!" shouted Anna.

At the other side of the picture, Erik and Jeromy had paired up along with Alice and teleported into a gush of air that left the cottage and landed right onto the arch playa of Berimme.

Their eyes opened under a wave of water.

"Look! Haha! I can't believe this, Jeromy!" Erik was quite happy for the far-reaching success of his spell to work, "The water is above us!"

"But I think we have a long way to go down there," Jeromy pointed down to the playa-of-a-water well.

"That's the way towards the Forest of Limbo."

By this time, all three groups were under trial and on their way towards the thunderbird entrance of Forest of Limbo which marks the end of the trial.

At another place, Denisse had been using a compass spell that she had learned in the Olta to find the way to the Hollow Caves of Lovesley. She was paired with Akwiraron for the journey, and they could now see a large tree in front of them.

As they proceed towards it, they see a passage in the form of a tree trunk, and upon entering it, they fall into a small corridor leading to three different alleys.

"Perform the spell again," Akwiraron said with a tone as soft as Denisse would not have expected, but then she heard a creepy, echoing voice from the cave and quickly turned to see what it was. It was a hollow '*Ooh*'ing sound, but the look on Akwiraron's face showed that he had heard nothing of the sort.

"What happened, Denisse?"

"Nothing," she ignored it and got the scroll out to perform not only the compass spell but simultaneously put the lantern spell on it as well, as she knew that her powers would not work beyond the caves.

"Ian! Ian!" Akwiraron started shouting and running towards one of the three cave alleys.

"You are going in the wrong direction!" Denisse tried to calm him down and grabbed his hand, stopping him from going. "What happened? Tell me!"

"I hear my little brother's voice!" He paused as his throat dried out, "He's calling me! I have to go!"

"Wait! This is a trick, Akwiraron!" Denisse put her hands on his shoulder, "I know… I know it sounds real, but it is not. Just a while ago, I heard my mother's voice as if she was drowning."

The door of the cave alley from where they were hearing voices closed immediately while they were talking, but then the scroll started to rotate in an unstoppable motion.

"What's going on?!" Akwiraron looked around, confused about what was happening.

"I don't know," Denisse responded.

"Wait! I sense danger!" Akwiraron saw something from the cave alley right next to the vanished one, but what Denisse saw had seized her breath midway!

"Aaaah!" She stumbled back and was about to fall when Akwiraron balanced her with his firm grip. She had seen human-size spiders from the one beside it that had disappeared now.

"I – I saw something. I saw large spiders there… in that one," Denisse pointed at the middle passage.

"Hmm.. another hallucination? Then I suppose that our destination is none of these doors. Do you know a spell that will show a hidden passage, Denisse?"

"Sing ora katon" shouted Denisse. A passage showed above the cave alley in the middle, and the two recruits enter it as they feel that it is the right one.

"Well done, Den!" remarked Akwiraron.

Suddenly, Denisse saw the huge spiders again in this alley as well. "We might need a defense… You never know when these hallucinations might be a reality," Denisse pointed out.

"Wait, you see it, too?" Akwiraron gasped.

"Uh oh, that must mean that they are real?" Denisse yelped.

"Pedhang Cayuga!"

Akwiraron quickly performed the spell, and a sword in his hand appeared as he chopped a few giant spider heads. Quickly grabbing Denisse, he jumped into the passage above their heads.

"We found the way, Akwiraron!" Both laughed with excitement, "This is the passage to the Forest of Limbo."

While they were about to reach their destination, Jeromy, Alice and Erik were proceeding as well. Jeromy looked down into the well and turned to Erik.

"I know your element is water," he said. "But do you mind if I do this?"

"Sure, Jeromy. If I'm right about you, you have more than one elemental power anyway."

"I never have… but somehow I know this." Jeromy paused and recalled a conversation with grandma when she told him

"Jeromy, you know you can make people travel through water."

"How ma?!"

"I remember now" He came back to the present,

Oh, Adam's Ale. Let me travel through the water like a whale.

He just thought this to himself as he said, *"Angat kula,"* and the water above their head came down to their feet, and they stood tall on its surface and, like being in an all-glass elevator, and it carried the three of them down to the mist near the Forest of Limbo.

"Outstanding!" shouted Erik.

"Holy Spirits!" exclaimed Alice.

As soon as the three reached there, they saw a portal that opened with Denisse and Akwiraron coming from it, and all five of them advanced near a boiling pond.

The portal suddenly turned reddish-orange with hot lava, and Akwiraron says while he's ready to cover himself up, "Guys, don't you feel like this is going to explode?"

But then, they started to feel a wave of heat around them, and they saw two shadows emerging. When the heat started to raise the air temperature around them, they saw two people coming and braced themselves, ready to fight. As they saw their faces, they relaxed their postures.

"Why? Wait!" Erik was shocked to see Anna and Alexa coming out of the pond.

So, Denisse rushed towards her friends, "Are you okay, guys?"

Anna stood up out of the pond but then fell to her knees to catch a breath and then smiled, after which she stood up again immediately. Alexa looked at her, and they both started laughing.

Alexa continued, "We reached the River of Cayuga, and then we performed the Earthing spell. That was how we were able to find the way to the blood moon beneath the river."

"Then we swam to find a catacomb beneath the south of the river, and when we entered it, I used a fire spell to boil the water out of the way and carry us to the one straight path we saw there."

"It was that easy for you guys?" Akwiraron asked with a confused expression on his face.

After hearing that, Alexa fell completely to the ground, and Anna answered for her, "Trust me! No!"

The seven were very happy to see each other. They decided to sit for a few minutes as they continued to share their trials. After several minutes, a foul breeze started blowing through the darkness.

"This air smells evil," said Anna.

"Yes, like death on the wind," replied Jeromy. "Let's get moving."

The troops looked in the direction the putrid air was traveling from and saw the mist parting to reveal the towering thunderbirds. Between them was an incredible blackness. Absolute nothing.

"Well, we know what that is," said Erik.

"Entrance to the Forest of Limbo…" added Anna.

"Yeah, as Jeromy said, let's get going," replied Akwiraron.

As all the troops moved away from the thunderbirds and forward to the mist in the forest, they came across an electric barrier from which they couldn't seem to proceed. It looked like blue-black barbed wires, like a regular barbed wire fence, but also had an eerie blue sleek ray of electricity swirling around each wire that glowed in the darkness of the forest and appeared to pop off white fireflies through the mist.

Denisse jogged forward to touch it, and she was electrified again. "Yeeooow! Why me?!"

They turned to see some people walking towards them. The recruits looked in their direction and saw that they all walked in a line as if they were marching.

"So… it's time for the recruits?!" said Erik, judging by the look of the scene.

"Yes," Denisse answered, "But I thought the trial was over?"

With that, the wind started to blow like a storm. The rustle of dried leaves on the ground made them all expect something big, something magical, to happen. The sky above them turned darker, and the view was taken as a surprise for all those who looked as four portals opened in midair above Jeromy, Erik, Akwiraron, and Anna.

As soon as they, along with everyone else, started to understand what this might mean, a levitating scroll dropped down to the ground from one of the portals and fell at Jeromy's feet. Immediately after they reached to grab the scroll, the portals became enlarged and teleported the four chosen recruits to the other side of the barrier.

Chapter # 6:
The Forest of Limbo

Confused, Jeromy, Akwiraron, Erik, and Anna walked through the mist in the forest. Turning back, they realized they were now on the other side of the electrifying barrier and noticed that Alice, Alexa, and Denisse stood there waving goodbye.

They stopped briefly, and upon looking deeper, the chosen recruits realized that the three on the other side of the barrier were discussing how they couldn't see them anymore and wished they could have continued.

"Where did they go?" Denisse cried out loud.

"I feel like they are on the other side of the wall," Alexa replied as she moved closer towards the barrier.

"Are we splitting for another round of tests?"

"I thought that this was the last one."

"No! I mean…" she trailed off.

"Yeah. You're right. Do you realize what this means?" She pondered.

Denisse walked towards the wall when she figured that she and Alexa had reached the same conclusion. The three girls were only inches away from being electrocuted and immediately turned back as they heard a loud screech.

It was a call for an announcement. They saw the crowd of all the natives and warriors who had made it this far. As the chosen recruits observed what was going on in confusion, the barrier disappeared from both sides, and Jeromy, Akwiraron, Erik, and Anna could not see them anymore. They could only see the forest's darkness where the barrier once stood before it vanished. And with it, all those people, including Alexa, Alice, and Denisse, vanished too.

Suddenly, the three who were behind heard a thumping rhythm somewhere nearby in the forest. Turning around, they saw a group of the tribesmen walking towards them, beating drums and cymbals in the traditional way. Then, from amongst them, one man stepped forward.

Denisse noticed how the group's clothes and physique were similar to that of Akwiraron, except they were all buffed up and had army-cut hair.

"Congratulations, young ones! You are among the people recruited for Chief Cayuga's army. I am general Wische." The man who stepped forward announced.

"I feel confused and left behind! If we're all recruits, how did they end up in the Forest of Limbo without passing the thunderbirds? And how did they pass through that electrified barrier?" Denisse whispered to Alexa, ignoring the announcement.

General Wische answered her question.

"The barrier that you see behind you is an enchanted wall to protect you from the Forest of Limbo and its dark entities. When your training is completed, and you are tested there, only then will I say we prepared you to be on the frontline of the battlefield. You have not yet witnessed and have no intimation of what is about to come your way. I believe the chosen four will prevail."

General Wische continued speaking as he turned towards the other side and started going towards a portal that opened and expanded by a very powerful spell that none of them had ever witnessed before.

"Nggedhekake Cakrawala!" He chanted.

Everyone, including Alexa, Denisse, and Alice, walked into the enchanted portal that looked like an elevator on a circular passage of purple and blue clouds from which they could hear thunderstorms.

"No matter which coterie you get selected for, remember, the common thing that led all of you here is not just your bravery, but the alliance that lives in each soul walking here." He explained.

"Quick! Alexa! Try the inscription spell. We need to contact Anna and the others!" Denisse whispered.

"What? You already know, I can't do it without…Oh…." Alexa trailed off.

"Okay!" Alexa put her hand in mid-air to continue as Denisse tried to read the spell.

"I hope they are alright in that dark, foul place. I am scared for them!" Denisse whispered worriedly.

"Don't be scared! You're supposed to be brave, remember?" Alexa reminded her.

Denisse made a rather eerie expression, almost as an amalgamation of being happy and upset at the same time. Of course, the three girls were delighted at being original recruits, but at the same time, they were wary of where their other fellows would be by now and whether they were okay or not.

"Oh, for God's sake! No, don't! Please, Denisse!" Alexa replied with a rather sarcastic tone, but as soon as she noticed that her comment would probably make her have a playa throat, she added, "You look like you're trying to laugh in front of a scorching sunlight afternoon. You're all red-faced. Calm down!"

Denisse laughed as they attempted to try the spell but felt an electric jolt through their veins to jinx it.

"Ouch!" They exclaimed as they realized that their spells were not working here.

In the meantime, on the other side of the barrier, Anna suddenly felt a pinch in her forearm.

"Ahhhh!" She fell on the damp forest ground.

"Are you alright?" Jeromy immediately held her hand. As he helped her get up, his gaze fell upon her arm.

"Wait! Look at your arm, Anna." He exclaimed.

"What?" She yelped just as a blurry message started appearing on her arm.

"Where are you?" The message read.

"I'm worried!" Another message appeared as the first one was erased.

"It's Denisse! I think she doesn't know we're here. She's worried about us." She said.

"I don't even know why we are here or where we are supposed to be," Akwiraron says.

"People are being...."

Anna grabbed Jeromy's hand for the continuation as she ran out of breath because of the continuous little shocks she was getting every time a message decrypted onto her skin.

"...assigned coteries."

"Wa-wait, Anna!" Jeromy pulled her up, "Erik! Akwiraron! I feel like this is some sort of test!" He exclaimed.

"Something we never studied or knew about? I don't know...." Erik added. "Are you certain?"

Jeromy nodded his head, glanced at Erik, and whispered in Anna's ear.

"Let me send them a message." He said.

He clutched her fist and performed the spell.

We're okay! Don't contact us right now.

Both yelled out in pain, bent forward towards the ground, then stood back up immediately.

"Guys, I don't know whether or not this is a test or conspiracy against the enemies," Jeromy said.

"Yes! Because if this were to be a test, we would probably have known for something like this to happen from the scriptures, or a hint or some sort of connection should have been made by now." He said.

"Guys! Do you smell that?" asked Anna, wrinkling her nose at the smell of death in the air.

"Guys! Do you hear that?!" Akwiraron gasped and turned to where he thought the voice was coming from.

A nebulous Osprey sprung out amidst the dark forest. It was shining from a distance, and as it got closer, they noticed something.

"Guys! Am I the only one who can see this? That Osprey is about my size." Akwiraron walked backward quickly with his eyes wide with fear.

"And its wings alone are about Jeromy's size." He continued.

Jeromy looked at him with a flat face as the three of them ran.

"No, wait! Guys, it's Cayuga's bird!" Anna announced as she noticed Cayuga's headband's feathers on it.

"Anna, he had a flock of finches as far as I can remember," Erik tried to remember.

"A flock of finches that will turn into a nebulous Osprey that will be seen and help those people in tranquility." Jeromy recited.

"Yes! Exactly!" Erik exclaimed.

"I'm still confused! Is this a test? Why are we only ones being tested?" Akwiraron added.

"Are we? Or are we in some sort of trouble? Why else would Chief Cayuga help?" Erik pondered.

"You are right! This is not a test, I'm sure!" Anna added.

A robust, foul gust made it hard for them to stand as the Osprey landed in front of them.

"Are you sure this isn't some sort of delusion spell? Someone may try to depict Cayuga's powers." Akwiraron whispered worriedly in Anna's ear.

"No! No one is as…." Jeromy tried to answer Akwiraron, but the Osprey walked closer to them. It illuminated as they heard a voice coming from within themselves.

"… *Strong as me. And no one can have the power to depict the ones I hold.*" The voice said.

"It's Chief Cayuga!" Erik exclaimed with a dry throat as the others almost started crying. The Osprey only smirked at seeing that.

My young recruits, you are in danger, but don't be afraid; I'm with you. Be strong!" He said.

The Osprey opened his left wing, and a scroll levitated from under it and flowed in front of them.

Take this! And remember: the Forest of Limbo is full of dangers. Don't rely on anything but each other. You will have to face the Dark Lord's black raven on your way out of this place.

"Has Blaine Keir blocked the way to the catacombs?" Anna asked.

"What? We are the medallions?!" Akwiraron exclaimed in shock, realizing his wish was granted.

Jeromy, Anna, Akwiraron, and Erik, the scroll was supposed to transport you to your final stage as the medallion recruits. But because the scrolls were effused in front of the thunderbirds that guard the entrance to the dark barrier, Keir transported you to the evil layer.

"How do we get out of here?" Erik questioned.

Follow the light…

Follow my voice…

Follow me, follow me, and come to my doorway.

Back at the recruitment camp, the girls were equally afraid of the unknown.

"Do you think we should inform General Wische?" asked Denisse.

"Yes! I can't exactly comprehend whether they have performed the spell to cut the connection or if they are in trouble!" Alexa replied as they went to the base camp of the General to inform him.

"You two were performing the interim spell in the portal?" He had a map in his hand to track all recruits for safety reasons.

"Not only is it dangerous, but it is prohibited." He scolded them.

"Sir, we had continuous shocks to perform it. We weren't being experimental. We are well-aware of the consequences." Denisse said, with her head bowed down.

"May I know the purpose?" He put the scroll of a map down, folded his arm, and raised his eyebrow.

Denisse sensed things were getting angst there, so she added, "Sir! Our friends are missing!"

"A portal opened above them, and as soon as they got into it, they vanished," Alexa added to the explanation.

"What?!" Both of them noticed the difference in his expression. Instead of being disappointed, the General looked concerned now.

"Where exactly did this take place?" He asked.

"Near the barrier!" Alexa answered.

"Uh…" He trailed off.

"No… that is not good." He inhaled as if he had just heard the bad news.

"What happened, Sir?" Denisse asked, concerned.

"They are in danger! They are far into the Forest of Limbo, and only Cayuga can help them now. We knew that something like this could happen. But we made the powerful barrier to…." He paused, "Ahhhh… hold on, girls! I'll look into this." He finally said.

At this point, they all figured that everything that had happened up till now was a fierce fusion of what was fated and that anything could happen. But they were unaware that their friends were only getting stronger as they faced challenges, and it was, in fact, part of their training to be prepared for such challenges.

Meanwhile, the four in Limbo gathered in a circle and put their right hands out up front to grab on to each other.

"Guys! Gather around!" insisted Jeromy. "We're performing the telepathy spell!"

"Nglacak lan maca sesanti." They chanted together. They had learned this in one of their standard classes in Olta, and now it was coming in handy.

"Do you see that, Akwiraron?" Erik asked with a smirk on his face. Knowing that Akwiraron's wish to be a part of the medallion had come true.

As the shield of their elements surrounded them, they could see their reflection on the shield and feel the energy circulating throughout their bodies.

Suddenly, before the spell was even activated, something strange happened. Among the glowing circle of elements around the recruits, something else appeared. The outline of Jeromy's body seemed to vibrate, sparkle, and transform. It was a rather dramatic change.

"Ummmm… guys!" exclaimed Anna. "Am I the only one who can see this?"

Jeromy's eyes were wide with alarm. He adjusted his heavy glasses up tight onto his nose and braced himself.

"Oh, my God!" the smile vanished from Akwiraron's face, and complete astonishment replaced it as he turned towards Jeromy.

"What happened, guys?"

The way his fellow recruits were looking at him confused Jeromy.

He felt a change in him within the past few seconds, and he felt stronger, more confident, and somewhat different, but he was not sure why the others were looking at him like that.

"Do you feel that, Jeromy?" Erik almost yelped.

Jeromy took a slow, deep breath, probably the deepest of his life. He suddenly felt calmer than he had ever felt before.

"Feel what?" Jeromy was unsure if the others could somehow tell that he felt changed. He didn't think it was possible.

"Your transformation…?" Akwiraron clarified.

"The metamorphosis." Adds Erik wide-eyed.

"Yes!" Jeromy exclaimed, as everyone confirmed his transformation. He looked around, but everything had become fuzzy. Removing his glasses to clean them, he noticed everything became crystal clear without the glasses.

"I can see, I mean, see clearly!" he exclaimed excitedly.

As the reflective shield reached from his feet up to cover his head, he realized what they were talking about. Shock took over him as he could see his reflection in the shield that encircled him.

"What…" Jeromy blurted out, "Just happened?" He couldn't believe that he had just undergone whole body-altering healing.

"Wow!" Anna exclaimed with a clear throat. "Jer, you got buff!"

"Holy Spirits!" exclaimed Akwiraron.

"Yeah, dude, you look like you just gained 25 or 30 pounds of muscle, too!" yelped Erik.

Jeromy looked back at Anna with a smirk as she looked away shyly.

"Umm… guys, we need to go." Erik said, bringing everyone back to the present.

"You know, guys, I think we should be more strategic with the paths we are going to take rather than fighting directly against the Dark Lord. This might as well be his strategy." Akwiraron thought out loud.

"For which we shouldn't fall for." Added Erik.

"Yeah!" Jeromy nodded. "You guys are right. And we need to think carefully about spells, too. They may go sideways here in Limbo." He turned to Anna, who was staring at him again with eyes wide open.

"Ha… Yes?!" Anna looked towards Erik and Akwiraron, "Yes, yes, let's do this, ah, I mean, let's go." She said, flustered.

Jeromy smiled and continued, as he knew the transformation still struck her.

"Remember, we need to find a way to the river of Cayuga." He reminded everyone.

"The portal that got us to this side!" Erik shrugged and continued. "Something like that might as well be on our way back."

"So, what should we do?!" Added Anna.

"Yeah, Jeromy! No matter how much we dodge danger, something is clearly planned at the last stage." Akwiraron sighed heavily.

"Don't you guys remember what Chief Cayuga said?" Jeromy rubbed his right hand on his head as he exhaled with new confidence.

"It's alright, guys! We'll find a way! I know we will." He said cheerfully.

The telepathy spell was already activated. Anna suddenly felt a minor shock in her arm and saw a message appear.

"Get to the other side of the barrier! That side is governed by the Dark." The words inscribed on her skin said, as Anna fell to her knees in pain.

"Are you alright?!" Jeromy grabbed her as she grunted.

"It was probably a message from Denisse," she said, trying to get up and balance herself.

"Yeah. Well, I think we should let them know we are trying to make it out of here, and we'll be alright. They would be worried for us, otherwise." Akwiraron suggested.

"I'll do it. I'll send them a message, but Anna needs to avoid sending or receiving any further messages now." Jeromy commanded, which made Anna feel protected and warm. She smiled at him, and he started the telepathy spell.

"We're okay. We're trying to find a way out. Don't worry". He sent the message to Denisse, who was standing in the General's office when she received the painful shocks in her arm as the words appeared on her skin.

"They responded!" Denisse announced with a painful grunt.

The General had allowed Denisse to send one message to the detoured recruits to warn them of the danger they were in so that they could prepare. At the same time, arrangements were being made to get them out of the Forest of Limbo. Upon seeing the message on Denisse's arm, the General smiled.

"Don't worry. Your friends will be alright." He said finally.

Chapter # 7:
Twilight in Limbo

"Do you remember 'The History of the Dark Spirits' classes?" asked Erik.

"Oh, my God! Why do I feel like I already know what you're talking about?" Anna exclaimed.

"Was I good at that class, or am I able to read your mind now?" She wondered. Erik shrugged while Jeromy just laughed and said.

"No, I think you were just good at that class. But I don't know!" He shrugged again and continued, "You might be stirred by the fact that you're a medallion."

Anna immediately whipped her hand on Jeromy's chest.

"Hey!" Jeromy said. "Just got super strength. Better not mess with me right now." He laughed.

"Okay! I wasn't expecting that." Akwiraron said awkwardly. He turned towards Erik, trying to bring the focus back on the issue at hand.

"And what are we missing out on?" He inquired.

"…Umm, there's a secret passage in the middle of the wood. North to the River of Cayuga, opposite to the mist from the Forest of Limbo. They taught us this in the Dark Spirits class, I think." Anna answered Akwiraron, thinking hard.

"Legend says that the portal is in a tree trunk of an invisible tree that appears in the dark only when the moon goes down, and is most prominent when there is an eclipse." Erik explained.

"And how exactly are we going to wait for an eclipse here?" asked Akwiraron.

Everyone whipped towards him like a bolt of lightning out of the blue hit them. It suddenly struck them!

"Akwiraron, you and Erik are thinking of Wakan Tanka Land?" Jeromy asked.

"Wow, Jey, that is creepy! Did you read their minds?" Anna yelped.

"It's okay, guys. Hey, don't you remember the Wakan Tanka land on the border? The land of the divine?" Erik replied while laughing.

"Yes! Oh, yes! That's what I was thinking! But how are we going there?" Akwiraron exclaimed.

"By…" Anna tries to tell him, but he cut her off.

"… the transportation spell. Yes, I know, but that's not what I'm trying to say. We're kind of short on time. Don't you remember the hourglass?" He said.

"Yes, that's true." Jeromy pointed out and continued, "We should split up!"

"So, here's the plan. Nobody is going to suspect us being at the Wakan Tanka land. That land has departed spirits and the lunar well. If we drink its water and pair it with someone whose powerful element is Earth, which in our case is going to be Akwiraron, we can control the moon's movement temporarily." Erik explains.

"It is done, then! Akwiraron and I are going to collect the water from the well from Wakan Tanka land, while you and Anna can find the tree and tell us by the telepathy spell. How does that sound?" Erik said as he laid out his well-thought plan.

"Yeah! You can – no, wait! Anna cannot afford more telepathy, so send any messages to me when you have to." Jeromy objected.

"Also, if you use the echoing spell, it'll make it obvious that this is a decoy attack." He concluded.

"Hmm. Yes, so I can use the earthing spell by the water in that land," says Akwiraron.

"There you are! Your brain is wor-"

"Shhh!... get down!" Akwiraron interrupted Anna, hissing as he pulled her down just as all of them heard a loud howling noise and Erik and Jeromy immediately ducked.

"Are those wolves?" asked Anna, whispering louder than necessary.

"Keep it down, Anna," Akwiraron whispered in her ears.

"These aren't any ordinary wolves. They're Calarodos! And clearly, they don't hunt alone!" Jeromy added.

"And why exactly are we sitting here?" Anna pondered as she added rhetorically to the entire gang, hinting at the action that was about to begin.

"Yeah! Let's get in action!" exclaimed Akwiraron. "Wait…Cala-what-so?" he paused, suddenly realizing how little knowledge he possessed about the situation.

"Calm down, tiger!" Erik pulled him back. "Jeromy, I think we need to use your shield to hide us all." He turned to Jeromy.

"Alrighty, Sir!" Jeromy obeyed.

"Ndhelik nganggo hawa!" Jeromy stood up and flicked his fingers.

"Calarodos are wolves that can shape-shift to an animal you like, or one that you are *familiar with*, as a disguise to attack you," Erik explained to Akwiraron quickly.

"Got it. About Jeromy, though, is it just me or the guy grew confidence that he missed out on entirely earlier?" Akwiraron said, glancing at Jeromy.

Meanwhile, Jeromy continued standing bravely in the face of the wolves while the rest of the recruits still crouched on the ground.

"That's kinda hot!" Anna exclaimed and stood up too.

"This… what the hell happened to this guy, man?!" Erik exclaimed.

"Yup! Exactly what I meant!" replied Akwiraron.

"Guys! Stand up!" exclaimed Jeromy, just as a blue shield surrounded and camouflaged them with the colors of the forest.

"Now wh –" Akwiraron tried to ask before getting interrupted by Erik.

"Shhh! Dude, the spell is to vanish from the naked eye. Doesn't exactly block the sound going outside from the shield." He explained.

"Oh, yeah! Sorry!" Akwiraron said guiltily, running his hand through his hair.

"Okay, now we have to perform the teleportation spell. Anna and I will be off to find the tree. Erik and Akwiraron, get to the Wakan Tanka land." Jeromy ordered.

"Celik Praraha!" The medallions chanted the teleportation spell together. Unfortunately, they were all transported to the riverside in a forest instead of where they had intended to go, and to top it all off, the sun was getting low on the horizon.

"I don't understand. Jeromy, what happened?" Erik panicked.

"Ndhelik nganggo hawa!" Jeromy immediately puts a spell to get the invisibility shield off.

"You're asking me? Shit! Erik. You guys need to... I think I needed to get the shield off of us for the spell to work." Jeromy realized.

"Yeah, I guess. let's find a safe spot." Akwiraron agreed, pointing to a small clearing in the mist next to the river.

Looking at the water, Anna reached down and touched it.

"Why does this water look like – ouch!" she exclaimed. "Shit! It's like acid! Guys, no! We shouldn't be here either."

"So much for Wanka Tanka land, guys," Erik sighed.

"There's something strange about this place," warned Anna.

"Akwiraron! Can you perform the Wektu spell?" Jeromy asked with a dry throat.

Akwiraron nodded and attempted to open a portal, but got electrocuted.

"I don't understand. It's not…." He trailed off.

"Guys, this is still Limbo and a timeless realm…." Erik pointed towards the sky. "We shouldn't be here. Can't you hear your heartbeat? And feel the thin air. It is all too similar as it was when we were going through that train that transported us to this age." He spoke.

"It's twilight!" Anna yelped. "We're stuck! It only gets darker from here, and we have no way out. God only knows what the night awaits!" She panicked.

Suddenly, all of them heard a dreadful howl, and Jeromy looked around at everyone in panic.

"Guys, this is what Chief Cayuga was talking about. We're being attacked by foulas. They warned us of these creatures in the Forest of Limbo while we were in the Olta, remember?" He remembered.

The foulas looked like shadows with glowing yellow eyes and were shaped like giant gorillas. Their existence was neither entirely physical nor invisible, but somewhere in between, like a gaseous, hulking shadow.

"Jeromy, there's no way we're ready..." Erik said breathlessly as the voice got closer.

"Please do something, Jeromy. I didn't really pay much attention in that class!" Anna said, stepping closer to Jeromy. She was shaking from fear, as she felt unprepared to combat the beasts that were now looking at them with an intense glowing glare.

These dark entities travelled only to this realm from the underworld after being called by the Dark Lord. They hid among bats but were always easily identifiable by those who are aware of their appearance. They couldn't even "poison" their prey, and enough poison could turn the prey into a Foula.

* * *

Meanwhile, back at the Mohawk Recruitment Bureau, the word had spread out about four of the recruits missing. As Denisse, Alice, and Alexa weren't the only people that witnessed the disappearance, and the General had sent orders to watch out for them, too, there was growing concern surfacing with time.

"Guys, don't worry, we'll find a way." Jeromy tried to console the others.

But the howling sound turned into a loud screeching sound that kept on getting closer and closer so much that Anna had to put her hands on her ears, screaming because of the pain. Jeromy became worried and grabbed her. He held her close and tried to help cover her ears.

When Jeromy was certain they would attack them, he prepared to form a defensive spell, but the sound ceased suddenly.

Anna pulled herself together and walked a few steps away as all four of them started looking towards the sky.

There was still a heavy presence around them, but they could see no enemies as they looked around.

"Anna, no! Look out!" Akwiraron shouted, breaking the silence.

Anna dove to the ground just in time as a huge foula flew by, trying to grab her. Several others were also circling overhead and shrieking loudly.

Anna jumped back up, tracking the flight of the attacking monster as it turned around to make another run at her.

"*Dibakar nganggo Geni!*" She shouted, pointing directly at the beast.

Immediately, her hand looked like a flamethrower with a 50-foot stream of fire that caught the foula by surprise. It caught fire, screamed, turned to ash, and then a blue-black dust and vanished with air.

But the other foulas dived at her while she was toasting the first one. One of them grabbed hold of her and attacked her with its very thin sharp needles into the front of her head. It immediately sedated her, preventing her from casting any more spells at her attackers. The attack was over in seconds, faster than the others could manage spells to assist.

Jeromy, Erik, and Akwiraron turned back to look as the demon raised her up in midair. It used its eyes to gaze within her eyes and extract everything good she ever saw and heard.

The foulas had the power to take away all the goodness one had in them, including all their good memories. After this stage of their attack, they left the preys with poison to make the preys become attackers themselves with no soul or humanity left in them.

"Jeromy, what do we do?" Erik shouted as he tried to perform the interim spell to speak to Anna. But her eyes blacked out as the foulas shrieked sounds like a thousand children screaming and crying as they were burning from inside.

Chapter # 8:
The Yandellion Forest

Before the foula could poison Anna as their finishing move, Jeromy barked out a spell. He bent air in the forest to cause a concentrated storm that attacked the foulas.

"Bledheg mogok udhara!"

Suddenly, the temperature dropped, and darkness fell. Air swirled everywhere like cyclones. Leaves and branches ripped from trees with shredding and tearing. A thunderclap of lightning struck a nearby stump.

With their panicking shrieks, the foulas fled the ferocious storm. Within a minute, the air warmed, debris settled to the ground, and the air became sweet to smell. It was light again.

The recruits quickly ran over to Anna and saw her lips and skin return to pink and no longer the earlier pale purple that the attack had inflicted upon her. She opened her eyes with a grunt, and her hand naturally went to her head that was hurting from the attack that she had just endured.

Meanwhile, Jeromy held her hand and laid her on his lap to allow her to rest before they could get up and get going.

"Hey!" Akwiraron exclaimed. "There's someone here! Some humans! I can tell by feeling the Earth."

"Maybe someone has come to save us?" Erik said hopefully.

Anna rolled her eyes before muttering, "Or maybe someone is stuck here like us…." She was tired of the attacks.

"Anna!" Denisse came running towards the riverside, and the group of recruits was surprised to see her. An older man dressed in military clothing was following her.

"General! These are the recruits, my friends, that I told you about." Denisse informed the General, who looked relieved to have found them yet tensed to be there.

"Guys, this is General Wische" Denisse added

General Wische saw Jeromy holding Anna.

"Chief Cayuga sent word to help. I brought Denisse to assist. You're not supposed to be here like this. None of us are. Let's get going now." The General ordered strictly. "Quickly, gather together in a circle! Which of you is Jeromy Whitefeather?"

Denise pointed to Jeromy and held on tightly to her friend Anna and the six of them gathered together.

"Jeromy, you are to perform the teleportation spell forward while I perform it backward. Do it Now!"

"Celik Praraha," shouted Jeromy.

"Praraha Celik!" the general commanded.

The last thing the six of them saw was them flying by the tall Thunderbird Totems. Then they landed softly onto a grassy knoll overlooking a primitive fort a short distance away.

* * *

"Everyone!" General Wische turned to the crowd of recruits at the headquarters, "Welcome the Medallion recruits."

Then he gestured the four recruits, Akwiraron, Erik, Jeromy, and Anna, to step forward. The entire Bureau and the young recruits started cheering.

"These four recruits are chosen to lead the coteries. These are Cayuga's Four-Leaf Clover Medallion Recruits!" The General announced.

Everyone applauded.

Although all of them were overwhelmed at the moment about whether they'd be able to handle being surrounded by people all the time. The one thing that was well-occupied in Jeromy's head was about how they were going to lead the recruits of all four coteries.

Once again, General Wische asked for everyone's attention.

"Jeromy Whitefeather... please step forward."

Jeromy walked toward the general with confidence while many clapped him on the back and expressed their admiration.

"Jeromy Whitefeather. You have mighty spirit magic. Even in the mist of the Forest of Limbo, the spirits have healed and strengthened you as a way of showing their approval of your heart, mind, and spirit. We also saw how you commanded the very weather without fear. This will be a huge advantage in the coming battles. The elders and I have been watching. We would like you to consider accepting an important name, a name that has been mentioned in the scriptures for hundreds of years."

General Wische unfolded a blanket to reveal a large white feather and leather band.

"Jeromy Whitefeather. It is your destiny to now be known simply as 'White Feather.'"

Jeromy bent his head forward slightly, and the general tied the feather onto Jeromy's head with the leather band.

"Everyone! I present to you – WHITE FEATHER!"

Applause, whoops, howls and cheers went up everywhere.

A few moments later, Denisse walked past the crowd and gave Anna a tight hug.

"I'm so proud of you. I can't believe you made it."

"Neither can I…" Anna was still confused. *Leading a coterie? ME?*

"Wow, what do you think of White Feather," Denise teased her.

Anna smiled put her hands on Denisse's shoulder, and then turned her towards the direction of where Jeromy was standing.

"What?!" exclaimed Jeromy and shrugged, as his face turned red with shyness.

"Oh, my Gosh! You know, at first, I didn't recognize you. What happened to you?" Denisse put her hands on her face while raising her eyebrows. "That's one hell of a transformation."

"I'll tell you all about it tonight." Anna looked flirtatiously at Jeromy, took her bag off her shoulder, and put it on Denisse's shoulder.

Denisse pulled her hair back from Anna's shoulder and whispered into her ear, "We got a cabin with Alexa, and I hope you don't mind."

"No, why would I mind?" Anna immediately yelped and continued in the same tone as that of her best friend, "Why'd you ask me that? Is everything alright?" She gasped as if suddenly worried. "Did I say something to make her feel bad?"

At that moment, Akwiraron interrupted their conversation as he put his arms on both of their shoulders, "Ladies! Why don't you save the gossip for later tonight? Right?"

Denisse and Anna laughed as both of them agreed with Akwiraron's sense of responsibility.

"Recruits! Please gather around!" exclaimed General Wische as he continued, "Verily, this moment is something worth celebrating. And White Feather, Anna, Akwiraron, and Erik, we are all very proud of you. And so is Chief Cayuga. Of course. After all, you are his Medallion Recruits."

The recruits start hooting to this again, even louder. But the celebration was short-lived as General Wische had more to say. "However…this is just the first phase of the challenges that are up ahead. For everyone who has gathered around here, remember to batten down your hatches.", He took a slight pause, after which he continued , "Tomorrow, all of you will be assigned to your coteries, after which the training will begin—starting with training your Wendigos. Bring something to cover your noses. Dismissed!"

"With that tone, I'm not quite sure if I should be excited or paranoid with General Wische taking the first class," said Erik as he joined Akwiraron, Denisse, and Anna.

"Am I the only one, or does this feel like we're back in school?" asked Akwiraron.

"And am I the only one, or is Mr. Hotshot over there getting more attention?" added Anna, looking at Jeromy, who was talking to one of the other female recruits.

"Why?" Denisse smirked and continued, "Are you jealous?"

"Okay, now I definitely feel like I'm back in school." Anna exhaled.

Later that night, everyone gathered around for a convention with a campfire. It gave everyone more time to bond further and process everything that had recently happened.

After all, four of the medallions had settled in their cabin, and they walked out towards the campfire area. It was quite late. And it was like the white thread of the dawn became manifested unto them from the black thread of night at the dawn break.

Anna stood alone near the cold forest, rubbing her upper arms up and down to keep herself warm.

"*Murup geni,*" Akwiraron tried to put on the fire where the woods were still warm from when the recruits were settled in, and they were fighting the dark entities in the forest.

"Well tried, medallion!" Alexa rubbed her hands and then blew on them as a minor fire orb released and levitated in the air. Alexa then directed it to the firewood and said, "*Murup geni.*"

"Impressive!" Akwiraron shrugged and continued, "Might as well be overwhelmed by now... Ah... I mean, I suppose."

"You don't have to...you just might as well be nervous...."

"Around you..."

"No, I meant by the situation at hand, Romeo." Both of them start laughing. "No, I am actually kidding... Um... I did mean by being around me. Although..." Alexa turned towards Akwiraron, "Why? Do you not find me aggressive?"

"Aggressive?" Akwiraron exclaimed, "For a minute, I actually thought that you are a Roh Jahat."

This time their laughter reached out to Erik, Anna, and Jeromy, who were coming in late to their secret meeting.

"I think the guy needs some time" Jeromy said.

"And I know that you will find it rather weird coming from me, but can we do this tomorrow. For now, I think we should all get some rest." Erik put his hand on his waist as he ran out of breath and stretched down to grab hold of his knees. "I am exhausted," he said with his head down.

"No!" yelped Anna.

"Yes!" said Jeromy at the same instance.

"Why would you say that?" Anna's pitch changed immediately, given that she wanted to spend some more time with him before just going to sleep.

Erik pulled himself back up and said, "Okay…you two love birds enjoy. I'm going to go take a nap." And he turned around to leave the premises.

Jeromy held Anna's hand, smiled softly, and asked, "Anna, would you want to go to the lake with me?"

"Yeah," She smiled at him.

"Cool, it's less than a mile from…." He began to say when she cut him off.

"Jeromy…" She smirked and turned towards him to say, "We're magical beings! We could go there at a snap… but at this time… the villagers…."

"Umm… no, actually. I really wanted to be able to walk with you. And… umm…" Jeromy shrugged and said, "We could be quiet."

"And…." A longer than usual *and* as she waited for a reply. Anna continued, "If not quiet! We could learn how to do that with our powers."

"You're a real enthusiast! The next class doesn't start until tomorrow."

"Yeah, I know! But…"

They started walking.

"Anna," Jeromy softly whispered her name and moved closer to her, "It was not your fault. What happened in the forest was…."

"No, no…" Anna began to speak, but Jeromy interrupted her.

"No…I am really sorry. My brain stopped! I couldn't see you like that. I just don't.…"

"Hey," She stopped and held his chin with her hand and turned his head toward her own.

Jeromy felt a thrill throughout his body but moved his face right and left, feeling shy about looking her in the eyes. Anna continued, "If anything happened, Jeromy, it was that you saved my life. And I am.…"

"Please don't say grateful…Because…umm…" He rubbed his hand through his hair and said, "I am grateful that I got to meet you."

They kissed. Long and breathlessly. Then, they chuckled as she bed grabbed his hand and turned towards the direction leading to Cayuga Lake.

* * *

"Where are they?" Akwiraron thought to himself.

"What happened?" Alexa asked.

"Umm…no, nothing. It was…" Akwiraron scratched the back of his neck as he tried to cover up their meeting.

"You guys were supposed to meet." Alexa nodded her head, and answered herself.

"Would you please give me a minute?"

"Sure."

Akwiraron stood up from in front of the fire and walked fast as he performed the interim spell, but Erik didn't answer.

"What's going on...? Did something happen to them? Ugh, not again. Where can they be...?" Akwiraron thought to himself.

He got worried and then performed the spell again, but he tried to communicate with Jeromy this time.

Jeromy and Anna had just reached the lake in front of the village, as his arm started to glow with a message: *Where are you guys?*

But then something rather strange happened.

"I am sorry, we didn't tell you. We will meet tomorrow morning, Akwiraron. Erik has gone back to his cabin." This loudly bawled inside both Akwiraron and Anna's heads.

"What was that?! Why could I hear that?!" Anna put her hand on her head.

"I suppose we just performed a spell. Because I intended for him to listen to this, instead of me "writing" this on my arm or mid-air." Jeromy chuckled.

"Ha," Anna said, "There is still so much to learn. I think we have a long way to go for such a short period. Tell me, Jeromy...." She looked dreamily into the horizon that surrounded their view. "Are you scared?"

"No, Anna, I was waiting for this time to come. And come as soon as possible." He immediately took a brief pause before continuing, "You know… I think to myself that I should have been scared, not for something like this to happen. But having to be the… a medallion. But for all of the things that I have been through up till now, it seems that I just need to embrace what lies in my fate. Be strong. And with this power, be able to look into the eyes of danger because we need to bring justice, and it shouldn't be easy." And then he held Anna's hand and put it on his lap, "But I am not scared. And neither are you. You're just curious."

She smirked, "Thanks, Jeromy… ah, I mean White Feather." She teased.

Jeromy smiled. "Not you. Just Jeromy, please."

"Now, would you want to tell me a little about yourself? About your parents…"

"And which Academy did I go to? Sure," Anna turned her hand upwards and continued, "Well, a foster family in French Quarter, New Orleans, Louisiana, raised me. And then when I got a letter from the Olta that said I should be preparing myself. I told my parents, so all of us decided to move to Deadwood. That's where I had a few Native friends that belonged to a very spiritually advanced family. After school, I studied spirit magic and controlling with those friends and their families."

"You're their only…." Jeromy began to ask, but Anna was pleased about sharing these personal details with him.

"Yeah! I have no siblings. They didn't have any kids, actually. I suppose that's why they adopted me…." She paused to see Jeromy's eyebrows shoot upwards in surprise.

"You're adopted?" He repeated but then instantly regretted saying it.

"You know, Jeromy, I don't even know how I ended up there. I don't even know about my birth parents. I'd like to believe that they told me the truth, that everyone is unaware of. But I still feel like they were hiding something from me."

"Why did they choose Deadwood?"

"Well, that's where they studied and met. And when they thought they couldn't have a child to… Umm… they moved to French Quarter." Anna explained.

"Oh, so they were from the ring of supporters?" Jeromy asked, impressed to know about her family background. The Ring of Supporters was a group of Natives. They had learned spirit magic and began a nationwide movement to pass on the Native American beliefs, ideologies, and knowledge of spirit magic to the younger generations. They had supported the growth of the Indian culture and strengthened their younger generations to keep the magic alive.

"Yes." Anna said, not really sounding impressed, "Jeromy… tell me something. How did you feel about having been able to carry a secret as old as time? Knowing that people will hate you, mock you, and never will be able to accept what the truth is. And what the truth about End Times is."

"Anna, you should know this isn't the end. This is the beginning, not for just us, but for everyone around the globe in need of restoring the right on this planet. Even people whose hearts are full of faith can't comprehend what is about to come their way, both good and bad. And as far as the secret is concerned. Haven't we reached the time when it will reveal itself to the people of the Earth?" He smirked, "It is not a secret! It is a legacy!"

* * * The night took over with complete silence, even the sound of other animals of nature had quietened. It was almost as if you could hear the owls yawning. Suddenly a spark rose and fell from somewhere in the middle of the Yandellion Forest.It was something that Jeromy woke up to see with his sleepy eyes as it would always break in this time of the dusk. When he was younger, he would call it the "witching hour," for it was during this time that many unexplainable things happened to him. For many visions did he get to see… verses did he get to hear.

"…after the nightfall on this fateful night, the doors to the secrets of the earthly realm will open. The secrets that have the two cosmos latched onto one another like threads on a wind chime will reveal themselves. And will be revealed to none other than Cayuga's apprentice for the End times."

"These young warriors will find themselves dwelling in the last place where the Savior was seen before going into occultation and will meet Kiehton when the ring of supporters gathered around will be in deep slumber…."

Hearing these words inside his head, he woke up Anna to what seemed like a vision. "Hey, wake up…look, Anna."

"Oh my God!" Anna partially yelped.

"I know… can you see that?"

"No…wait, see what? I'm just shocked we slept out here."

"Oh, I'm sorry…I mean, you did, and I did not want to disturb you. I just knocked out for a small instance while I still had my eyes over there." Jeromy pointed to the other side of the lake.

Anna immediately sat up straight and put her hands on her hips, looking at the bright trail of light in the sky above them, "What do you think? Is it a meteor?"

"No! Why would it constantly fluctuate then? I think I may already know the answer." He stood up straight, "Let's go find out."

"What if it's something dangerous, Jeromy?" Anna asked.

"You already know it isn't."

"Let's call Erik and Akwiraron?" Anna shrugged which made it look like less of a question and more of a request.

"Or… we can go back to the headquarters instead of calling them over here" Jeromy answered.

Chapter # 9:
Angel Along the Pathway

Anna and Jeromy performed the teleportation spell to return to the headquarters and marched towards Erik and Akwiraron's cabin.

"Guys!" Anna aggressively whispered. "Erik, wake up!"

"Anna, let me try," Jeromy offered.

"No, wait!" She smirked as she looked back at Jeromy.

It was as if he read Anna's mind as she said, *"Celik Praraha"* while he performed the Wektu spell to teleport them to the lakeside immediately.

"What…Ugh," Akwiraron attempted to fight thin air due to the paranoia of being mysteriously transferred to the lake while Erik was still snoring. But as soon as he saw Anna and Jeromy, he woke up confused, "What are you guys doing?" He looked around in surprise as he did not recognize the surrounding area.

"How did I get here?! You gave me a heart attack!"

"Now I know more than ever what this training is all about," Anna said as she sat down to wake Erik up, politely this time because Jeromy had requested.

"Akwiraron, do you see that?" Jeromy put his hand on his shoulder.

Akwiraron was still upset about what happened as he turned his face towards the Yandellion forest, and his expression changed.

"Is it the…" He smiled ridiculously and in wonder.

"The portal." Jeromy completed, "Yes, there is a great chance for that to be true."

"Okay, let's go find out, then." Erik, in his fluctuating tones, added.

"How…" Akwiraron took a brief pause to rub his hand on his forehead and then continued, "…can you not be angry at them?" He was now wondering if Erik was still too sleepy to realize that they were teleported by their fellows.

"Guys, let's go!" Anna exclaimed as she saw the night fading out.

Jeromy, along with Anna, was stopped in the attempt to perform the Wektu spell.

"Guys, wait… I think… Erik and I got this." Akwiraron said to them.

"Levitasi banyu, supaya kita tekan wates kasebut". The two recruits combined their elemental strengths to create a path.

They used their powers to make a passage so that all four of them could walk on the lake to reach the other side.

As they reached the Yandellion Forest, they notice that from far away, it seemed as if the light was coming from the corner, but only after they took their first step they realized that the source of the light was coming from deep inside the forest.

"Why is the light fading?" Anna asked.

"I didn't expect something like that to be asked from you, Ann." Akwiraron said, "That's usually me."

"Yeah, I have a feeling this isn't the doorway itself" Jeromy stated.

"Someone is directing us to that place." Erik completed.

"How does this guy function even after being disturbed in his sleep?"

"Ay, what a wonderful slumber did I have! One like never before." Erik replied while he was still yawning.

"And that's why he made it till here." Anna chuckled, "Don't know about you yet, though."

"Hey…"

"Guys, look, the light has stopped fluctuating." Jeromy was lost in the moment as he only focused on where it was coming from. He was genuinely concerned that they might have just stepped into a trap of some sort.

As they walked up to the place between the long banyan trees, the trees naturally parted to make space for them. And from between those trees, a doorway showed itself, and the static light was being drawn from it.

The Medallion recruits walked past the area that seemed to have been a few feet above the ground, levitating. They detected a sparse image of what seemed like a hollow or cave, but… it was still a blur. The scene looked somewhat incomplete in its appearance. A three-dimensional image stretched out in front of their eyes.

The place seemed similar to what Erik and Jeromy had witnessed before in one of their visions. Jeromy thought that maybe it was their spiritual guides giving them hints rather than a trap. The floor of the passage fell away beneath the water, but the water would have gone above their heads if they stepped in. Erik read out a spell to make the water in the passage such that they could walk down and through it with an air bubble around them to allow them to breathe even under the water. But it wasn't a cave at all.

As they got past the thin, watery passage and onto the dry ground once again, it was as if a shift in a spacious dimension had occurred. Before them was a tall, beautiful creature standing with long wings that could take over the horizon.

As they moved forward, the creature turned around.

"Who are you?" Anna asked.

"I suppose you are well aware, Anna. And so are all of you. Jeromy. Erik. Akwiraron."

And although they could see the beautiful creature, they could not see its lips moving as it spoke to them. There was nothing but a smile on its face. Yet they heard its silky, baritone voice in their minds.

"You're an angel…." Akwiraron added, his mouth still open in wonder.

The sight of this legendary creature had the recruits struck with awe. The glowing creature, the archangel, was one of the chief angels of the army of Kiehton, the Great Spirit and creator.

"Yes, and I have come here to serve my master - the Great Spirit of both realms. And also the Chief who many call Lord Cayuga."

"And your purpose is…." Anna tried to ask.

"It's the archangel, Raphael." Interrupted Jeromy.

The angel smiled as he heard Jeromy say that.

"Very good, White Feather. And my purpose is to blow the trumpet soon. And so, the portal has revealed itself to the medallion."

The angel opened its arms to show them their birthstones and handed them over to the four recruits. Taking their names as he handed them over one by one, *"Jeromy, the opal that will serve as the map of Earth, and all dimensions to the "other side" from it."*

Jeromy performed a protection spell on it, as he kept it to himself in his waist bag.

"A diamond for the lady. A diamond that controls space and time." He said and handed it to Anna.

"An emerald that brings earth over water, and water over the earth in any space, time, and place in both realms." He gave it to Akwiraron.

"Do you guys know that Chief Cayuga has made time freeze for us to be in this dimension?" said Akwiraron.

"Yes, or a thousand years on Earth would have passed. Which means way past End times." Erik completed. "Tell me, Angel Raphael. What is my stone?"

"Yours is an amethyst, Erik. A rare stone that has the power to amalgamate the powers of each one of you altogether. You can use two of any of these stones together, with the right spell and energy, and fuse their powers for an attack or defense spell."

* * *

As soon as the angel handed Erik his stone, he covered himself with his wings. The luminous glow around his exterior diminished as he became an owl and began flying away. A short distance later, the owl flashed brilliant white and was gone.

The recruits talked to each other on their way back from the forest and discussed what they had just experienced. Being met by an archangel of Kiehton's army was indeed a miracle for any recruit. Because the four-leaf medallion recruits had received their birthstones, they were stronger and more potent than the other recruits.

While they were talking and were close to the forest's exit, a mighty wind started to blow. Suddenly, all the trees and darkness surrounding them began to appear as they were moving around. With an intense light suddenly blinding the recruits, they were now back to that side of the Lake of Cayuga, where they began their journey. And the threads in the night sky were still the same. The time of the headquarters where they left was still the same. But the journey back was as if they had traveled along all of the cosmos at bolt speed, strangely, safe inside a thunderstorm that got them back here.

Chapter # 10:
The Olta of Sihir

The Olta of Sihir, Wyoming, South Dakota

General Wische

(Third Ring of the Savior, Supreme Court of Black Hills. International Confed. at the Island of Java)

Dear chosen ones,

We are pleased to inform you that you have been accepted at the Sihir Olta for learning about the nature of the Natives' history, tribal spirit magic, and animism. You will learn spirit magic and repentance, control over the four elements, and combat against black magic.

This is to inform the candidates that there are four coteries, each of which you will have to study, and each in accordance with the respective element listed as below:

1.   Telik Inadi – Air – Classes for Intellectual Training

2.   Kekuwatan – Earth – Classes for Physical Strength

3.   Alas gedhe samun – Water - Classes for the Awareness of the Wilderness and Limbo

4.   Roh jahat – Fire - Classes to nurture strength to combat evil within you and entities in the physical realm or traveling through the warm holes, the same way angels do.

You are to report among the other recruits to attend the training sessions to be undertaken at the secret location disclosed through the Juhi spell.

Yours Sincerely,

General Wische

* * *

"Hey, look what I found," Alexa shows her acceptance letter to Denisse.

"You studied at Wyoming in your life before this journey began… right…?" Denisse adds.

"Yeah. Hey, Jeromy will be there, too," Anna says as she prepares her bag to leave like the other recruits. But after that statement, there was a rather eerie silence in the room that seemed absolutely uncalled for.

To break the silence, Denisse says, "Let's get going. We may have been late for classes. But for training… Yeah, I don't think it's a good idea for you."

"Especially with General Wische around." Alexa shrugs and heads outside at a faster pace.

"Well, everything seems to be alright," Denisse smirks and seems relieved, but she is now lamenting that she was not chosen to be in the Four-Leaf Clover Medallion which she had so desperately dreamed of.

"What do you mean?" Anna was confused.

"No, well, when we came in…." Denisse shrugs and finds it hard to put things together.

"Hey, you can talk to me. Is everything alright?" Anna shrugs and smirks as she continues to say, "A hunch?!"

"Wait, no. Ever since we've met her… I'm talking about Alexa - I have had constant fluctuations, in my opinion. Don't get me wrong, Ann."

"No, no, go on." She said, keeping her bag aside for a while and seating herself beside her.

"I haven't drawn a conclusion yet either. But when we reached here, and she got to know that you guys were in trouble – you know, you were lost at the other side of the forest of Limbo. She even argued with General Wische to take us seriously. And I was like, she really does care. But then again…" Denisse paused and looked confused about whether she should go on with the story. "I can't seem to forget how agitated she seemed when she got to know that you guys are the medallion. Her attitude had changed suddenly. I mean… I'm sad that I didn't get chosen, but Alexa is livid. Really mad!"

"Hey, listen to me," Anna softly says, "Denisse, maybe you are just overthinking. Even if whatever is going on in your head may be true, you don't have to be the bad person here. And you should trust the fact that none of us here, any of the recruits are! That's the reason why we're here. Not everyone would have had the same reaction. Not everyone would have known that we would have been granted to be at this position. We didn't either. Just be prepared with where things are taking you." Anna paused and smiled at Denisse. She continued, "I know that you already have a good feeling about this. Now let's go."

"Yeah!" Denisse smiles as more than anything, she realizes that she is being overprotective of her best friend. The Olta of Sihir was the final training ground for the armies of recruits. Of course, the four-leaf medallion recruits held a special place in the school. They were given the most intense training, but all the other recruits were also being trained in this school according to their respective tribes, coteries, and elemental strengths.

When the recruits arrived at the Sihir Olta after a short journey, they were each assigned their classes and training grounds by a famous Native man. He was in his 50s and was known to be one of the strongest members of the Ring of Supporters.

"Cayuga's chosen ones… follow me," he said after the other recruits were sent to their training grounds in Sihir alongside their Native trainers. Denisse, Alexa, and Alice turned back to look at Anna, Akwiraron, Erik, and Jeromy as they walked separate paths. Before the groups of warriors proceeded towards their grounds, Denisse ran back to give Anna a quick hug. They were told they would not meet again before the uprise against the Dark Lord now, which was a long time ahead.

"I'm so proud of you, Ann. Stay safe," Denisse said with a warm smile as she turned to join her group and disappeared into the corridor.

The Native man leading the four chosen recruits talked to them on their way as they walked through a rugged pathway within the hugely built Olta of Sihir.

"You have learned most of what you needed to know at the Olta. But now, here in Olta of Sihir, you will learn the tactics and skills needed to make you true warriors…."

The recruits listened to him as he went on.

"The mission that is chosen for you is not of ease. It is a journey of sacrifice and struggles before any victory can be expected. It is a pathway of thorns on which you must be prepared to walk, and your preparation, our chosen ones, is not one of the bodies alone. Your preparation exceeds the limits of physical strength – your soul and mind are to be prepared for war and whatever may come."

The recruits felt motivated by what they heard. They wanted this spiritual growth promised to them, and they were ready to work hard towards its achievement. The man leading them stopped when they reached a sizeable cave-like room at the bottom of the Olta of Sihir. "This is where you will live for as long as you are here with us. Chosen ones, I must tell you, that your discipline and punctuality are of extreme importance to your training, growth, and success, so be present there," he said, pointing his finger towards another tunnel beside this large room leading to the training ground. "Your mentors will await you there tomorrow morning."

The recruits felt great. Their room was lined with four soft beds made of leaves and cotton, with lanterns hung on the walls in the distance between each bed.

Jeromy and Anna looked coyly at each other as they sat on two adjacent beds to mark them as theirs. It was late, and they had already had dinner earlier with the rest of the recruits. So, without wasting any more time, the four recruits took off their waist bags and took turns going to the bathroom and getting into their night attire to sleep.

"Psst… Jeromy!" He woke up with someone hissing his name in the near distance. As he opened one eye and squinted to see who it was, he saw Anna crouching beside his bed.

Jeromy opened both his eyes and looked at her as she had a broad smile that looked beautiful on her face, especially with her hair tied back into a high ponytail. She lightly grazed his arm with her fingers.

"Wake up! We should get ready for the training!"

Her excitement was evident in her body language that morning. The boys woke up one after another groaning at the Sun for rising up so quickly. They had gotten to sleep late last night, so they were probably not feeling the freshest this morning. Anna pulled Jeromy out of his bed, and as he stumbled a little before balancing on his feet, the group laughed. They were eager to learn the powerful skills that would be taught to them. This was nothing short of a reward – being chosen as Cayuga's medallion recruits.

After breakfast, the recruits found themselves being led into their designated training ground by the same man who had led them here last night.

"Welcome, chosen ones. Before we begin teaching you the advanced war tactics using spirit magic and elemental strengths, we will first conduct a small test to see if you are well-trained in the basics." He said, and the recruits noticed two other quinquagenarians standing there, noticing their every move. They looked amazingly fit for being nearly 60 years old.

"Meet your mentors: Adahy and Catori." The man gestures the mentors to come forward and introduce themselves.

"Chosen ones… Cayuga's chosen ones…." Adahy, a man with a broad built and immense manly charisma, smiled as his gaze traced each of the four recruits with an impressed expression.

"I am Adahy, and I am known for my ability with survival in the wild. Among many things, I will teach you about converting to your spirit animals and using those powers. You will find yourself immensely powerful once you master this skill."

His way of talking was encouraging, and the recruits were surprised that they were going to learn one of the most challenging spirit magic skills, i.e., turning into your spirit animals. They could already feel that the Olta of Sihir was going to be their most significant transformation of power and control.

The woman also stepped forward to introduce herself, "I'm Catori," she said in a warm, motherly tone. "In my youth, I was raised by witches and taught by a Shaman. With my knowledge of totems and nature, you will learn to utilize different elements of the Earth to create spiritual effects of medicinal and protective purposes."

The recruits were amazed. They had been living in the cities before they came on this life-changing journey and had been so caught up in their regular modern city lives that despite knowing the spiritual and magical family backgrounds and tribes they came from; they never explored these strengths.

The Native man who was leading them so far announced that their test was going to begin now. Over the next three hours, the recruits were tested in several aspects of what they had learned in the Olta earlier. The test began with the easiest skills, i.e., starting a fire, communicating with fellow Indians through the telepathy spell, implementing the transcription spell. Then, it proceeded to the more difficult abilities like the teleportation spell and the protection spell in which Jeromy formed a protective dome around them.

"Well done, medallion recruits! You have proven that you are truly Cayuga's chosen warriors!" The Native man had smiled for the first time since they had met, and the recruits could not help but notice how his stern features immediately softened as he smiled.

"You are now ready for your first training session at the Olta of Sihir, and I must remind you that because you are chosen by Cayuga to be his medallion warriors, more is expected of you than of others. So, more responsibility lies on your shoulders than the other recruits." With this statement, the Native man nodded at both the mentors and left.

A few days had passed, and every morning, the four recruits would meet Catori and Adahy to learn something new. Some days would be theory, and some days they would practice of what they were learning.

Adahy had identified the spirit animals for each of the recruits. Anna's Native American totem was a woodpecker – driven, persistent, and strong. Erik's totem was a bear, and people affiliated with the bear are known to be very passionate and loyal to their fellows. Akwiraron was identified as the deer, quick to think and act. Jeromy was the wolf – an enormous white beast – brilliant, courageous, independent, and leader of the pack.

Each of them embraced their native totems as their identities. Through a period of three more weeks, the medallion recruits had mastered the skill of converting themselves into their spirit animals, using the animals' abilities when they needed to, and even communicating with the animals in the wilderness to help them.

"However, animals that are possessed by dark energies, especially those that live in the dark forests, will not understand you when you call for them," Adahy warned them. He knew what evil spirits awaited them in their journey.

Similarly, by the end of their training session, the recruits had also learned how to use different elements of nature to stir up potions and create different effects. In one of their last classes with Catori, they learned to make a healing medicinal bag.

"You will need the charm to represent each of nature's elements: air, fire, water, and earth. To represent air, find a feather. Feathers are powerful charms, dear recruits. They represent divine wisdom and a strong connection to the Spirits. An eagle's feather would be best for a strongly effective medicine bag, but any bird's feather would do." Catori started teaching them one of her most popular works. She was known in her tribe to be the healer of the sick and the armor of the warriors.

"Then," she went on as the recruits listened to her attentively, memorizing each of her words because they knew how important this medicinal skill is going to be on their journey and on the battlefield. "You will need a red acorn from the red oak tree to represent the fire element. The acorn also represents life, growth, and wisdom. Lastly, you will need a seashell to represent water and a stone to represent the earth. Each of these charms has its own spiritual effects and strengths that aid in healing and strengthening the person using the medicine bag."

This was all very interesting for the recruits, especially for Dr. Jeromy Whitefeather, whose Ph.D. education program would never agree to all of this making any sense, but it made sense to him. He knew that science is not just in labs or textbooks but rather in the spirits and energies of each living or non-living object that surrounds us. Everything has a spirit. Everything has an effect.

"Now, once you have all these four charms, you can either go straight to the procedure or do an additional act to strengthen the medicinal effect further: If you can find sandalwood oil, lightly sprinkle the four elements with it. If you cannot find it, you can go on anyway and make your medicine bag," Catori was an excellent teacher who had trained far and wide. She made sure to give each detail, each alternative. She paused in between stages of each lesson to see if the recruits had any confusion or questions.

"Covered in sandalwood oil or not, this is how you make the medicinal bag," She had the four elements laid out in front of her: a stone, an eagle's feather, a seashell, and a red acorn. "You take a bag, any bag," Catori held up a small drawstring bag made of jute, "and one by one, you put the elements in it in the order and manner that I will now show you."

Catori held the bag open in front of her and started to chant:

"Blessed be the elements of earth, air, fire, and sea."

Then, she picked up the stone and put that in the bag while chanting, *"Blessed be the earth element."*

She proceeded to put the eagle's feather into the jute bag and said, *"Blessed be the air element."*

Similarly, she added the red acorn into the bag. As she chanted, words naturally escaped from Anna's mouth as well, *"Blessed be the fire element."*

They both said in unison, and Catori smiled at Anna impressively. Then, she dropped the seashell in the bag and chanted, *"Blessed be the water element."*

Catori then proceeded to close the drawstring bag and hold it in both her hands, extending it into the air and saying,

"Blessed be this bag of medicine...

By the elements of earth, air, fire, and sea...

Shower me with divine energy...

So be it! Blessed be!"

The jute bag started to dimly glow in green color for a few seconds before returning to its usual look.

"Now, here we have a blessed medicine bag. One of you may keep it. As long as you have this bag touching your skin, you will be able to ward off severe damage to a good extent and have stronger attacking skills."

She held the bag out for any of them to get it, and the four recruits looked at each other to decide who would take it.

"Let's let Anna have it? If any one of us would need it at any given time, we can get it from her?" Jeromy suggested, and Anna found that very sweet. She smirked, impressed by his selflessness. The other men agreed, too, and Anna stepped forward to take the bag from Catori.

"You're well prepared, chosen ones. Very well prepared." Catori concluded the session, but not before asking to speak with Jeromy.

"White Feather, there is another training we will ask you to undergo."

"Yes, Catori," Jeromy responded.

Please say goodbye to your fellow recruits. You will not see them for a few days.

After a brief goodbye, Jeromy and Catori proceeded to walk toward the wood and onto a path.

"Catori?" Inquired Jeromy.

"Yes, White Feather."

"I am thankful for your teachings. I did notice that some of them do not appear to be traditional Native American."

"Ahhh, you noticed that, didn't you?" she replied.

As they walked, Catori began singing and chanting in a strange language. She began gesturing her staff in what appeared to be blessings upon the trees, birds, and animals as they moved along. Jeromy had never heard just a rhythm or song in either his experience or education. Finally, after about 15 minutes, a light went off in his mind.

"Catori, is that ancient Hopi that you are speaking?"

"Yes, White Feather."

She stopped and, once again, had a good look at Jeromy.

"You are very wise for your years, White Feather. The Spirits have chosen wisely."

"Spirits?
"Yes… behold!"

Just around the next turn in the path, there was a wide clearing and in the middle of the clearing was an enormous stone circle.

Then, as if from nowhere and everywhere, drums started beating..

Chapter # 11:
Imperial House – Darkness Arrives

The villagers of Little Kekuwatan still called it "the Imperial House," even though it had been several years since the Skahonhi family had lived there. The large, old estate stood on a hill overlooking the village. Some of its windows were boarded, tiles were missing from its roof, and ivy spread over its face. Once a fine-looking manor and easily the largest and grandest building for miles around, the Imperial House was damp, derelict, and unoccupied. The Little Kekuwatan all agreed that the old house was haunted, or as they would say, *'creepy.'*

Years ago, something strange and horrible had happened there, something that the older inhabitants of the village still liked to discuss when topics for gossip were scarce. The story had been picked over so many times and had been embroidered in so many places that nobody was quite sure what the truth was anymore. However, every version of the tale started in the same place: Twelve years earlier, at daybreak on a fine summer's morning, when the Imperial House had still been well kept and impressive, a maid had entered the drawing-room to find all three of the Skahonhis dead. The maid had run screaming down the hill into the village and roused as many people as she could.

"Lying there with their eyes wide open! Cold as ice! Still in their dinner things!"

The sheriff was summoned, and the whole of Little Kekuwatan had seethed with shocked curiosity and ill-disguised excitement. Nobody wasted their breath pretending to feel very sad about the Skahonhi, for they had been the most unpopular inhabitants there. Elderly Mr. and Mrs. Skahonhi had been rich, snobbish, and rude, and their grown-up son, Tom, had been if anything, worse. The villagers did not feel saddened by the *loss*. *Still,* all that they cared about was the identity of their murderer — for plainly, three apparently healthy people did not all drop dead of natural causes on the same night. The Hanged Man, the popular village pub, made a roaring trade that night; the whole village seemed to have turned out to drink beer and discuss the murders, turning the bar's tables into conference meetings. They were rewarded for leaving their firesides when the Skahonhi family's cook arrived dramatically in their midst and announced to the suddenly silent pub that a man called Norman Bryce had just been arrested.

"Norman?!" cried several people.

"Never!" Norman Bryce was the Riddles' gardener. He lived alone in a rundown cottage on the grounds of the Imperial House. He had come back from fighting with the English at the French Fortress of Louisbourg in 1745 with a very stiff leg and a great dislike of crowds and loud noises and had been working for the Skahonhis ever since. There was a rush to buy the cook drinks and hear more details.

"Always thought he was odd," she told the eagerly listening lagers, after her fourth sherry. "Unfriendly, like, I'm sure if I've offered him a cuppa once, I've offered it a hundred times. Never wanted to mix, he didn't."

"Ah, now," said a woman at the bar, "He had a hard war, Norman. He likes the quiet life. That's no reason to —"

"Who else had a key to the back door, then?" barked the cook. "There's been a spare key hanging in the gardener's cottage far back as I can remember! Nobody forced the door last night!

No broken windows! All Norman had to do was creep up to the big house while they were all sleeping..."

The villagers exchanged dark looks.

"I always thought he had a nasty look about him, right enough," grunted a man at the bar.

"Strange man... War turned him funny if you ask me," said the landlord.

"Told you I wouldn't like to get on the wrong side of Norman, didn't me, Dot?" said an excited woman in the corner.

"Hell, yes, you did! Horrible temper," said Dot, nodding fervently. "I remember when he was a kid...."

The night's silence drowned in the murmurs at the pub. By the following morning, hardly anyone in Little Kekuwatan doubted that Norman Bryce had killed the Skahonhis. But over in the neighboring town of Great Skahonhi, in the dark Sheriff's Office, Norman was stubbornly repeating, again and again, that he was innocent and that the only person he had seen near the house on the day of the Skahonhi' deaths had been a teenage boy, a stranger, dark-haired and pale. Nobody else in the village had seen any such boy, and the lawmen were all quite sure that Norman had invented him as a fragment of his imagination to get out of here.

Then, just when things were looking very serious for Norman, the report on the Skahonhi's bodies came back and changed everything. Two doctors had examined the bodies and had concluded that none of the Skahonhi had been poisoned, stabbed, shot, strangled, suffocated, or (as far as they could tell) harmed at all. In fact (the report continued, in a tone of unmistakable bewilderment), the Skahonhis all appeared to be in perfect health — apart from the fact that they were all dead, of course.

The doctors did note (as though determined to find something wrong with the bodies) that each of the Skahonhi had a look of terror upon their face — but as the frustrated Sheriff said, "Whoever heard of three people being frightened to death?!"

As there was no proof that the Skahonhi had been murdered, the Sheriff was forced to let Norman go. The Skahonhis were buried in the Little Kekuwatan's churchyard, and their graves remained objects of curiosity for a while. To everyone's surprise, and amid a cloud of suspicion, Norman Bryce returned to his cottage on the grounds of the Imperial House.

"As far as I'm concerned, he killed them, and I don't care what the lawmen say," said Dot at the Hanged Man. "And if he had any decency, he'd leave here, knowing how we knows he did it."

But Norman did not leave. He stayed to tend the garden for the next family who lived in the Imperial House, and then the next — for neither family stayed longer than a few months. Perhaps it was partly because of Norman that the new owners said that there was a nasty feeling about the place, which started to fall into disrepair in the absence of inhabitants. The wealthy man who owned the Imperial House these days neither lived there nor put it to any use; they said in the village that he kept it for "tax reasons," though nobody was sure what that was all about. The wealthy owner continued to pay Norman to do the gardening, however. Norman was nearing his sixty-seventh birthday now, very deaf, his bad leg stiffer than ever, but he could still be seen pottering around the flower beds in fine weather. Even though the weeds were starting to creep up on him, try as he might suppress them.

Weeds were not the only things Norman had to contend with either. Boys from the village made a habit of throwing stones through the windows of the Imperial House and stomped all over the lawns that Norman worked so hard to keep smooth. Once or twice, they broke into the old house for a dare. They knew that old Norman's devotion to the house and grounds amounted almost to an obsession, and it amused them to see him limping across the garden, brandishing his stick and yelling croakily at them, "Hush! Hush, you bastards!"

Norman, for his part, believed the boys tormented him because they, like their parents and grandparents, thought him to be the murderer of the Skahonhi family. So, when Norman awoke one night in August and saw something very odd up at the old house, he merely assumed that the boys had gone one step further in their attempts to punish him. It was Norman's bad leg that woke him; it was paining him worse than ever in his old age. He got up and limped downstairs into the kitchen with the idea of sticking the bed warmer in the fire for a bit to help ease the stiffness in his knee. Standing at the fireplace, he looked up at the Imperial House and saw lights glimmering in its upper windows. Norman knew at once what was going on. The boys had broken into the house again and judging by the flickering light, they had started a fire. He grunted in frustration but was prepared to get ready for an encounter. He could not let the house burn down.

Norman deeply mistrusted the sheriff ever since they had taken him in to question about the Skahonhis' deaths. Besides, there was no way to get help right away.

He hurried back upstairs as fast as his bad leg would allow and was soon back downstairs, fully dressed and removing a rusty old key from its hook by the door. He thought about grabbing the hot bed warmer but instead picked up his walking stick, which was propped against the wall, and set off into the night. The front door of the Imperial House bore no sign of being forced, nor did any of the windows. That was strange... *how else would the boys break into the house?*

Norman limped around to the back of the house until he reached a door almost completely hidden by ivy, took out the old key, put it into the lock, and opened the door noiselessly. He let himself into the large kitchen. Norman had not entered it for many years; nevertheless, although it was very dark, he remembered where everything was. He walked to where the door into the hall was, and he groped his way toward it, his nostrils fully active in search of the smell of decay, ears pricked for any sound of footsteps or voices from overhead. He reached the hall, which was a little lighter owing to the large, mullioned windows on either side of the front door. Starting to climb the stairs, he blessed the dust that lay thick upon the stone because it muffled the sound of his feet and stick. On the landing, Norman turned right and saw at once where the intruders were.

At the very end of the passage, a door stood ajar, and a flickering light shone through the gap, casting a long sliver of gold across the black floor. Norman edged closer and closer, grasping his walking stick firmly. Several feet from the entrance, he could see a narrow slice of the room beyond. The fire, he now saw, had been lit in the grate. This surprised him. Then he stopped moving and listened intently, for a man's voice spoke within the room; it sounded timid and fearful.

"There is a little more in the bottle, my Lord - if you are still hungry."

"Later," said a second voice. This, too, belonged to a man — but it was strangely high-pitched and cold as a sudden blast of icy wind. Something about that voice made the sparse hair on the back of Norman's neck stand up.

"Move me closer to the fire, Asmodeus."

Norman turned his right ear toward the door, the better to hear. It was obviously not the village boys but rather two grown men. There came the clink of a bottle being put down upon a hard surface and then the dull scraping noise of a heavy chair being dragged across the floor. Norman caught a glimpse of a small man, his back facing the door, pushing the chair into place. He was wearing a long black cloak, and a bald patch was visible at the back of his head. Then he went out of sight again.

"Where is he now?" said the cold voice.

"I — I don't know, my Lord," said the first voice nervously. "He set out towards the Dark Forest; I think. It was last we heard of him..."

"Are you certain it was him? What was his name again?" The cold voice asked as Norman listened intently to their conversation with piked curiosity.

"I'm certain, my Lord. His name is Jeromy White Feather, and he is among Cayuga's medallion recruits and his army of warriors...."

The nervous voice echoed in its high pitch.

"White Feather? Damn! You will get him before we retire, Asmodeus," said the second voice. "If I don't see him beg for his life at my feet while I cut off his head, I will cut off yours instead."

There was silence for a few seconds before the cold voice echoed in the dark again, "I will need feeding in the night. The journey has tired me greatly."

Norman inclined his good ear still closer to the door with furrowed brows, listening very hard. There was a pause, and then the man called Asmodeus spoke again. "My Lord, may I ask how long we are going to stay here?"

"A week," said the cold voice. "Perhaps longer. The place is moderately comfortable, and the plan cannot proceed yet. It would be foolish to act before the recruitment is over. Let them do what they are doing, and we will do what we are doing."

Norman inserted a gnarled finger into his ear and rotated it. Owing, no doubt, to a buildup of earwax, he had heard the word 'Recruitment,' which was not a word at all – not at least for him at the time.

"The - the... what, my Lord?" said Asmodeus. (Norman dug his finger still more vigorously into his ear.)

"Forgive me, but — I do not understand — why should we wait until the recruitment is over?"

"Because, fool, at this very moment, the Indians are pouring into the Olta from all over the country under Cayuga's supervision and instruction, and every meddler from the tribes will be on duty, on the watch for signs of any unusual activity, checking and double-checking identities. They will be obsessed with security, lest the Kekuwatan or Alas Gedhe notice anything. So, we wait."

Norman stopped trying to clear out his ear. He had distinctly heard the words "*Olta*" and "*Alas Gedhe*." Plainly, each of these expressions meant something secret, and Norman could think of only two sorts of people who would speak in code: spies and criminals. Norman tightened his hold on his walking stick once again and listened more closely, still unsure of what move he could or should make at this point.

"Your Lordship is still determined, then?" Asmodeus said quietly.

"Certainly, I am determined, Asmodeus." There was a note of menace in the cold voice now. A slight pause followed — and then Asmodeus spoke, the words tumbling from him in a rush, as though he was forcing himself to say this before he lost his nerve.

"It could be done without that Jeromy White Feather, my Lord." Another pause, more protracted, and then....

"With someone close to him instead, like Anna?" breathed the second voice softly.

"I see . . . You don't think that I know that you tried to get her already?"

"My Lord?"

"You sent foulas. She torched some of them but, in the end, got away. It was Jeromy White Feather that stopped them!"

"I do not say this out of concern for him!" said Asmodeus, his voice rising squeakily. "He is nothing to me, nothing at all! It is merely that if we were to use another of Cayuga's recruits, the thing could be done so much more quickly! If you allowed me to leave you for a short while — you know that I can disguise myself most effectively — I could be back here in as little as two days with a suitable person —"

"Hmm... I could use another Indian recruit," said the cold voice softly, "that is true..."

"My Lord, it makes sense," said Asmodeus, sounding thoroughly relieved now. "Laying hands on Jeromy White Feather would be so difficult; he is so well protected and armed with his knowledge and skills —"

"And so, you volunteer to go and fetch me a substitute? I wonder . . . perhaps the task of nursing me has become wearisome for you, Asmodeus? Could this suggestion of abandoning the plan be nothing more than an attempt to desert me?"

"My Lord!" The high-pitched voice squealed. "I — I have no wish to leave you, none at all —"

"Do not lie to me!" hissed the second voice. "I can always tell, Asmodeus! You are regretting that you ever returned to me. I revolt you. I see you flinch when you look at me, feel you shudder when you touch me..."

"No! My devotion to Your Lordship —"

"Your devotion is nothing more than cowardice. You would not be here if you had anywhere else to go. How am I to survive without you when I need feeding every few hours?"

"But you seem so much stronger, my Lord —"

"Liar," breathed the second voice. "I am no stronger since the imprisonment, and a few days alone would be enough to rob me of the little health I have regained under your clumsy care. Silence!"

Asmodeus, who had been sputtering incoherently, fell silent at once. For a few seconds, Norman could hear nothing but the fire crackling under the chimney. Then the second man spoke once more, in a whisper that was almost a hiss.

"I have my reasons for using the boy, as I have already explained to you, and I will use no other. I have waited long, long years. A few more months will make no difference. As for the protection surrounding the boy, I believe my plan will be effective. All that is needed is a little courage from you, Asmodeus — courage you will find unless you wish to feel the full extent of my wrath —"

"My Lord, I must speak!" said Asmodeus, panic in his voice now. "All through our journey, I have gone over the plan in my head — my Lord, ever since we kidnapped Bertha Skahonhi from the Olta, right from under Cayuga's supervision, I have been thinking this. Bertha Skahonhi's sudden disappearance from the Olta will not go unnoticed for long, and if we proceed, if I murder —"

"If?" whispered the second voice. "If? If you follow the plan, Asmodeus, the Indians at the Olta need never know that anyone else has died. You will do it quietly and without fuss; I only wish that I could do it myself, but until I am freed from this curse that has cut off my powers... Come, Asmodeus, one more death, and our path to Jeromy White Feather is clear. I am not asking you to do it alone. By that time, my faithful servant will have rejoined us —"

"I am a faithful servant," said Asmodeus, the merest trace of sullenness in his voice.

"Asmodeus, I need somebody with brains, somebody whose loyalty has never wavered, and you, unfortunately, fulfill neither requirement."

"I found you," said Asmodeus, and there was definitely a sulky edge to his voice now. "I was the one who found you. I brought you Bertha Skahonhi to make the blood sacrifice to get you out of the earth."

"That is true," said the second man, sounding amused. "A stroke of brilliance I would not have thought possible from you, Asmodeus — though, if truth be told, you were not aware how useful she would be when you caught her, were you?"

"I — I thought she might be useful, my Lord —" Asmodeus tried to define his place, his importance to the Dark Lord.

"Liar," repeated the second voice, with more pronounced cruel amusement than ever. "However, I do not deny that her information and power were invaluable. Without it, I could never have gotten this far or formed our plan, and for that, you will have your reward, Asmodeus. I will allow you to perform an essential task for me, one that many of my followers would give their right hands to perform..."

"R-really, my Lord? What —?" Asmodeus sounded terrified again.

"Ah, Asmodeus, you don't want me to spoil the surprise, do you? Your part will come at the very end... but I promise you, you will have the honor of being just as useful as Bertha Skahonhi."

"You... you...." Asmodeus's voice suddenly sounded hoarse, as though his mouth had gone parched. "You... are going... to kill me, too?!"

"Asmodeus, Asmodeus, Asmodeus," said the cold voice silkily, "why would I kill you? I killed Bertha because I had to. She was fit for nothing else, quite useless. In any case, awkward questions would have been asked if she had gone back to the Olta with the news that she had met you on her holidays... and I would not be here where I am now. People who are supposed to be dead would do well not to run into Indian warriors or serpents at wayside inns..."

Asmodeus muttered something so quietly that Norman could not hear it, but it made the second man laugh — an entirely mirthless laugh, cold as his speech.

"We could have duplicated her? But implanted memory charms can be broken by a powerful Native, as I proved when I questioned that Skahonhi girl. It would be an insult to her memory not to use the information I extracted from her, Asmodeus. Besides, she was such a delicious individual." He snorted and laughed.

Out in the corridor, Norman suddenly became aware that the hand gripping his walking stick was slippery with sweat. The man with the cold voice had killed a woman. He was talking about it without any kind of remorse; instead, there was amusement in his voice. It was clear that he was dangerous — a madman. And he was planning more murders — Anna, or this boy, Jeromy, whoever he was — was in danger. Norman knew what he must do. Now, if ever, was the time to go to the sheriff. He would creep out of the house and head straight for help in the village... but the cold voice was speaking again, and Norman remained where he was, frozen to the spot, listening with all his might.

"One more murder... my faithful servant at Sihir... Jeromy is as good as mine, Asmodeus. It is decided. There will be no more argument. But, quiet...." The cold voice suddenly sounded alert. "I think I hear...."

And the second man's voice changed. He started making noises such as Norman had never heard before; he was hissing and spitting without drawing breath as if muttering an evil spell of some sort. Norman thought he must be having some kind of fit or seizure. And as he stood still outside the door, unsure of what to do, he heard movement behind him in the dark passageway. When he turned to look, he found himself paralyzed with fright.

Something was slithering toward him along the dark corridor floor. As it drew nearer to the sliver of firelight, he realized with a thrill of terror that it was a gigantic snake, at least fifteen feet long. Horrified and transfixed, Norman stared as its undulating body cut a wide, curving track through the thick dust on the floor, coming closer and closer — *What was he to do?* The only means of escape was into the room where two men sat plotting murder, yet if he stayed where he was, the serpent would surely kill him. But, before he had made his decision, the snake was level with him, and then, incredibly, miraculously, it was passing; it was following the spitting, hissing noises made by the cold voice beyond the door, and in seconds, the tip of its diamond-patterned tail had vanished through the gap.

That was close! There was sweat on Norman's forehead now, and the hand on the walking stick was trembling. He realized that his breath was stuck inside him – and he quickly exhaled and tried to breathe. Inside the room, the cold voice was continuing to hiss, and Norman was visited by a strange idea, an impossible idea that this man could talk to snakes. Norman didn't understand what was happening, but he sensed impending trouble.

He wanted more than anything to be back in his bed with his bed warmer. Standing for so long had only worsened the pain in his bad leg. For a moment, he thought, '*Who cares who these men are?! No one lives in the Imperial House anymore for them to harm.*'

The problem was that his legs didn't seem to want to move. As he stood there shaking and trying to master himself, the cold voice switched abruptly to English again.

"The snake has interesting news, Asmodeus," it said.

"In- indeed, my Lord?" said Asmodeus.

"Indeed, yes," said the voice. "According to the Snake of Mischief, an old person is standing right outside this room, listening to every word we say...."

Norman's heart was beating louder than ever, and he could literally feel the man behind the voice smile mischievously. He didn't have a chance to hide, then, though. In what seemed to be the tiniest fraction of a second, there were footsteps approaching, and then the door of the room was flung wide open.

A short, balding man with graying hair, a pointed nose, and small, watery eyes stood before Norman, a mixture of fear and alarm in his face.

"Invite him inside, Asmodeus. Where are your manners?"

The cold voice was coming from the ancient armchair before the fire, but Norman couldn't see the speaker. On the other hand, the snake was curled up on the rotting hearth rug, like some horrible travesty of a pet dog. Asmodeus beckoned Norman into the room. Though still deeply shaken, Norman took a firmer grip upon his walking stick and limped over the threshold. The fire was the only light source in the room; it cast long, spidery shadows upon the walls. Norman stared at the back of the armchair; the man inside it seemed to be very tall but even uglier than his servant, for Norman couldn't even see his face yet. Still, the skin of his sides appeared rotten.

"You heard everything?" said the cold voice.

"Y – Yes. What's that you were calling me?" said Norman defiantly, for now, that he was inside the room, now that the time had come for some sort of action, he felt braver; it had always been so in the war. When the situation arrives, when you can only face it and not run from it, one must face it bravely.

"Old man? I am also calling you an intruder," said the voice coolly. "I am here now, and that means that you are trespassing…."

"I don't know what you mean by trespassing," said Norman, his voice growing steadier. "All I know is I've heard enough to interest the sheriff tonight. I have. You've done murder, and you're planning more! And I'll tell you this, too," He added on a sudden inspiration, "my wife knows I'm up here, and if I don't come back —"

"You have no wife," said the cold voice, very quietly, as if amused with how this situation was unfolding. "Nobody knows you are here. You told nobody that you were coming. Do not lie to the Dark Lord, for he knows... he always knows…."

"Is that right?" said Norman roughly. "The Dark Lord, is it? That's a fancy title for someone like you. Well, I don't think much of your manners, *my Lord*." He said sarcastically, surprising himself by the sudden boast of courage he had. "Turn 'round and face me like a man, why don't you?"

"But I am not a man," said the cold voice, barely audible now over the crackling of the flames. "I am much, much more than just a man. I only took the body of Magua's son for my convenience. However… why not? I will *face* you... Asmodeus? Come turn my chair around. This old man here wants to *face* me."

The servant gave a whimper.

"You heard me, Asmodeus."

Slowly, with his face screwed up, as though he would instead have done anything other than approach his master and the hearth rug where the snake lay, the small man walked forward and began to turn the chair. The snake behind them lifted its ugly triangular head and hissed slightly as the legs of the chair snagged on its rug. And then the chair was facing Norman, and he saw what was sitting in it. His walking stick fell to the floor with a clatter.

"Now, Asmodeus," ordered the Dark Lord.

Asmodeus' arms and legs quickly retracted into his body, and within seconds, he transformed himself into another enormous serpent.

Norman opened his mouth and let out a scream.

"I am *Nun'Yina'Wi,* and I am very hungry for human flesh." The Dark Lord added, but Norman was screaming so loudly that he never heard him or the words the thing in the chair spoke as it raised a staff. There was a flash of green light, a rushing sound, and Norman Bryce crumpled. He was dead before he hit the floor.

The serpents all fed well.

Chapter # 12:
Wankan Tanka Land

Jeromy proceeded slowly to the edge of the enormous circular stone. As he approached the edge of it, he crouched down to take a closer look but was profoundly shocked at what he saw before his eyes. It was so perfectly formed it almost looked manufactured, and yet, it also looked ancient with a patina of green and brown in areas on top of the slate-gray stone. The giant circle had to be at least a hundred feet across, was perfectly flat, looked precisely level, and must have weighed hundreds of tons.

The drumming continued…

"Jesus! This is amazing." He gasped. "It can't be real!"

He looked around him, and everything else appeared pretty normal… except for the strange cloud layer just above the treetops over his head, that is. However, as he took a closer look, he realized that there were carvings in the stone. There were symbols etched into the solid stone surface around the outside in a ring about two feet wide. Inside the outer ring, another ring also had carvings, then another inside that, and so on.

Jeromy couldn't believe his eyes and was aghast with disbelief.

"I'm no expert on petroglyphs, but these look old Catori. Really old. Thousands of years old! Man, I wish I had more science guys here." He muttered.

"No, I wish Issabelle was here… I wish Anna could see this!"

He appraised the circular mass carefully but wasn't sure he should be stepping on it, so he slowly walked forward around the outside while observing and studying what he was looking at.

Stopping from time to time, he started thinking that some of the symbols looked familiar. He would bend down, trace a hand or finger along the grooves and lines, stand up and inch sideways around the circle a few more feet before repeating the process over and over.

I know these symbols, he thought. *These look tribal.*

Now examining them almost forensically, his face began lighting up into a big *Aha!* Moment.

"They are tribes… actual tribes!" He said out loud. "And there are hundreds of them! There must be at least 600."

Jeromy was mesmerized by the beauty and meaning of the carvings in the stone; he almost forgot about the drums and singing. He stood up and looked around once again. Catori had resumed singing, but otherwise, there was absolutely no one there. He was utterly alone.

Now looking toward the center of the circle, he decided he would get a closer look at other carvings he could see. He paused for a full minute, thinking carefully about what he was about to do. Then, he took a small, gentle step onto the rock surface… and like testing the water of a pool, he first touched his toe and then tapped his foot onto the nearly smooth surface. First with one foot, and then with both feet. Then he was standing on the rock.

He felt funny. He sensed vibration of some kind, and his feet itched and almost tickled. It wasn't a bad feeling. In fact, the vibrations appeared to follow along with the drumbeats he was still hearing.

So, he stood perfectly still for another minute, enjoying the sensation. And then again, he looked around.

When he looked down again, what he saw almost took his breath away. He was standing on a very familiar symbol. He knew it well. In fact, he had known it all his life. It was the symbol for the Oglala Sioux Tribe... *his* tribe.

"Oh, my God." He blurted out to no one. "I can't believe this. This is my tribe. And these symbols are all the other tribes. This is sacred ground."

To say he was in awe would have been an understatement. He not only felt amazed; he felt a deep sense of pride right down to his bones.

"My tribe!" He excitedly repeated.

Looking once again at the stone table's entirety and smiling from ear to ear, Jeromy looked over at Catori. He proclaimed, "It's time to see what's in the center."

He proceeded to walk carefully, respecting the stone circle while inching forward toward the center. As he walked, the sound grew louder and louder the closer he came to the stone's middle point. Looking down again, he noticed that the symbols had changed. Now, instead of tribal symbols, there were animals of many kinds carved into the stone circles.

"These symbols must be Spirit Animals," he thought. And then he looked for and found the symbol for the wolf.

"Ah-ha. Found my Spirit Animal, the Wolf."

He stood up and listened more carefully because it seemed as though other voices had joined Catori's. He could now distinguish what sounded like hundreds of voices singing in unison to the drums. Many hundreds, maybe even thousands.

"Singing!" He said out loud.

He looked all around, confused. "Where are these voices coming from?"

His feet were now measurably vibrating on the rock beneath him. And he found himself humming to the repeating song he was hearing.

He advanced further and, as he got nearly to the center, he stopped dumbfounded once again.

"There is a Medicine Wheel in the center?" he said out loud. And although the colors were subdued or faded, he could make out black, red, yellow, and white.

"These represent the four directions in our tribal beliefs, west, north, east, and south."

However, inside the Medicine Wheel, in the exact center, what he saw, was even more unbelievable. Carved deeply into the hard surface was a simple, very light feather almost 2 feet across. It was much lighter than the rest of the surface... almost white.

"It's a feather. It's a White Feather." He realized with amazement.

Jeromy stood there, and for what seemed like an eternity, he simply stared at the feather before him on the rock. He was lost for words... almost apoplectic.

"What is this, Catori? What is this all about?" He asked in earnest.

"They are waiting for you." She replied.

Feeling a gentle breeze against his back, he felt pushed or drawn to stand on the feather. The feeling made him excited to see what happens next.

"Who is waiting for me, Catori?" Jeromy asked with childlike enthusiasm.

"Everyone" was the one-word reply he heard in his mind.

Jeromy smiled and took a deep breath. The stone beneath his feet was really vibrating strongly now... and almost humming, and he felt it through his entire body. It wasn't a bad feeling. In fact, it felt natural to him as though it was vibrating on precisely the right frequency... his frequency.

Smiling with his head held high and listening to the singing, he took in another deep breath.

"Audentes Fortuna Juvat," he announced. "Fortune Favors the Bold."

With a measured, deliberate move, he stepped forward onto the feather with both feet. That is when he heard a familiar deep voice. He used to hear very often in his dreams a long time ago.

"Welcome, White Feather."

The air around him began to feel thick and heavy and seemed to take on form. It enveloped him like dense water or jello to the point where he was sure he was losing control of physical movement. He felt nearly weightless, helpless, and found it difficult to breathe... so he held his breath.

Stars? It had become darker around him, and it appeared as though stars were spinning in a vortex and drawing him in.

Feeling a little unsteady, he fell to his knees. But suddenly, it was over.

Instantly, he felt strong and balanced and stood up once again.

He could still hear the drumming. In fact, it was almost deafening with voices singing clearly. And they sang together but in many different languages.

The light was a brilliant white. Focusing was a bit difficult.

The drumming and singing continued for several moments longer and ended with one loud thunderous beat. Boom!

Jeromy snapped to attention.

Then that familiar male voice spoke to him again.

"Welcome, White Feather."

This was followed by what sounded like a million voices loudly echoing the same greeting... all in unison.

"Welcome, White Feather!"

"Welcome, White Feather!"

"Welcome, White Feather!"

Startled, he gasped and caught his breath because standing less than 10 feet from him was the most magnificent American Indian he could have ever imagined.

"Wow, what a trip!" He blurted out.

The tall, ancient native man smiled. It was then that Jeromy noticed that the extraordinary man was glowing – no sparkling! In fact, he looked otherworldly.

It was then that a different, old, and much more familiar voice spoke to him. It was a female voice that he had not heard in many, many years and one that he had loved throughout his childhood.

"Jeromy," she said.

Jeromy hesitated for a moment, then slowly looked over in the direction of the voice.

It was then that a multitude of new realities set in. He could now clearly see the man standing before him was supernatural, and standing right next to him was what looked like his dear long-departed Grandma Blossom smiling from ear-to-ear... and looking young and healthy.

Jeromy felt a convergence of shock and exhilaration and joy all at the same time.

"Grandmother Blossom, is that you? It can't be you…. Is that really you? What is going on?!" He could barely get the sputtering words out of his mouth.

"Yes, my little White Feather. It is me. I am Grandmother Blossom... I'm your Grandma."

Jeromy froze solid like a breathless statue. Overcome with emotion, he began softly sobbing, and tears started streaming down his face.

"Oh my God." He whispered softly.

"It can't be you. You are dead. I'm sorry, but you died, and I went to your funeral. We buried you, Grandma."

And then another thought splashed onto the chaotic canvas of his mind.

"Am I dead?"

"No, Jeromy dear, you are not dead." She replied.

He kept his focus on his Grandma Blossom. On the one hand, it seemed to comfort him; on the other hand, he was standing and speaking to his dead grandmother.

Taking a deep breath, he pulled his shoulders back to steady himself. Then be turned his head around to get a good look in all directions. There was far more going on here than he could process. To say he was overwhelmed would be the understatement of the millennia.

It was then that Jeromy looked back at the magnificent man.

He was definitely Indian… and absolutely spectacular. He was wearing a breathtaking, formal ceremonial dress that looked as ancient as him, but it wasn't gaudy. In fact, it was the most intricate and splendid clothing or costume he had ever seen... like something out of a portrait in a museum. Beads, feathers, and sequins adorned him like a king, flowing and moving in the gentle breeze that Jeromy now realized was comforting his own flushed face.

The Chief's head was crowned with an incredible headdress or bonnet made of furs, feathers, and beadwork that flowed to the ground and extended out behind him like a royal train. Obviously an outstanding Chief, he was, in fact, the most astonishing and amazing-looking Indian that Jeromy had ever seen.

In the Chief's hand, he held a staff.

The three of them stood on the same solid stone circle, but the woods were gone, so was Catori.

Instead, there was only a slightly elevated hill… a soft plateau where the stone circle now was. The stone circle he was still standing on.

He had transported.

He looked out even further and beyond the circle and plateau was the vast, open green plain of his dream that stretched out for miles and miles in most directions, except for the also familiar green forest off to one side.

And there were Indians. Millions. Perhaps even billions.

Their sheer numbers confused his mind. Millions upon millions surrounded him endlessly and filled his field of view as far as the eyes could see and beyond. And they were all extending their arms and waving their hands in welcome.

Jeromy smiled and, once again, gasped. It was then that they all raised their voices together once again:

"Welcome, White Feather!"

"Welcome, White Feather!"

"Welcome, White Feather!"

"Yes, yes... Welcome, White Feather," the great Chief declared. "Welcome, indeed."

In his right hand, Jeromy could see that the staff the Chief was holding was very intricate and ancient-looking. It had to be at least 7 feet long and nearly 3 inches in diameter. It appeared to be crafted from a gnarled and twisted natural wood branch or tree; however, nothing about it looked natural overall. In fact, it looked otherworldly… supernatural.

His heart was racing a bit, but the scholar in Jeromy kicked in, and he took one slow, careful step closer toward the man and stared inquisitively at the staff. Throughout its height, it was detailed with small twig and root-like protrusions. It was carefully carved with incredible glyphic detail.

"Was it alive?" He thought.

At first glance, he could see what looked like various nature and religious symbols, and there was also gold inlaid and a strange orb-like crystal at the top. It also seemed incredibly ancient... perhaps as old as time itself.

It was then that the man adjusted his grip on the staff and raised it a couple of feet off the ground. He turned away from Jeromy and looked out across the assembled legion of Indians. He held it in the air for several seconds. Then, with a sudden thrust downward, he struck it to the ground with a loud thunderous concussion that shook the very rock they were standing upon. Like canon fire, the sound reverberated and echoed everywhere, shaking the very air itself.

And with that... all of the many millions of people waved to Jeromy one more time and then turned, and all walked away.

Jeromy turned to face the great Chief and the woman who appeared to be his grandmother. He took a few slow, careful steps forward to get a closer look.

The great Chief's face was a dark reddish-brown with deep lines and creases crossing his leathery face like a roadmap of his life's travels, triumphs, and sorrows. His eyes were dark and deep-set, but not ominously so. And yet, they gave Jeromy a gut-twisting feeling that this was a gravely serious man who should not be taken lightly.

The woman standing next to the chief indeed looked like his Grandma - only a much younger version. She was smiling the same loving smile he remembered, and it gave him great comfort and made it possible for him to relax.

This Chief, his Grandma, this place, his dreams from his childhood… everything continued to be surreal. In his mind, he definitely had questions.

"Wow," he said. Then he paused for what seemed like a very long time, just staring at them before continuing to speak.

He opened his mouth to begin asking questions; however, the great Chief held up one hand with his palm toward Jeromy.

"Please wait, White Feather. I know you have many questions. This is normal and to be expected. What you need to know right now is that a great gift and responsibility are about to be bestowed upon you. And, we have all been waiting for you."

The Great Chief paused for a moment and then stated, "You will stay with us."

Jeromy was about to speak again, but it was his Grandma's turn to hold up a hand, clearly cautioning him to hold his questions for now. So, Jeromy decided that it might be a wise idea. He may be 36, but he still respected his Grandma, alive or dead.

The Great Chief turned and started walking away.

Jeromy was trying his best to remain silent but felt he needed to ask one more question.

"Chief. Is your name Chingachgook?"

The Great Chief smiled, turned to the Grandma, pointed to Jeromy, and remarked, "He is brilliant - this one."

Then, looking over his shoulder as he began to walk away, he replied to Jeromy. "Yes... I am Chingachgook. I was the last of the Mohican people to walk upon the earth until my lost son Cayuga came back."

He continued to walk away with the train of his long headdress trailing behind him. As he did, he made one more comment.

"Welcome to the Spirit World."

Jeromy and his Grandma stood for a few moments and watched the great chief walk away. It was his grandmother who then continued the conversation.

"Grandson, I am sure you have many questions."

"The Spirit World?" Jeromy replied.

"Heaven? Wankan Tanka Land? The Great Myst? The place of the dead? How can this be? I mean, I always thought there must be an afterlife; at least that is what you taught me and what the elders were always teaching us when I was growing up. But… how is it that I am here? Am I dreaming?"

His grandmother smiled and looked at her grandson lovingly.

"Jeromy, we will walk, you will ask questions, and I will give answers."

As they started to walk, Jeromy began.

"Okay, to start with: are you real?"

"Yes, Jeromy… I am real." And with that, she stretched her arm forward and gently caressed his cheek with the palm of her hand.

Again, Jeromy took in a quick breath.

"Oh my God, I can feel the warmth of your hand. It really is you, Grandma. Can I touch you also?"

"Yes, of course." She replied, smiling. "By the way… how long is it going to take for you to give your ole' Grandma a hug?"

Jeromy laughed nervously but reached forward and pulled her to him and hugged her firmly and long. With that hug, most of his cares subsided, and he felt both invigorated and relaxed.

Releasing her, he continued his questions.

"Am I dead?"

"No." She replied. "As I said before, you are not dead. You are merely a visitor. When your visit is completed, you will return to join the others."

"Is everyone else here dead?"

"Yes, their walk with the living ended. Some of them arrived recently. Most of them have been here for hundreds and even thousands of years."

Jeromy took a deep breath and let it out. *Alive is good*, he thought.

"Are all the dead Indian people here in the Spirit World?"

"There are many people from all tribes that exist or have ever existed," she replied. "In the living world, some tribes simply are no longer. However, they continue here."

"Do they all come here when they die?"

"Most do. Some were not believers or not worthy. They are in other places."

"Does the Dark Lord know or see this place?"

Grandma Blossom smiled. "No, he is a non-believer."

"Where are we walking to?"

"We are going to the villages of our Lakota peoples." She smiled and looked up at her grandson with pride. "There are many tribes that are waiting to welcome you. In fact, millions have anticipated your arrival."

"Many tribes? Me? Our tribe and others? Millions?"

"Yes, Jeromy." She responded. "We will first visit all the Lakota peoples, but over 600 tribes have been waiting. But let's talk more about that when we arrive. Okay?"

"And… why are they waiting to meet me?"

"In time, grandson. Please be patient for that answer for just a while longer."

"Uhh…" he hesitated. He wanted answers, but he never disrespected his grandma in life, and he sure wasn't going to start now. So, he decided to wait on that for now and took the conversation in a new direction.

It was then that Jeromy noticed something funny about his left hand – the hand he had broken as a child. A surgeon had to repair it, and there had been a slight deformity and deep scar for nearly 30 years.

"What is going on with this hand?"

Once again, she smiled and looked into his eyes. "The Spirit World represents perfection. Your hand was not perfect. Now it is. You will also find that any other physical imperfections have also been corrected. You have been physically healed in all ways."

Jeromy paused to let that sink in. After about 30 seconds, he remembered his surgery when he was 12 and lifted up his shirt to inspect his abdomen.

"The scar from your appendectomy is gone." She said as she pointed to his stomach.

Jeromy checked his right wrist and knee too.

"Ah, yes… you were always climbing like a monkey and always falling down and skinning your knees or getting cuts. Those scars are gone, too. In fact, if you check, your wisdom teeth have returned, but they are straight, and there is plenty of space for them now. Even your hair is thicker."

Jeromy rolled his tongue around in his mouth. He felt the hair on his head, and she was right. It felt thicker! Then he even put his fingers into his mouth and looked at her with astonishment.

"Wow…" He said.

His Grandma let out a big laugh, and they continued walking. Looking out across the vast expanse, Jeromy found himself intellectually breathless. The immaculate, vividly green grass was gently waving and appeared alive. The light seemed pure white and danced between gently waving, full, and very green trees. Everything was aglow – almost providing its own internal radiance. In fact, looking again at his Grandma, she appeared to be glowing too.

"You are glowing, Grandma. And you look so much younger than when you died."

"We all glow here. This is the brightest and happiest place in the universe. Everything has a vibration and is alive. You see the love and joy within."

"Do I glow here?" He asked.

"No. You are still alive."

"Why do you look so young?"

"I can choose how I look. Watch."

Jeromy's Grandma stopped walking for a moment. She placed the palms of her hands in front of her facing upward. She smiled and, within seconds, she looked 75 years old again.

Jeromy jumped back about a foot and let out a gasp. "Jesus, grandma. Can you do that anytime you want?"

"Yes." She replied. "Would you prefer I stay like this?"

Jeromy paused in thought for a moment and then replied. "No, I want you to look like whatever age you prefer. I am good with that."

Once again, Grandma Blossom smiled.

"You always had a generous heart, dear. That is part of the reason why you are here."

Once again, she stretched out her hands with palms up and quickly morphed back to a 30-something look.

The two of them continued on their walking journey for some time… talking and catching up on the past 10 years… switching back and forth from Spirit World to Living World and back again as they enjoyed each other's company. Time flew by, as it does in the Spirit World. In fact, before long, Jeromy had no idea just how much time had transpired since he first arrived.

With the point of his arrival many miles behind him, a more profound realization settled into his heart and mind. What a blessing it was to have the opportunity to visit his Grandma and his people. She had mentioned that he would be visiting all tribes and getting to know all the native peoples. He decided to focus further on that single idea for a while.

Remembering the massive numbers of people who welcomed him, he asked, "There are many spirit people here. Won't it take a very long time to visit them all?"

Smiling a bit like the Cheshire Cat from Alice in Wonderland, she winked and replied, "Yes, you are right, and you only have three years for your education and training."

Jeromy stopped and looked shocked.

"Grandmother, this is an honor, but I cannot leave my life or the cause for three whole years!"

She laughed, "Do not worry, Jeromy. Time works differently here."

"How? What do you mean?"

"Three years here is as three days in the living world.'

"What?"

"Yes, grandson. You will only be gone three days from your life. And in the three spirit-years that you will be here, you will become even more enlightened and courageous, cunning, stronger, faster, skillful, and wiser. You will be fully Indian in ways you have only read and imagined. You will also gain the knowledge and experiences you will need for what is to come."

"Three days?" He asked again.

"Yes, Jeromy, three days."

Jeromy held up an index finger asking for a pause. He thought his head was about to explode, and he had to think. After a short time had passed, allowing all the thoughts flying around in his head to settle down just a bit, he turned once again to Grandma Blossom. When he spoke, his tone was more serious now.

"Grandmother, what is to come?"

"You are about to find out. Please be patient for just a bit longer. As soon as we reach our Oglala Lakota people, the whole story will be presented to you."

"Grandma, you remember Issabelle? You have not asked about her."

"Do not worry," she replied. "I watch after both of you all the time. I am very proud of Izzy, too." She smiled.

So, they continued their walk and spoke about everything they encountered for at least another hour. Jeromy felt like a student again - very excited. Along the path, he learned that everything in the Spirit World environment was controllable. With a simple few words or hand gestures, they could change the temperature, cloud cover, wind, rain, animals, birds, terrain, and so much more. Simply put, it was mind-blowing.

At first, it seemed a little challenging. For example, when he simply said "wind," he was nearly blown over. However, he soon learned to be specific: If he would say "warm, gentle breeze," the effect was much more desirable and controllable. And so, it went.

To his smiling Grandma, Jeromy looked and behaved like a child in a candy store. It took him no time at all until he had rainbows forming across a cloudless sky, trees blowing in many different directions at the same time, birds flying backward, and streams flowing uphill. That last one, in particular, made him laugh so hard he thought his sides would split open.

Before long, he felt that he totally understood the magnitude and possibilities and was happy and content to listen to what his visit was all about.

The two of them continued walking until their path took them over a modest rise. They paused at the highest point and, on the other side, spread out for miles and miles, they could see a vast open circular prairie, and around the outer circumference of the grand round prairie were hundreds and hundreds of enormous TeePees, the size of which Jeromy had never seen or heard of before.

Over the entrance of each teepee was a flag or symbol. Jeromy figured that the prairie must be many miles across, and Indian people gathered everywhere in small and large groups visiting, talking, and laughing. Children were running and playing in the prairie's gently waving, foot-deep emerald grass. All forms of wildlife could be seen walking, running, flying, and even interacting with the human spirit people. It was peace personified.

"We call this place the Green Sea." His Grandma said.

Jeromy and his Grandma smiled at each other, and then, without a word, everyone looked in their direction and waved to them. Thousands waved their greetings and shouted their hellos.

Then, walking in all directions toward their respective tribal teepees, they dispersed.

"Why are they leaving?" Asked Jeromy.

"They are all happy to meet you, but they know that they must all wait their turn." The grandmother replied.

They walked a short distance down the slope and across the massive open circular plain. As they approached one of the enormous teepees, Jeromy could see the flag of the Oglala Sioux Tribe with eight white tipis arranged in a circle with their bases inward, so they form a star on a red field.

They walked up to the entrance and stopped. Jeromy could see that the access was open; however, he could not see inside. There only appeared to be blackness in the opening.

"Grandma?" He simply asked.

"It is time for another trip, Grandson. Are you ready?"

"Ah, well, yes, I guess. Will it be like the last one? He said excitedly.

"Well, that is entirely up to you." She replied. "I recommend that you walk through quickly with confidence. Or, if you are really enjoying the trip, pause, and wiggle for a while."

"Hmmm…" he replied. "Quickly with confidence or pause and wiggle, eh?"

They both laughed.

"Yes." She simply said.

Jeromy hesitated for about 10 seconds but could see that Grandma Blossom would wait for him to take the initiative: the first step.

"Very well, then." He replied. "Let's see what's on the other side."

And with that, he touched his grandmother's arm, giving her a caress with his hand, and then lowered his head a bit like getting himself ready and quickly marched forward into the darkness.

She was right. Even though he could tell the stages of the transition were there, they all occurred in just 2 or 3 seconds. There was vibration, some vertigo, thick air, and then… arrival.

On the other side, he immediately saw thousands and thousands of new teepees and an enormous number of Oglala Sioux tribe people.

His Grandma Blossom arrived only two seconds after him.

"Welcome to the Oglala Lakota Nation and all Sioux Spirit Lands." She said.

"Welcome, White Feather!" A few dozen people nearby shouted.

Jeromy smiled and waved his hand while he took it all in. The sight of so many of his people all in one place, albeit vast and spread out for miles, was very exciting.

They walked forward into what looked like the center of a massive village, and Jeromy could see many, many individuals… all very busy with one thing or another. Some were simply talking or laughing. Others were working together on handicrafts and other projects, grooming horses, or caring for other animals.

"Grandma Blossom." Said Jeromy. "Are all of the Oglala Lakota Sioux people here in this village?"

"No. This is just one of the countless villages within our spirit nation. There are over a thousand other villages just like this."

"How come so many?" He asked.

"Remember that our people were around for thousands of years. The spirits tend to mostly gather with spirits from their time. But that is not important because villages can be made, changed, or combined in any way we desire. And we are all free to go wherever we want, whenever we want."

"So, the giant teepee that we entered through into the Oglala Lakota Nation here contains over a thousand other villages? It must not be proportional, right? I mean, it was big, but it was really just a portal, wasn't it?"

"Yes. That is right. Our lands here go on for hundreds of miles."

"And that means that all the other native tribes have hundreds or thousands of villages between all their tribal spirit lands that each goes on for hundreds of miles too?" He concluded.

"Yes, Jeromy. That is correct."

When the spirits saw Jeromy approaching, many stopped what they were doing and ran forward to greet him.

Then many more started talking and asking questions at once.

"Is it true? Are you the White Feather?"

"We've waited so long to meet you."

"It is an honor, White Feather."

"You don't glow, White Feather."

"Did you eat?"

"Are you hungry?

"Were you the one making the trees dance in different directions? Was that you?"

So went the questions, one after another. Truthfully, Jeromy was a bit overwhelmed and without words. There was so much he did not understand that he just didn't know where to begin. His pulse was racing, and he felt an apple-sized lump in his throat.

"Grandmother, what is going on?"

Then she turned to address the people and remarked, "Brothers and sisters, we will let White Feather rest for the evening. No more questions today."

Jeromy was about to speak again when she turned to him and, anticipating his next question, she replied, "Our people can ask you questions tomorrow after your own questions have been answered. Let's sit and talk now."

So, they both found a very comfortable place to sit alone. Everyone else gave them space as they needed it.

"Grandson, as we have said, you are being given a great gift and responsibility. Please listen."

This indicated she would speak, and Jeromy would listen.

"For thousands of years, our people, all Indian people, lived in balance and mostly in harmony. There was a natural order to our lives, and the outcomes were for us to choose and live through. But that all changed when the white European arrived.

"Many millions died from terrible diseases brought by the newcomers. Violence and suffering were also waged upon us, and millions more died. Soon, we became nearly extinct as the white man re-made our lands into what they had left behind in Europe.

"We tried to defend ourselves and our lands to no avail. Along that path, the white men made hundreds of promises in treaties - all of which they broke. They lied and lied and lied… while we died and died and died."

Jeromy was listening intently. He nodded frequently. This was well-known to him, and he taught this to his students.

"Jeromy, since you were very young, you were always passionate about our people. From an early age, you began asking why our people do not live in the comforts that white Americans enjoy. You were always asking questions; the right questions. You even went to college to learn more, and today… today, you teach our real history to people yourself.

"We have all been watching you. We have seen your passion, care, intellect, and call for justice. Our people here in the Spirit World have wanted a way to correct how badly things have turned out in the living world, but there needed to be a warrior leader or champion among the living to make that happen."

Jeromy swallowed hard, but continued to sit silently.

"Jeromy, my grandson… you are that champion."

Jeromy appeared both confused and astonished beyond words.

"Grandma Blossom. You know me. You know that, in my heart, I would run into battle, or whatever, to make a better life for our people. But… I am just a teacher."

His grandmother smiled.

"Actually, you are precisely the right person. You showed everyone you were witty and sincere and had a big, humble heart from an early age.

"We have also given you a new, stronger body and increased your confidence and courage. As far as the rest of it goes, three years will be all that you will need."

"Grandma, I hear you, but think about all the great warriors of history like Red Cloud, Crazy Horse, and so many others. I want to see things change for the positive for our people; I just want to understand… why me?"

"None of the great warriors of history had your extensive education, Jeromy. And none of them really knew the white people the way you do. We know you have a brave heart; you just need the physical strength and training to pull it together."

"You said 'we.'" He asked questioningly.

"Jeromy, I didn't choose you; that is not my place. I was asked if I thought you could do this, and I said yes."

"Last question, Grandma. Who asked you?"

"Chingachgook and his son Cayuga. They said you had already been chosen from a long time ago. Predestination, they called it. Chingachgook simply came to me to let me know and hear what I had to say."

Then she looked at him with the most serious face he had ever seen.

"Jeromy Whitefeather, this is your destiny. You are already known to all of us. You are *White Feather*."

His grandmother's reassurances began melting any remaining doubts away.

"Now, you know why you are here." She continued. "You will be trained into a Sioux warrior. You will use all the knowledge you already have and all the skills and knowledge that we can provide you. Indeed, you will become the champion and leader of a great spirit army, grandson."

Jeromy sat with his mouth agape.

"You are the one, Jeromy." She said.

Jeromy stared at her for a moment and then replied.

"I hear you, and I believe you."

"And now," she continued. "This evening, we will have fun."

And so, they did. Hundreds of thousands of Oglala Sioux filed past Jeromy to say a simple hello as he sat with his Grandma Blossom. Together they all watched the sun setting and painting the sky crimson and gold while they sat or strolled around visiting hundreds of campfires.

Several played drums, and many danced in joy, elated that White Feather had arrived. Everyone wanted to pay their respects, but the questions and interactions were kept to a minimum so Jeromy could eat and simply relax and watch tribal activities.

Jeromy mostly watched the children at play. He was amazed and saddened at the vast number of children present, indicating they had died before ever having the chance to become adults. Many were killed as babies and toddlers. However, there was no sadness or despair in the Spirit World, neither among adults nor children. Everyone was at peace, and they were incredibly happy and excited about Jeromy's arrival at long last.

On the first night, children were playing inyan onyeyapi games (using slingshots). Although boys usually played this, the girls were having just as much fun and were sometimes better than the boys at hitting targets. At one point, several children wanted Jeromy to join in, but Grandma Blossom kindly told them no. They were to wait until tomorrow. She wanted him to simply relax and take it all in, and he did...

Adults were just as eager to speak with Jeromy. However, they were also urged to wait until the next day, so they mostly filed past waving hello and then returned to their fires to chat and share stories, jokes, or dances, old and new.

Fireflies danced slowly through the air, intermittently glowing... almost in unison. Children chased after them, caught them, and released them.

An occasional wolf's howl could be heard eerily singing to the rising, brilliant silver moon. Strangely enough, the man-in-the-moon looked at peace, too.

He could see all kinds of fun and activities off into the distance. Everyone was very content and enjoying their eternal peace.

The people in the Spirit World were indeed at peace. It was the living that continued to suffer.

And so, the first night went. Jeromy was the only one eating; no one else needed to eat, although he soon found out they could eat if they wanted to. It didn't matter to their immortal souls, so they mostly didn't bother. But Jeromy really enjoyed the food brought to him in abundance. And, when he was finished, they simply took it away and offered what was left to the birds and animals, who also had the option of eating or not eating.

When he was tired, Grandma Blossom took him to a teepee and laid down to rest.

"What a day!" He thought.

The three days he spent with his own tribe were priceless to him. He got to meet hundreds and hundreds of great Oglala Sioux leaders and elders from the past. He also got to spend time with more contemporary elders such as Russell Means, a great American Indian actor and one of the leaders of the American Indian Movement or A.I.M. He had met him as a boy and was pleased to see him so content and happy at long last.

Among them were Chief American Horse and his father Old Chief Smoke, an Oglala Lakota head chief and one of the last great Shirt Wearers. They were considered highly prestigious Lakota warriors. Old Chief Smoke had five wives who were all present with him. Old Chief Smoke's sons had carried the Smoke People legacy of leadership into the early 20th century. In addition to his five wives and son, Chief American Horse, several of his other children were present, including Spotted Horse Woman, Chief Big Mouth, Chief Blue Horse, Chief Red Cloud, Chief Bull Bear III, Chief Solomon Smoke II, Chief No Neck and others.

Then, there was Chief Crazy Horse, who Jeromy was thrilled to meet. They discussed many of the battles he was involved in during the 1800s, including the Battle of Little Big Horn. He found Chief Crazy Horse to be very passionate and remarkably intelligent. When they were finished, Chief Crazy Horse placed a hand on Jeromy's shoulder and said:

"We see you. We are here with you. Train hard. Learn everything you can. We will be with you when the time comes."

And although Jeromy still felt anxious by the responsibility given to him, he was honored. He took great comfort in the reassuring words.

On the last day with his tribe, over 40 of his tribe's chiefs from across the ages sat in a circle with him. They gave him counsel, wisdom, and praise. They also gave him their blessing and told him they would be with him when the time arrived.

Chapter # 13:
Training with the Ancestors

In the first year in the Spirit World, Jeromy visited nearly 600 native tribes. Sometimes, he spent a day or two with a particular tribe, and sometimes, he visited 2 or 3 tribes in a day.

Every tribe had its own dialect or language; however, Jeromy could miraculously understand and converse with everyone. It didn't matter whether he spoke Lakota or English, and it didn't matter what they spoke. It was as though a language and dialect translator was in universal operation. Every word and meaning were understood completely by both man and spirit.

Each tribe rolled out the red carpet with greetings and food and was genuinely excited to share their history and stories with White Feather. They also shared their techniques for making and using tools and weapons. However, actual training would not happen until the second year.

Jeromy knew many tribal backgrounds due to his extensive college studies; however, many new details came to light, and some misunderstandings were corrected too. He especially treasured all the new information he had never known about precious pearls of the past lost over millennia.

There were also graphic visions and accounts of the suffering and death at the hands of the whites. In all cases, the accounts that were shared were told without pitched emotions or sadness. Those negative feelings did not exist here, except for within Jeromy. Tribe after tribe, every story cut his soul with sorrow for the sufferings of the native peoples. They also built up his resolve.

Women did much of the heavy work in the villages, including farming, building, skinning, and butchering. They were also experts on tanning and sewing leather into shoes, clothing, and other apparel. In the afterlife, men also helped make things, unlike during the days of their lives. All these activities were optional and only continued because they brought joy to the souls who enjoyed making things with their hands.

Occasionally, spirit people would also cook, bake, gather firewood, weave, and make all kinds of arts and crafts. Men and women alike enjoyed the work. It was yet another opportunity to sit and talk and enjoy each other's company.

Out of an abundance of love, genuine concerns for the living were expressed by most. They saw the living conditions, disease, and poverty, and they wanted the suffering of Indian peoples in the United States to come to an end. They all longed for fairness, equality, and justice to be realized by the living. Still, year after year and century after century, they continued to witness the deplorable living conditions and prejudicial treatment by the American leaders back in the living world. Promises kept being made, but their living relatives kept suffering and disappearing, and justice wasn't coming… At least not without White Feather.

Although there wasn't sadness expressed per se, there was high expectation and excitement about Jeromy's arrival because he was *"the one."* The White Feather was longed for to lead the way for justice and life-correction among the living. Some had been waiting for him for a very long time.

And so it went; Jeromy went on to the other Sioux tribes and got to know the countless number of men, women, and children. He was able to ask questions and learn from them. Valuable stories were told: stories of their lives and stories of their deaths. He then went on to other tribes and repeated the same, asking questions, learning, and listening. And at every gathering, he was given reassurances that he wasn't alone. They would all be with him when the time was at hand — the time to take back their heritage.

During the first year, Jeromy was given great knowledge but few skills aside from becoming an excellent equestrian. He quickly graduated from riding old nags to the most athletic horses in the afterlife with daily exercise.

When he left his tribe, he was given a gift – a beautiful chestnut thoroughbred that stood 16.2 hands tall or about 66 inches at the withers. In fact, when he first saw the magnificent animal, he doubted he could ride him, imagining how much it would hurt falling off of him. But, as soon as the thought entered his head, he heard the thoughts of the horse enter his head, too. He didn't receive words, not exactly. He actually received images in his mind. The images were of him riding with confidence and the horse always staying under him. And so, it became a reality. Jeromy quickly became an excellent rider because his horse made him so, if for no other reason.

He named his magnificent horse 'Red Thunder.'

* * *

By the time the second year arrived, Jeromy's fears and anxiety were nearly a thing of the past. He was already becoming stronger and more confident with a better diet and physical exercises, including walking, running, and riding.

Physical endurance was paramount with endless running and horseback riding. He learned hand-to-hand combat from some of the best warriors who ever lived. Wrestling was considered an art. It went on endlessly and included some martial-arts style strikes, kicks, and grappling that made him more comfortable and very effective in a fight.

At first, it was grueling.

And he got hurt - a lot, and very often.

He also got wounded and injured - a lot, and often.

But he also healed almost immediately.

In the beginning, the pain was almost intolerable. He wasn't used to pain and had tried to avoid it at any cost. To put it simply, in the past, he had always thought of himself as timid and fearful most of his life; That was fading into his past.

He also underwent one-on-one weapons training with Chingachgook during the second year. In life, the Great Chief was an expert with a double-bladed gunstock war club, the weapon he had used in battle and the weapon he had used to kill the evil Huron named Magua. It was an absolutely vicious-looking weapon. On the gunstock's ends were mounted opposing knife blades capable of slashing in either direction. Jeromy remembered watching old episodes of the TV show 'Star Trek' and thought it looked like a weapon the Klingons would have used.

Chingachgook indeed was a master of the weapon, and he trained Jeromy until he was very proficient with it. Using the weapon required quite a bit of strength and agility because of its weight and because the total effect of its fierce capability required speed and momentum, including centrifugal force. Chingachgook was so effective with it that he could leap, spin, and bring the weapon around with such velocity that it was able to cut down a 3 to 4-inch diameter tree.

"White Feather, when the time comes, you must be one with the weapon. Be strong. Be fast. Be fearless. Deliver justice."

"I will, Great Chief. I will call it Battle Blade." Jeromy responded.

So, Jeromy practiced repeatedly with the instruction of the Great Chief for over a month. He was told to take it with him and carry it everywhere he went to bond with the weapon, and that is precisely what he did. Then he moved on for additional weapons training by other tribes. With each tribe, he also played games with the warriors. This helped to build his war skills. At first, he was very ineffective - clumsy, actually. He tripped over his own feet and fell more times than he could remember. He even broke his arm twice, but it was healed soon.

He persevered.

There were also activities like shooting arrows through rolling wooden hoops while racing his horse at a gallop. It gave him exceptional balance and trained all his senses. At first, he was uncoordinated and ineffective. Eventually, he became one with the course, and he did very well. During all of his training, he also practiced the Spirit Magic he had learned at the Olta.

He persevered.

After he was trained to hunt, he spent some time hunting alone and stalking prey, although he couldn't hurt them, and they were always able to get up afterward. At first, he was reluctant. Unsteady. Eventually, he became so good he knew that if the day ever arrived, he could survive out in the wild.

One training required him to stalk and kill a bear. The bear didn't give him a break either. It took an entire day to track him down. Finally, he came upon the bear at twilight before the moon could rise. The bear charged through the brambles, over and over again, growling and roaring so fiercely Jeromy nearly relieved himself in his pants. When the bear won, Jeromy got a swat from the massive paws and claws that hurt and cut, but like his previous wounds, he healed immediately. Eventually, Jeromy learned to move and lunge and thrust in a rhythm that matched the bear's movements. He actually took down the bear to his amazement and attacked. The bear was surprised, too.

In addition to the making and use of weapons, some tribes also showed him how to make and set traps long distances apart and find his way back to them. He learned how to navigate and track his route through the wilderness.

Then there was the constant practice with all the wide variety of weapons, including the combat use of war clubs of all descriptions, the throwing of various spears of various weights and sizes, and thrusting, jabbing, cutting, and slicing with all kinds of knives.

Most of the knives were made in the old ways depending on the tribe with chunks of obsidian or flint. Some with metal, some more resembled swords, and then there were battle axes, hatchets, tomahawks, and more knives. There were no firearms that he saw.

Jeromy completed his second year feeling very much like a master at arms.

* * *

There were battles and battle strategies in the third and final years of his training. The afterlife had no intention of sending White Feather into the struggle with knowledge and training only. He needed experience in combat.

The Return of the Mohicans

Before the arrival of white Europeans in the 1500s, there were some wars and conflicts between various tribes on the continent. They were considered unfortunate, but natural. And they were resolved one way or the other between tribes.

However, the Europeans' arrival brought with it an era of more significant tribal conflicts and warfare due to the intensified competition for resources and the newcomer's greed for land and riches. Mounted Lakota Sioux warriors attacked the Blackfeet and Crow westward. Other tribes felt the pinch as well. Since they had little chance to beat back the Europeans (and eventually new Americans), they took to warfare as a means of survival.

This is where Jeromy's tribal ancestors came in. Since the Sioux were very effective in battle and battle strategies (remember Custer), they and the Blackfeet and Crow all came together to organize war games.

They would come together in harmony each day, welcoming each other and White Feather to the war game. Chingachgook helped with the plans and strategies.

They organized military units that protected and patrolled and other military units that were to be the attackers. Every day was a new scenario in a different situation, location, or terrain.

Sometimes, the attacks came on horseback and sometimes on foot. Some attacks were launched at night, while others were against very large villages and others were out in the open. There were attacks made in the rain and in the snow and in blowing and howling winds.

The raids and defenses went on for nine months. With some of the attacks, Jeromy was a part of the raiders. In other scenarios, he was on defense, protecting a camp or village. Some attacks involved small numbers, and others became massive warfare by legends of warriors.

In the last month of the war games, he was designated the Chief. Taking what he had learned and with Chingachgook's consultation, he launched several very effective and surprising attacks. He also mounted several outstanding defenses.

As with everything else in the Spirit World, he and everyone else healed instantly from wounds inflicted on the battlefield. And, after the daily conflict was over, everyone came together and had a great time reenacting and retelling the story of the war, often laughing and teasing each other if they had fallen in battle. In the final months of the third and last year of his training, he was taken to a place prepared by the Great Chief ahead of time.

He awoke early to the smell of coffee. He always found it a fantastic favor that someone would prepare coffee for him in the mornings. For nearly three years, he had been continuously made to feel welcomed in that way.

On this particular morning, the person entering the teepee with his coffee with the Great Chief Chingachgook himself.

"Good morning, White Feather."

"Good morning, Great Chief."

"Here is your coffee," said Chingachgook as he handed the stoneware mug to Jeromy. "Are you ready for the final planning and training?"

Jeromy stood up, took the mug, and thanked the Great Chief. Wearing only a breechcloth, he stretched and yawned and took a big, welcomed sip.

Chingachgook stared at Jeromy, bronzed and rippled with muscles. Jeromy could sense he was about to say something else.

"Uh… Is everything okay, Great Chief?"

"Yes, White Feather," he replied. "Everything is perfect. I was just observing and thinking."

"Observing and thinking? Really?"

"Yes. I observed how you look since you have been with us for nearly three years. You came to us, less brave in your heart, mind, and spirit. Now I see you looking like one of the biggest, fastest, and most formidable braves that I ever trained. You are strong in Spirit Magic – smartest, too. Look at you. We are all very pleased."

Jeromy felt almost embarrassed, but he knew the words of the Great Chief were true. He had, indeed, changed dramatically and looked and felt very strong. *How would Issabelle take all of this*, he thought.

"Chief, do you think that my sister, Issabelle, will be okay with all of this?" He used his hands to point to the changes in his size.

"Yes. Issabelle is a wonderful sister and loves you very much, White Feather. Besides, I have been giving her dreams, so she will not be so shocked or surprised.

"Anna will be pleased, too." He smiled and added.

"Wow, thank you. I appreciate that very much."

"We are all family, White Feather. All of us. I am happy to do this."

Jeromy took another sip from his coffee mug and then replied to the original question.

"Great Chief. I am ready. What is next?"

"We plan and train for the battle to come. We have a surprise for you, White Feather. I think the expression you will understand is… *'you are not going to believe this.'*"

"Really? Well, you have me very curious. I have gotten to know many of our people. I have trained with weapons and in hand-to-hand combat. And, I have been a part of the war games, which was a great experience. So, I am inquisitive to see what is next."

Jeromy finished his coffee and finished dressing. Chingachgook gave him some bread and meat and then walked out of the teepee with him. As soon as he emerged into the daylight, he gasped.

The Great Chief's own horse was named Red Fury. Both Red Fury and Red Thunder were standing outside the tent, ready for their riders. So, both Jeromy and Chingachgook mounted their horses and began riding toward the tree line.

They followed the edge of the forest for several miles at a canter. The morning was a little brisk and very sunny, with a light scent of flowers in the breeze. Chingachgook had dialed the weather perfectly.

Jeromy focused and tuned his senses to the smell of the flowers. There was something in the air that Jeromy recognized.

"Am I smelling apples or apple blossoms?"

"Yes. In fact, why don't we have a few apples this morning?" Said Chingachgook waving his hand, and some apples appeared in front of them.

They enjoyed their apples and continued riding along the tree line until the woods on their right side stopped. As they reined their horses to the right to continue riding, they rode up to the higher ground and stopped on the rise.

Jeromy was blown away with surprise.

Below them was a 19th-century city, but it was not just any city; it was Washington DC.

Apple Blossoms! Everywhere around the Spirit World town of Washington DC were fragrant apple trees in full blossom.

"That is one beautiful town, Great Chief," Jeromy said.

"It is Washington DC in the year 1830. The United States Congress has just passed President Andrew Jackson's Indian Removal Act...." He said solemnly.

"Which began the Trail of Tears, land theft, and forced relocation for dozens of years," Jeromy interrupted.

"That is right, White Feather. You will train your army to attack Washington, DC, in May of 1830 right after the passage of the law."

Chingachgook smiled. He pointed the large staff at one end of the town, and a few of the trees morphed through the cycle of shedding blossoms and growing apples.

"Now, that is really cool!" Remarked Jeromy.

"Yes, it is cool. White Feather. Real *cool*." He said funnily, trying to sound like Jeromy.

And they both burst out laughing. But when they finished, Chingachgook pointed the staff to the other side of town and said one word.

"Now."

Suddenly, there was a thunderous sound. A cloud of dust started rising on the other side of the town, and the loud noise became discernible.

"Horses?" Jeromy asked.

"Yes, White Feather. The Sioux Warrior Riders are coming.

"Really? You're kidding, right?"

But he wasn't kidding, and seconds later, a massive Indian cavalry rounded that end of town and came into sight. They kept coming and coming and coming. In fact, it took ten minutes for all 50,000 of them to clear the edge of town to ride toward Jeromy and the Great Chief.

"Wow," said Jeromy.

"White Feather, I give you the Sioux Warrior Cavalry. 50,000 warriors on horseback."

"Oh, my God…" Replied Jeromy. "They look magnificent."

Then he paused to think for a few seconds while the cavalry approached. He had a concern.

"Great Chief. Will this be enough to defeat the enemy soldiers and take Washington, DC?"

"No. Not nearly enough." Replied Chingachgook. "That is why we have legions of warriors practicing all over the Spirit World. When the time comes, you will first lead the main army. The other Medallion recruits will lead three more armies, take orders and follow your command."

Chapter # 14:
The Blackness of Oneida

"There is a thing about darkness," Erik teases the conversation. At the same time, the rest of his companions watch him staring away in the distance.

"How brilliantly it hides all that remains pronounced and reveals all the subtleties." He concludes and maintains his silence, having his companions watch him in awe. Dakota led the way into the darkness, which swallowed them into blindness.

"Never knew the dark could mean so much to someone. It could make someone so wise." One of the other companions remarked about the surprising suggestion lent by their friend.

"And it somehow actually gets people into very serious troubles in this middle of the forest," another voice registers his complaint, somehow bringing it to others' knowledge that they were in the pitch-black part of the forest. They could only recognize and identify each other in the void of light from the voices. Even the slightest silhouettes were masked; the dark spared nothing to be seen. Together, they slowly and blindly treaded on the forest grounds, hoping that they wouldn't step or fall into a trap or somewhere from where they couldn't be discovered.

"Toes first, guys. We need to walk the native way silently." Akwiraron whispered.

"Whose idea was it to take this route?" Anna whispers loudly from some distance. They all proceeded in the dark, taking one careful step after the other.

"And who advised to take this route at this hour, without even exploring it when the light was ample?" The invisible Erik continues with the snide backhanded remark.

"Some brilliant person said so, and we followed him, and we are still following him, strangely." Akwiraron expresses with sarcasm the discontent with following the path that seemingly led to nowhere but the darkest part of the forest, the only part no one prefers exploring and being lost at this hour.

"It was Catori. She told us to go this way. She wouldn't steer us wrong." Commented Dakota.

Together, the quiet footfalls gently press the earth and proceed along the path through the Oneida Forest. Each footfall lifted cautiously and rested with sufficient care; each following the one preceding it.

"You know, there is a good reason we all are headed this way?" Dakota suggests, hoping it to be received the way he wanted it to. "The dark is not just a path. It is an inspiration. I'm not leading anything or anyone here…."

"Yeah, we know. But you should have at least given us the idea about such blinding darkness. It is actually scary dark. You realize this, right? Like, we don't know if there are trees around us or whether they changed into something, we can't even see. We are practically blind right now," said Erik breathlessly. Either that shakiness could be out of fear or from the rage of being dragged into this apparent mess.

"Well, that has to be the silliest thing I could hear from you. And you aren't the only one going into all this. We all are in this together." Akwiraron whispers back.

"Guys, can you all stop being such babies? We are here for a reason. We are on a mission here, and from what I know, Cayuga would not choose us as his medallion recruits if we were not capable of dealing with some darkness. Geez!" Anna shuts the complaining voices down.

The light footsteps continued, barely audible in the thickness of foliage. The trial ended when the leading person halted right where the slightest hint of the light seeped through, merely lending the sight to see the faint silhouette of the standing structures and the ones surrounding all. All that was immersed in the monotonous black.

"So... We stop here?" Erik whispers, almost wary of disturbing someone or something nearby. "Are you sure we are safe here? Like we won't be discovered from here?" The concerning inquiries rest.

"I second him. Can we be sure about this place?" The ones following raise their apprehensions. The inquiries rest, letting those who questioned follow and halt where his steps rest.

The four of them halt together, where the forest grounds appear to be evened out; the four exploring recruits turned, hoping to see what else the dark has to give away. However, the utter darkness lent nothing to the eye but absolute blackness stretching out to reach the unknown.

"So, we stop here?" A pronounced concern echoes in his voice again. The three recruits lined up, turned to inspect how far the voice reached; it became louder for a while and then deadened where the extensive woods stretched far beyond.

"Yes, it is the ideal place, I guess," Dakota stands at the front, with the remaining following him. All in the queue, they stand, awaiting the order of the one leading them through all the guidance and direction.

"We will start by taking turns." A relief resonates in his tone; hushed footfalls resume in the same direction, convinced they were, knowing where they wanted to be. Every step was taken in a similar direction, at a similar pace, by the other three.

Sensing the leading recruit's body language and confusion, one of the recruits realized that he was waiting for someone or something.

"Are we going to meet someone else here?" A worried tone from Erik replaces the quiet in the deepest part of the forest. "The quiet is playing around with us," the worried tone continues with foretelling all that was granted.

"We have been searching for the safe place; the place where we could see all yet never be revealed to the world. It will be the safe place where nothing at all threatens or poses a challenge." The one leading them assumed the very front position, facing the ones eagerly waiting for the next set of instructions.

Quite surprisingly, Dakota, the one leading them, somehow knew that he had to make others understand the very choice he made; to be in the darkest, to let no light reach them, just to be in the light for the final time.

A few hushed words. The weakest spark escapes. The spark sent by the one leading them reaches a farther tree, lights it up with a yellow glow outlining it, and allows a few birds chirping around it to leave their homes.

"What was that for?" asked Akwiraron, more like condemning the act of bothering those who peacefully rest in the foliage.

Suddenly, footsteps were heard trampling the dry leaves nearby. The three behind the one leading them stepped back hesitantly, wondering who was there. It was difficult to fight an enemy when they could not even see their friends.

"Hey?" There was a whisper in the air.

Even though the voice sounded very familiar, the forest's darkness was suffocating and any sound at all, even their own heartbeats, sounded like a threat.

"Is someone here?" Anna whispered at the silhouette that had led them to this point. The outline of the group's lead stood with exhilarating confidence, as if he knew who was there with them. There was definitely a fifth person there. The four recruits were not alone there. They could feel the presence of another, but the presence was not making any more noise, as if whoever it was there was trying to hide.

"*Okupljanje,*" Dakota, the leading silhouette, said out loud, addressing whoever was there. He was the only one amongst the four who had not stepped back upon hearing the fifth person's voice and footsteps.

Behind him, Akwiraron, Anna, and Erik stood confused. *Is that a codeword?* They couldn't help but question the unprecedented situation being presented to them.

"Dakota?" Erik hissed as if scolding him for leading them here but received no response. His voice had a clear tone of disapproval – he really wanted to be out of there now. In his mind, a lot was going on, including the many important tasks they needed to do to fulfill the responsibilities on their shoulders.

Anna was just thinking about grabbing Erik's arm and pulling him back to walk in the opposite direction when the bushes under the huge tree in front of them rustled. She held her breath.

The rustling grew louder, and with the very little moonlight that fell upon the spot they stood in, the four could see the outline of a man emerge from behind the bushes. It was a human-shaped figure, so that was a relief.

"Yeah, it's me, Jer…." The fifth voice reappeared in the dark and gradually faded out as if it was unsure about revealing further details yet. Akwiraron squinted his eyes, trying to figure out who was there. Anna had had enough of the suspense. She did not like waiting around for answers, and now that she could tell it was a man, she wanted to see who it was, especially after hearing his voice. *Well, I'll be damned if this is who I think this is!* She thought to herself excitedly.

Dakota stepped forward, farther from the three following him and closer towards the blue outline of the fifth person who had just emerged. Anna decided to ask no more questions and get answers, anyway.

"*Cemlorot,*" She said the fire spell under her breath, and a flick of fire emerged, floating above her palm. She moved closer towards the fifth person. The flickering orange light fell upon his face, lighting it up as Anna's eyes met his honey brown eyes. The ball of fire in her palm immediately vanished as a surprised gasp escaped her lips.

"Shh! Anna! You're not to light up the fire! We do not want to attract any attention here," Erik hissed at her.

When the flame had lit up only briefly before it disappeared, the three recruits were glad to see the fifth man's face. It was Jeromy there. He had been away for days ever since Catori brought Chief Cayuga's order for him to go for advanced training.

Jeromy wasn't yet aware that the Dark Lord had his servants looking actively for him. The other Medallion Recruits had no idea where exactly Jeromy had gone.

This deception worked to their advantage because none of the Dark Lord's henchmen could discover what no one else knew.

"This is why we came here. I was communicated to lead you all to this dark forest to reunite with Jeromy. Apparently, a dangerous entity is after our boy here. He will now tell you where he has been," Dakota explained to the rest of the group, who were still unsure whether they could ask any questions now.

Jeromy looked around and saw a small hollow in a nearby rock outcropping and motioned for everyone to follow him there. The five of them were able to comfortably duck into the opening.

"I have been training in the Spirit World for three years." Jeromy began.

Anna was the first to laugh.

"Very funny, Jer. What happened? Did you hit your head or something while you were away?"

The others were also smiling, but they held their comments as Jeromy, with complete sincerity, proceeded to share his three-year training.

"So, you see," Jeromy concluded. "Three years in the Spirit World is the same as three days here."

"Wait, who's this guy? Who are you?" Jeromy asked, referring to Dakota.

"He's one of us. Chief Cayuga appointed him as one of his medallion recruits ever since you were gone." Anna explained. "Do you remember him from the Olta?"

"Yes! That's right. I remember now. I remember that he was cool and quiet."

The other four recruits laughed.

"So, are you trying to replace me, Dakota?"

"No! You're the lead of Cayuga's Four-Leaf Clover – I'm just a bonus medallion recruit because…." Dakota was cut off midway through his sentence as Erik chimed in.

"Because Chief Cayuga deems him as talented and trained as us. He was in Olta a little longer than us and was undergoing training to lead a coterie, but when the Dark Lord's search for your blood was heard of, and you were hiding, Chief Cayuga added him to our group."

"I have a good knowledge of the playa and all these forests. I know my way around these places, so I was given the task of joining you. Good to see you again, White Feather," Dakota smiled.

"Oh, alright. But please call me Jeromy," Jeromy scratched his head.

"How have you all been?" Jeromy addressed everyone when he asked this, but the response only came from the voice he had missed the most and longed to hear.

"We've been good. But look at you! You are even more buff than when you left!" Anna observed. "And you've been training with armies of Spirit Warriors?"

"Thanks, and yes."

"So, three years. Eh?" continued Anna. "You didn't forget about us in three years?"

Jeromy stared into Anna's warm and smiling eyes.

"No, Anna, I definitely didn't forget about you."

There was a noticeable pause. The others rolled their eyes in the darkness at the cheesiness of the moment.

"Chief Cayuga had telecommunicated to me that my training was complete, and it is time to join you all. Something huge is cooking. Something is happening, and we will be taking care of what it is," Jeromy explained.

The five recruits gathered around, thankful for each other's well-being, and tried to formulate a strategy for the upcoming stages of their long, long journey.

"Well, I have my birthstone - the opal with me. It shows the maps on Earth and of the other dimensions, too, remember?" Jeromy hinted at his friends to get moving from this dark place that just did not feel comfortable for any of them.

"The birthstone that the archangel handed to you?" Akwiraron confirmed.

Jeromy nodded in affirmation, to which Dakota replied, "Brother, sorry to burst your bubble, but none of our birthstones or spells seem to be working to their full potential in this forest. It is as if our powers are suffocated here; I don't understand why, though."

"Well, only one way to find out!" Jeromy responded, and murmured a spell under his breath to bring the opal to appear in his palm. The magical black opal glowed with a luminous blue that gradually faded and reappeared with a bird-eye view of the dark forest to serve as a map.

"It works!" Anna was delighted. The group of young recruits cheered as quietly as they could and stared into the map displayed on the opal in Jeromy's hand.

The map seemed complicated, of course, because they were in a forest where light rarely entered, and any light that did enter faded away in a spark. Obviously, there were no paths marked with exits or signs, but there was at least direction in the map. There was a yellow dot somewhere in their northwest direction. Even though nothing was visible around them to the naked eye except a thick mist of darkness that slithered in circles, they tried to make the best sense of what they could see on the opal.

"I – umm, I'm not sure if we should head for that yellow marking on the map. I mean, who knows what it could mean?" Akwiraron was hesitant. Not afraid, but just doubtful if that was the way towards the exit.

"I'm not sure either, but I see nothing else on the map that we should head towards…." Anna thought out loud.

After a few more dialogues, the group of the recruits decided to be on their way to the yellow marking. On the opal-shaped map in Jeromy's palm, the yellow spot appeared luminous; as if it was a light source in the forest. That was strange because the forest was known to literally swallow light, so how could any luminosity be there?

Regardless, that was the only way that seemed like a way at all, so the group decided to proceed towards it anyway. They all adjusted their packs, and as they walked, Dakota fell back with the others. Jeromy led the way as he had the map. Not surprisingly, his personality had developed, making him a natural leader, especially since his transformation.

The five individuals walked in utter darkness led by an opal stone that guided them. Their footsteps treaded with more determination now than before. The dried fallen leaves crumpled under their feet as they walked, and the sky above them was almost invisible with the thick, dark trees hovering over them.

As they reached nearer to what appeared to be the yellow spot on the forest's map on the opal stone, they began to see a flickering light somewhere in the distance in the woods.

"It looks like a bonfire from here," Erik pointed out, looking at the dimmest rays of light emerging from between the trees.

The five recruits pushed twigs and branches out of their way, stepped over stones, and walked closer towards the light. It was the yellow spot on the map, and they were no longer looking at the map now that they could see the light in the forest themselves. As they closed in towards the light source, it was not a fire but what appeared to be something floating in mid-air.

"Is that…" Akwiraron's eyes twinkled.

"Yup, I guess. That must be Chief Cayuga helping us through another golden script!" Jeromy smiled and jogged towards the script to grab it.

Dakota noticed something off about this script. "It looks different than the previous scrolls we had gotten… I'm not so sure. I don't know if it's…."

He had not finished speaking when Jeromy's painful gasp interrupted his speech, and they all became suddenly alert.

The golden scroll, luminously exhibiting a bright golden light in the middle of the darkest of the forests ever known to humans, had burnt Jeromy's hand and sent an electric shock through his body, jolting his body as he fell over sideways and shouted in pain.

Anna leaped towards him and fell to her knees as his face scrunched up in excruciating pain.

"What the hell! Help him, guys! What just happened?!" She called out to the others who were still shocked to see the scroll's unexpected impact.

Jeromy was summoning all the strength he could muster to just kneel erect. The opal stone in his hand was no longer luminous, and Anna noticed that he had turned pale. Erik moved closer to inspect his friend, who was no longer writhing in pain but had fallen to his knees due to the high impact of the shock.

Anna's intense black eyes had welled up at the sight. She picked the magical opal stone and placed it in the bag that Jeromy had always worn around his waist. The other recruits gathered around him, too, wondering what could be done to make him well again.

"*Kesehatan*," Akwiraron said a spell that he had known earlier to presume health to some extent. He was taught this spell by Denisse, who had learned it at the Olta of Sihir.

The deafening silence of the forest was broken by Jeromy's cough. He inhaled sharply, shook his head, and stood up quickly as if waking from a bad dream.

His fellows all stepped back to give him some room to breathe and relax while Anna stayed there. He gave her a confused look, as he did not remember what had happened earlier.

"The golden scroll burned and shocked you. Maybe it was not meant for you to read?" Anna suggested, glad to see him up again. She reached into her waist bag and took out the medicine bag that their mentor, Catori, in the Sihir of Olta had given her. It was a small bag – almost the size of an egg, and Anna quickly tied it loosely around Jeromy's neck with a string to help him heal better. A tear left her eye and rolled down her cheek as she bit her lip to prevent the whimper that was finding its way from her throat to her mouth. Jeromy looked into her raven eyes and gently cupped her face with his palm to wipe away the tear.

Their short-lived romance was interrupted by Erik as he cleared his throat. "If you two lovebirds are done, let's move on?" He teased them as they quickly distanced from each other in an awkward movement.

"Should any of us try to read the scroll?" Dakota asked the group, and they agreed in unison that Dakota should do it since it was his idea.

"Careful, buddy," Akwiraron warned him as his steps moved closer to the golden scroll floating in the middle of that opening in the dark forest.

When he attempted to grab the scroll, he moved with light, steady steps and pushed his hand closer to it with the most careful movement. No adverse reaction happened as his hand touched the scroll's parchment paper. All five of them took a sigh of relief as they had all been holding their breath.

"Great, so it was probably meant for me?" Dakota was glad that he was not lying unconscious on the ground right now, but he was also confused.

Jeromy cleared his throat and spoke up.

"This was not sent by Chief Cayuga. It was sent by the Dark Lord, who somehow knew who the four Medallion Recruits were. But… he didn't know about you, Dakota."

Dakota opened the scroll, and unlike the previous scrolls that they had received, it was not empty. No message appeared glowing on any of their arms, and the message was clearly just written on the scroll with what seemed to be ordinary ink.

"This forest does not forget, nor does it let you forget. Be warned. Evil forces are at a leash here."

Dakota read the message out loud and then looked up from the scroll to meet everyone's concerned gazes.

"Oh, the darkness is not so inspiring now, is it?" Erik teased Dakota, referring back to the remarks that he had said when they had entered the dark forest.

The luminous glow of the script started to fade in Dakota's hand. As they watched it, the scroll turned into ashy dust and vanished into nothingness.

"I think Jeromy was right, guys. It does not seem like Chief Cayuga. This is not how he sends us help," Akwiraron points out.

"Well, maybe he was just warning us this time so that we would get out of here sooner?" Anna said her opinion rather unsurely. "But yeah. I do have a bad feeling about this whole thing."

The group of medallions was debating whether or not they should trust the source of the golden scroll that they had just found when they heard loud footsteps in the distance. It sounded almost as if someone was running. They all became quiet and tried to focus on the sound that seemed to get closer and closer.

Jeromy gestured his four companions to gather behind him. They obliged to only gather but refused to stand behind him.

"We are all in this, Jeromy. You are not our human shield, man," Dakota said on behalf of all others.

The footsteps grew closer now, and the recruits felt their heartbeats growing louder with every step.

"Help!" A man came running into the glade where the five recruits stood, waiting for someone or something to show up.

The five recruits relaxed. *It was just a man.*

"There is evil in this forest! I had come here to seek protection in the darkness, but I was attacked and fooled by the wilderness and the evil energies here!" The man exclaimed.

It was almost impossible to make out his face or appearance in the darkness, mainly because he was standing at a distance. Still, the outline of his body could be seen. He seemed to be in good shape but appeared to be injured as he limped and fell to the ground. The five medallions went closer to him, and Jeromy asked the man what was happening.

"Evil! There is evil here!" was all he could say.

Jeromy asked who he was.

"Have you heard about the Dark Lord?" He said in a weak voice.

"Yes, the cruel dark ruler, but you're not-" Jeromy replied, but was interrupted.

"No, I am one of his former commanders. He is an evil devil's son! A master of serpents. I escaped! I – I do not think I will make it alone in this dark forest. I am lost and starving! Please help me," the man cried out in pain.

Dakota knelt down beside him and held up his head to help him drink water from Dakota's bottle.

"Here, have this," He also took out a sandwich from his bag and handed it to him.

"When you feel better, you can continue forward with us until we exit the forest. Right, guys?" Dakota looked back at his fellow recruits, questioning if helping this man would be too much trouble to ask for. They all agreed it was a good idea. After all, they may get more information from the man about the Dark Lord's plan.

"But we do have some questions," stated Jeromy firmly.

As the man tried to sit up and eat the sandwich that Dakota had given to him, his eyes grew wide in horror.

"I – I – I feel it! The dark energy! It's here! Help!" He whimpered.

The five recruits found it strange to see such a big and strong-looking man whimper like this in fear. *Could he be hallucinating?* They wondered, but before they could tell him to get back to his senses, they heard a loud hiss that sent shivers down their spines.

The hiss seemed to be coming from the same opening in the area from which the man had come, and it grew louder. The trees around the area were bustling with movement, and they could all sense trouble coming their way.

Uh oh.

Dakota quickly got up and dragged the commander towards the group so that they could all stay together and be farthest from whatever was heading there. As they all stood with their feet ready to run or attack, a large pair of gleaming eyes could be seen.

Anyone who looked in those eyes faced utmost terror. Without any orders coming from any of them, all the five recruits quickly averted their gazes as soon as they felt the impact of those eyes. They just stood alerted, hearing for any movement around them.

Suddenly, the commander began shaking convulsively and started screaming. "No! No, it's Asmodeus! Someone save me! God help me! Help! HELP!!"

Then the commander's body felt heavier under Dakota's grasp of his shirt's collars. When he looked down, the man had fainted from fright and dropped to the ground with his eyes wide open as if he had seen something that had shaken him to his very core.

A giant snake slithered towards the recruits, and as hard as Dakota tried, he could not move the commander with him.

"Dakota!" Anna shouted. "Let him be! Run! We need to save ourselves first!"

Dakota realized how close the creature was to him and quickly ran in the direction of the others. He glanced back only once and saw the giant snake swallowing the man whole, and a black fume was released from his mouth.

"Teleport! Teleport!" Dakota shouted at the group as he tried to catch up with them and felt the giant snake coming closer behind them.

"Celik Praraha!" Anna and Jeromy shout in unison, and a large blue bubble forms around all five of them. The giant snake is only inches away from Jeromy when they disappear.

Chapter # 15:
Wild Wood

Jeromy opened his eyes and saw nothing but suffocating clouds of darkness surrounding him. He felt the ground beneath him and could tell that he was lying on rocks and grass. It smelled like the dry sand of a desert, and just as he came to his senses, he felt the worst headache.

"Ugh." He sat up with a grunt as his head spun, and so did the dark silhouettes around him.

"Guys?" He voiced out, waiting for a response from his fellow recruits, hoping that they were there, too. The last thing he remembered was a huge snake ambushing them.

Am I bitten? He wondered, quickly checking his body for any signs of injury or venomous injection.

"Wh – where are we?" He heard Dakota grumble from somewhere around him.

Jeromy's eyes were now adapting to the darkness, and the pain in his head slowly faded to a dull throbbing. He heard the grass around him rustle, and a twig cracked as someone stepped on it.

"Are we all here? Are we all okay?" Jeromy said into the dimming darkness.

"I'm alright. Just feeling like I fell down a story," Anna said with a tinge of exhaustion and pain in her voice.

"Yup, I'm here," Erik's voice echoed. "I'm almost okay. Scraped my elbows and landed on a twig, I think."

Soon, Akwiraron also voiced his presence, and they all took a sigh of relief that they made it out alive and in one piece. The heart-wrenching view of the monstrous snake devouring the commander made still made them all shudder.

"Asmodeus? What the hell was that?" asked Anna.

"Must be a weapon or servant of the Dark Lord," Jeromy replied.

"Yeah, um, we're alive *for now,* but there's definitely nothing good here. Don't you think we have to get out of this place?" Dakota proposed to the rest of the group.

"I have got to say, it does feel weird here. Where are we, though?" Anna responded.

This place that they had teleported to was different. It did not look like the dark forest that they were in earlier. This place was hilly and rockier than the forest. And, as some time passed and the five recruits treaded on an upward slope, they realized that there was a patch on the surface of what was presumably a hill where moonlight lit the ground.

"I'm tired," Anna panted. She was never a fan of hiking.

"I suppose we can rest for a while there," Jeromy said, pointing to the moonlit area.

The recruits climbed towards the opening and put their bags down.

Ah, finally. They all sighed, relieved that they could finally breathe away from the suffocating darkness for a while. This was the range of hills at the edge of the dark forest, where nights never turned into days. They called the Oneida Forest the Dark Forest for a reason.

The five medallions laid on the hill's surface, looking up at the sky that they had missed for a long time.

"Feels like I'm watching the sky after ages," Akwiraron whispered to himself as his eyes adored the moon above them.

Anna had laid down closer to Jeromy, and as she closed her eyes to rest, she felt Jeromy's fingers entangling themselves with hers as he held her hand gently, but in a firm hold. She kept her eyes closed and smiled, making Jeromy do the same. He had not felt like this with anyone before, not even Chumani, and for all that mattered, this was a moment that he would remember till his last breath.

It was not long before the recruits of Oneida lost themselves to a sweet slumber. They did not toss or turn but laid still, with their chests rising and falling as they breathed under the open sky.

Suddenly, a soft rustle woke Anna up. She had not slept in two days and groaned at whatever had made that noise to disturb her sleep.

Detangling her fingers from Jeromy, she sat up to inspect the source of the noise. She looked around and saw all her fellow recruits sleeping peacefully but noticed that there was an unidentifiable silhouette moving near a tree, just seven feet away from her. Leaping to her feet, she slowly walked barefoot towards the silhouette.

"Anna?" A warm voice of a middle-aged woman echoed in the misty air of the moonlit hilltop.

Anna froze. *Who was there?* She contemplated between replying and staying quiet to avoid trouble, but finally decided to give in.

"Who – who is there?" she stuttered.

"It's me, my sweetheart," the female voice sang. "Your Mama."

Anna could feel a nervous lump forming in her throat. She fought to gulp down and find her voice again.

"My – my Mama? But –" She was taken aback. Her mother could not be here. "Am I dreaming?" She whispered out loud without meaning to.

"My baby! I came to see you. Look how grown you have become." The plump female silhouette said, hidden away from the moonlight behind a thick tree.

"This can't be happening. My mom – you cannot be my mom!" Anna stuttered like a child. It was very unlike her to show such emotions. Her eyes welled up, and it took all her strength to not let her tears fall, yet, they still did.

"You look just like me when I was your age, my sweet daughter. Your raven black hair. Your big, beautiful eyes. You're a warrior, my child. Just like your mama used to be before they took you away from me." The silhouette whispered.

"You – you were a warrior? What kind of –" Anna's throat felt like it was closing upon itself as her eyes gradually adapted to the dimness of the light, and she began to see some features of the silhouette, claiming to be her biological mother.

"The kind of warrior that you will be. I was your age when I had you. Young and hot-headed, yet, your delicate existence in my arms had made me weak in the knees. I was afraid that I would hurt you, and I could never –" The female voice behind the tree had a mesmerizing tinge of pain flowing with her words.

"Could not what, *Mom?*" Anna almost spat the last word angrily.

"*Mom!* Should I even call you that? You, who gave me away when I was too young to even remember what your face looked like!" Anna's voice broke as she spoke.

She always felt rejected ever since she had known that her biological mother abandoned her, and now here she was, trying to make Anna feel *loved?*

"Honey, our tribe has a matrilineal kinship system. My child, you were not safe there, so they sent you away," the misty figure explained in a broken voice.

"Lord knows how I felt like my soul was being ripped out of my body when I had to let you go." She continued.

Anna sobbed uncontrollably and fell on her knees with her face buried into her palms. She cried silently for a long while before her soft sibs turned to wails of pain. She forgot where she was and what she was doing. Everything around her vanished until she felt a hand on her shoulder.

"Anna?" It was Jeromy's voice. He was concerned and crouched beside her, and she finally realized that she was with her fellow recruiters. Her teary eyes immediately darted in the direction of the tree where her mother's silhouette had been.

"Mom?" She let out another weak sob, and her question hung in the air, gaining no response whatsoever. The silhouette was no longer there.

"Anna, what's going on?" Jeromy asked again.

"My mom…" Anna immediately stood up. "She – she was here! My mother was here, and now…" she trailed off.

Anna looked like a lost child in a crowded store. She was looking everywhere, running around, shouting for her mother to come back or respond. The other recruits woke up as they heard the disturbance around them, wondering what was happening.

Anna began to sob again as she felt defeated. "Again!" She whimpered as Jeromy held her.

"She left me again! Abandoned me again!" She cried into Jeromy's chest, staining his cyan blue shirt with her tears.

He cupped her face in both his hands and looked into her eyes.

"Anna, come back to reality. You must have had a bad dream." He tried to help her come back to her senses.

"Was I sleeping when you woke up?" She questioned, determined to prove that it was not a dream.

"No…" Jeromy trailed off as he realized that Anna indeed was fully awake when he woke up. He had woken up to see her crying in front of a huge tree.

"See, none of us had any sleep in days, sweetheart. It is very normal to hallucinate, too." He tried to make sense of the situation.

Anna sighed, understanding that she was being a bit illogical. *How can my dead mother come back to life?* She thought.

"You know what she told me, Jer?" The ends of her lips curved up into a slight smile.

"What?" He asked softly, hoping whatever it was had not hurt her.

"She said that she was a warrior, just like I am going to be," Anna whispered.

By now, all of the warriors had gathered around Anna. The world around them was tinged with a sense of sadness as they sat there and comforted Anna before finally deciding to continue their trek.

"I'm all right," Anna's composure returned. She felt almost guilty for letting her friends see this side of her, especially when they were on a journey that required them to be fearless and strong.

"Let's go?" She motioned for Jeromy to move forward and continue the walk uphill. The others followed them quietly, knowing that Anna was still in pain.

As they moved towards the peak of the hill, which seemed to be the only way beyond the edge of the forest, they heard a loud crack and then thump, followed by an ear-piercing scream.

Jeromy, Anna, Dakota, and Akwiraron turned around and realized that Erik was not behind them anymore, and it was his scream, apparently.

"Erik?" Akwiraron shouted.

"Ugh, I'm here," Erik's voice echoed around the empty area.

The four recruits immediately walked towards the source of the voice.

"Where?" Dakota asked again, hoping to get another response from him.

Erik said, "Down here. I fell into a hole. It appears to be a tunnel of some sort. I am trying to get up, but I can't."

The others followed his voice and saw a dark hole in the ground that could be the tunnel that Erik was talking about. Dakota knelt down, held out his hand to touch the ground, and observed the tunnel's steepness. It felt steep to some extent, which was why Erik must have stumbled into it.

"Should we...?" Jeromy asked Erik. "Should we come down, Erik? Can you see a way out?"

"I suppose it does lead downwards," Erik shouted. "I don't know if it's the right way. I mean, it feels rather suffocating here, and I don't see a way up either."

"I – I think just one of us should try to crawl downwards to get Erik out of here," Dakota suggested.

"I suppose that might be the sensible thing to do." Jeromy agreed as they all looked at each other to decide who should step into the tunnel.

"I'll go down," Akwiraron proposed as he sought a nod of approval from Jeromy and took out a rope from his bag. He tied a knot at one end of the rope, twisted it around his waist, and handed the other end to Dakota, who quickly tied it around a tree and secured a knot.

"All good." Dakota signaled to Akwiraron.

Akwiraron had only stepped a foot into the tunnel when he heard Erik's voice echo through, "Hey! Guys?"

"Yes, buddy? We hear you!" Akwiraron gasped, feeling his lungs work harder to catch air in the suffocating darkness of the tunnel that he was now engulfed in.

"I – I think, I see some sort of light at the bottom! It is probably coming from the opening of the tunnel! Do you think we should go through?" Erik's voice echoed, and all the recruits froze.

Well, that was unexpected. They all thought to themselves.

Of course, they were not hoping to jump down dark tunnels, but since it was not entirely dark anymore, maybe it was a sign to go into it? The recruits looked at each other as Akwiraron continued crawling deeper into the diagonally vertical shaft to get to Erik.

"Well, I don't think that is safe based on our previous experience with luminous rays of lights leading to mysterious scrolls or openings," Jeromy remembered the painful electric shock he had suffered when he had touched the golden scroll earlier.

Then he recalled the snake encounter, too, so jumping into a tunnel that would not lead the way back onto the upper surface seemed like a suicidal mission to him.

"But –" Akwiraron interjected, "We were told during training that we will find our destinations in the most unexpected places."

"Yeah," Anna chimed in, "And come on – nothing about this whole journey or mission is safe, anyway, so we cannot really worry for our safety now."

Jeromy inhaled sharply, thinking whether it was the right thing to do.

"Um, okay! So, we're going in! Let's all be careful, though?" He instructed.

As the recruits standing outside the tunnel quickly checked their bags and extracted their ropes, Jeromy slid his arm behind Anna's waist.

"I'm not worried for my safety. I'm worried about yours. I can't let anything happen to you." He whispered in her ear.

Anna chuckled at the cheesiness in Jeromy's words, and he smiled. Both knew he utterly meant the words he just uttered.

Meanwhile, Erik crawled deeper towards the light that was emerging at the end of the tunnel. Akwiraron could hear the rustling underneath him and warned Erik, "Hey! Erik! Mind waiting for me before you go farther?"

"What for? You're all coming down anyway, right?" Erik responded and continued crawling on his belly towards the tunnel's luminous opening.

Akwiraron sighed but continued climbing downwards, and soon, he began to see the light, too. It was a pale, dim glow that appeared as the sun's rays when they penetrated the room through net curtains.

"I see the light, too! I think we're close to the opening!" Akwiraron informed the others as they started their journey downwards, too.

"Maybe this is where we would find what we were looking for!" Anna cheered and felt glad that there was an ending to this suffocation.

She was referring to the second portal, the one they had been searching for since the beginning of their journey in the dark forest.

As they climbed deeper down the hole in the ground, they all began to see the light one by one. Erik had already reached the end of the tunnel. He crawled out of it and gasped. It was unbelievable.

Whoa! He thought.

The underground tunnel led to an opening completely opposite of what they had seen in the dark forest and the hilly ranges. It was sunny here, with birds chirping and flying across the sky.

Erik stood to a side, breathed in the fresh air but still felt suffocated.

That is weird. He thought to himself.

The rest of the recruits eventually found their way out into the open and saw the scenery that took their breath away.

"Whoa!" They all said in harmony.

With smiles on their faces, the first thing they wanted to do here was breathe fresh air. Still, strangely enough, none of them could feel anything fresh in the air around them, even though the sky above them was open and free.

They saw green trees flowing with the wind and a place they could call heaven, especially after all the darkness they had witnessed, but something about it felt off. Something was just not right.

"Thankfully, there is no electrocuting golden scroll here. Just the same old sun that we wanted to see!" Jeromy sighed in relief.

The five recruits rested for five minutes as they were tired from the exhausting climb downwards, between walls that felt they were closing in on them.

"Is this the way out? I don't see how it could be; I mean, we came here through an underground passage, and I was expecting to still be underground at this time, you know?" Dakota voiced his concern.

"I know what you mean. I was expecting the same. But magic is nothing new to us anymore, is it?" Akwiraron responded to him.

All of them felt strange. Maybe it was because of how exhausted they were, or perhaps they had just grown accustomed to seeing strange things that a scene from the regular world made them feel like something was not right.

"I – If I say something, you would all call me crazy, but I am not." Anna clarified her standing before proposing her opinion on the riddle of this place's strangeness.

"I think that this place might be haunted? Or cursed? I don't know, I am not sure, but something is definitely not good here. I can sense it," she explained as the others looked at her.

"What are you suggesting?" Erik asked.

"I think this may be the place I heard of in a story told around a campfire. They called it 'Wild Wood.' I think that we are all just hallucinating. I mean – I was, earlier, when I saw my mother, and that was not normal for me!" Anna was worried that she might be right, and she had never in her life wished for herself to be wrong so desperately.

"How can we all hallucinate the same thing? I mean, we are all seeing this beautiful place and an open, sunny sky, right?" Dakota argued logically, to which Anna just shrugged.

"That's the thing about Wild Wood. Whole groups of people can hallucinate the same thing. But I just don't know. I just feel that there is something evil around here, or at least, something paranormal. It's in the air around us." Anna said hesitantly.

She turned to Jeromy, who was looking at her with confidence like he believed everything she was saying.

Chapter # 16:
Lining up the Birthstones

The five recruits found themselves in a setting that was too good to be true. They remembered what Cayuga had told them about how they might be tested in various ways, and sometimes, things would not be as they seem. With doubts still clouding their hearts and minds, they finally set out to find a portal.

"If nothing is what it seems to be, we have to find another way out. I mean, the trees are not the trees, and the sky probably is not the sky, anyway. The grass that we are now walking on is probably just a rocky corridor in an underground tunnel," Erik talked to his fellows who were listening keenly to him.

"So, what are you saying?" Anna questioned on behalf of everyone. They were not sure where he was going with these realizations.

"So, I am presuming that fire is probably water in this misleading world that we have dropped into." He clarified his point of view as they walked on the sandy ground.

"I suppose so," Akwiraron agreed with what he was hearing. The place did look like it was just a setup.

"You know that I belong to the *Alas gedhe samon*. I am aware of what is around or underneath. I can tell that there are evil forces around us. Anna was right." Erik explained to the other recruits as they continued to walk towards a large apple tree.

"If that is how it is, then I do not think we should eat those apples from that tree. Right, guys?" Jeromy realized.

"Yeah, we probably shouldn't," Akwiraron agreed, and the others nodded in affirmation.

"Then? Where should we head now? Honestly, I feel very lost at this moment," Dakota said.

"So do we, Dakota. We *are* lost." Anna responded.

The recruits were unsure of what to trust in this place and what to steer clear of. It all appeared beautiful, like a dream. It was a beach with sea waves that glittered under the sun's lights, but there was no sun in the sky. Just light.

After several minutes, as everyone was still looking around to detect a way out of the trippy place, Erik's eyes fell on what appeared to be a small hut in the distance.

"Let's go there? That's a hut, I think." Erik suggested.

"Okay, but we need to exit this place rather than finding a shelter here," Jeromy reminded them as they started walking in the hut's direction.

"I know, I know. But, since we have not found any exits yet, exploring what is already here won't hurt. Maybe, it will lead us to find a clue or something?" Erik had a point, and the others agreed.

As they walked closer to the hut, Anna looked at Jeromy and whispered in his ear as she held his hand, "I don't know what is real here and what is not, but I know that you and I are. And since we are here, why don't we enjoy the view?" She winked at him, smiling as her hand grazed out of his grip, and she hopped towards the sea.

"Come on!" She waved at the others to join her. The boys exchanged some concerned looks but finally decided to let go for a while, too.

Erik, Dakota, and Akwiraron started running, racing to the beach to see who would reach the waves first, while Jeromy walked closer to Anna and put his arm around her shoulder as they looked at the others run.

Seagulls flew above their heads, and as the boys raced, Erik was the first to reach the waves. But just as feet splashed against the sea's water, his laughter turned into screams, and he ran out of the water and fell on his side on the sandy part of the beach.

The other quickly ran to him as he lay there groaning in pain. As the others tried to figure out what was wrong, Dakota saw that the skin on Erik's feet appeared severely burnt.

"Holy sh –" He put his hand on his forehead in worry.

When the other recruits saw his feet, they realized that it was definitely not a regular beach's water.

"It burns! It burns like acid!" Erik was screaming in pain as he rubbed his feet wildly on the ground restlessly. Even though the breeze was cool there, Erik was now sweating due to the agitating pain that his body was in at the moment.

All of them suddenly got worried because there was nothing to aid his pain at the moment. As they tried different methods to heal Erik's pain through various spells, Akwiraron detected a few mushrooms growing at a little distance. He quickly ran over to pick them up because, apparently, the psilocybin in some mushrooms could minimize feelings of pain and anxiety.

But as soon as he touched one of the most oversized mushrooms, he immediately gasped and fell back.

A large eye on the mushroom's surface opened and looked at him. It was red and looked almost satanic, and all Akwiraron could think of doing at sight was to run back to his group.

By now, however, one of the healing spells had worked, and Erik was feeling much better.

"I'm okay now. Thanks." He said, picking up his water bottle to take a few sips.

"Yeah, well, I'm not! I just saw a huge human eye on a damned mushroom!" Akwiraron blurted out, his face still red from the shock.

The five recruits were still discussing what to do when Erik proposed, "Well, Jeromy, maybe we can look into your opal stone for some help? It can show us the map around this place."

The idea appealed to everyone, but when Jeromy slipped his hand into his waist bag, he realized it felt lighter and emptier. His heart jumped to his throat as he realized that the stone was missing.

"My – my birthstone?!" Jeromy panicked.

"Um, is it not there? I had put it in your waist bag when you had fainted earlier in the dark forest." Anna explained, hoping that the opal stone was there because if it was lost, it would mean that Jeromy was in for a lot of trouble.

Jeromy opened each one of his six-pocket cargo pants and scrabbled around to find the special stone that was not there. The other four recruits stood worried because apparently, the opal stone was lost, and not only was it the epitome of Jeromy's power and strength in this journey handed carefully by Chief Cayuga, but it was also their only hope out of this maze.

"I can try something. I don't know if it will work, though," Dakota said to his fellows while Jeromy was still searching for the stone everywhere he possibly could. He emptied his backpack completely on the sandy floor, which had everything but the opal stone.

"Where could it go? I – I had it with me the whole time! I checked my waist bag before sleeping on the hill's surface the last time we were resting there, and it was there then! Where could it go now?" Jeromy's face was red and sweaty. It was one of the most precious things he had been trusted with, and he could not bear losing it. *Was it an evil force that took it away?*

"*Peru vinay les!*" Dakota said the spell of truth. It was the spell that could clear the mind and help them see the truth. All of a sudden, the place started to change.

The sun in the sky was no longer bright. Its sunlight started to die out and eventually turned into a dark gray stone with rugged edges. The sky above them shifted in color from a beautiful calm blue sky to an ash grey roof of stone.

The recruits gazed around in horror. The trees were black and looked petrifying. The sparrows and birds that were previously chirping around were now just scary-looking bats hanging upside down from the stony roof of this dark place.

Eventually, the whole place, apparently a beautiful beachy land once, turned into an underground tunnel of mind games and misconceptions. Seeing the spell work, Dakota let out a sigh of relief.

He had only learned this spell but had never tried it before. Jeromy was still sitting on the ground with his backpack, and its accessories opened and spread around him; the waist bag was still attached to his waist and was open. Suddenly, Anna Noticed something sparkly peeking through the opening.

"Um, Jerry?" Anna came closer and knelt down beside him before extending her arm and reaching out to his waist bag. She opened it to find what had attracted her attention and was very confused to find the opal stone sitting there, just as she had left earlier.

"Whoa! Where did that come from?" Jeromy gasped upon seeing the opal stone being extracted from his waist bag.

"Wild Wood," was Anna's only reply.

The situation had changed drastically in the past few minutes, and the group was perplexed about what was happening. Of course, there were some forces playing tricks on their minds, and they had to have a strategy to escape this mind-wobbling cavern as soon as possible.

Jeromy rubbed the opal stone's surface, and a map appeared on the luminous blue birthstone. The map showed a dark brown tunnel that led to a dark sea at the east and another moonlit opening at the other end. The sensible decision was obviously to go towards the opening, and that is what they decided to do.

"Man, this is a messed-up place, isn't it?" Akwiraron said as they followed the map's direction. It was a long and boring journey.

The recruits fully expected the twists and turns on the trip, but nothing much happened until they reached the tunnel's exit.

"Mmm, I can *finally* sense the fresh air! I can finally breathe," Anna was delighted as they approached the end of their journey through the darkest forest and tunnel, which opened into an abandoned little village. The dim, warm light of the sun scattered around and touched their faces as a cool breeze grazed their hair.

Ah… finally! They all thought.

All of them smiled and looked at each other, glad that the suffocating feeling was over. Suddenly, the ground vibrated, and the five recruits stopped in their steps and turned around to see the source of the noise.

"Whoa…" Anna stepped back in awe.

Chief Cayuga had appeared there. He had not sent a message or a golden scroll – but was there himself, and it was an honor. At the same time, it meant that something huge was going to happen because Chief Cayuga never appeared to the recruits for just about anything.

"My medallions! You have passed the first test towards finding the second portal," Chief Cayuga's voice echoed as the sun gradually rose. The warmth of the sunlight toned down from being reddish-orange to a bright yellow.

The medallions lined up in front of Chief Cayuga as he addressed them. He told them that the second portal was now ready to be opened, but it would be unlocked only when the recruits could find the key.

"And, the key is not actually a key, but a gesture. An alignment. A riddle." He gave a hint.

"Yes, Chief Cayuga," Jeromy responded on behalf of all when Cayuga asked if the instructions were clear to the recruits. Before Jeromy could process the information and ask some crucial questions, Chief Cayuga faded into thin air of the abandoned village that was now lighting up as the morning sun came up.

"Some test this was." Erik shrugged.

"Trials followed by tests?" asked Akwiraron.

"Yeah, more tests to come, guys. Buckle up!" Jeromy announced.

As the five recruits walked towards the abandoned village that looked lonely with its destroyed and corroded buildings, their stomachs grumbled with hunger.

"We should definitely have lunch, or breakfast, or whatever! I'm starving!" Anna announced.

"So am I! Let's get closer to the village and find ourselves a spot to settle for the day." Jeromy walked in front of the other recruits as they all now saw the village closing in.

"What do you think the second portal does?" Akwiraron wondered out loud.

Suddenly, all of the recruits stopped thinking about their hunger and started wondering the same thing.

"Good question. I wonder, too," Dakota responded. "Anyone has any idea what this portal is supposed to do and why is it so important for us to open it?"

"I don't have a clue!" Erik shrugged. "I just hope it does not unleash some evil souls on us!" He chuckled.

"Yeah, as if we don't have enough experience fighting evil off by now," Akwiraron said sarcastically.

The five recruits could now see the village just a few feet away from them. It had mossy, unfinished houses that looked like they were built from wet sand and corroded by water.

"There might have been water here earlier," Jeromy said as he came to a halt suddenly, feeling his boots somewhat sink slightly into the damp ground.

"The sand is pretty damp here," Erik examined the ground underneath him. "Let's just hope that it is not the wet sand that could swallow us whole!"

Anna and Dakota looked at each other with wide eyes. Of course, stepping into this village was nothing short of a risk.

"Well, there is only one way to find out about that," Jeromy said as he walked carefully towards the village.

"Stay back, guys! I will test to see if it is safe to go further," he ordered his team members.

"Be careful, Jer," Anna warned him as she watched him step forward.

Jeromy's footsteps were careful and calculated as he was determined not to cause any harm to himself or others. He did not step on it but approached it close enough to drop a large stone onto it that he had picked up from a nearby spot.

"Okay, let's see if this is just wet sand or quicksand," he threw the stone onto the puddle-like sandy area and stepped back to avoid any dirt splashing on his clothes.

The large stone did not sink but definitely showed that the sand had some depth. So, judging from how deep the rock went, the deepest that a human can sink into this will be ankle-deep, even in the wettest areas.

"Looks good! We might need new boots after we cross this village, but other than that, none of us are drowning in this sand," Jeromy called out to his friends who were watching his experiment with intent.

"Great! Let's go, then!" Erik gestured the others to move forward.

"As I said, I am starving! We are stopping at the first safe place we find to sit and eat," Anna announced as she skidded with quick little jumps towards the village.

A two-foot wooden sign board at the village's entrance might have spelled out the village's name once long ago. Now it showed only some eroded red paint and the corners of a few letters that could be read as the remains of an 'A' or 'W.'

The five recruits walked with their booted feet splurging in the wet sand as they passed the board. The first thing that caught their attention was a little barn that looked like it was in better condition than most other accommodations nearby.

"That looks fine. I mean, we could use it to stop and eat and maybe even rest for a while if any of us need to?" Akwiraron proposed.

"Yup, that's what I was thinking, too," Erik agreed.

The five recruits moved into the barn, and its door creaked open as if it had not been used to perform this function for years. The barn had a lot of webs and dust that made Jeromy and Anna cough.

As the medallions found a sturdy spot on the wooden floor of the barn to lay their mats on, they sat there and withdrew their meals from the packs they carried with them at all times. There was a little stone stove in the barn that was covered in cobwebs, too. Anna dusted it off with a handkerchief that she had withdrawn from her bag.

"*Cemlorot.*" She said in a quiet whisper and exhaled onto the stove to light it up.

"Woohoo! Warm food, finally, eh?" Jeromy cheered as Anna brought the stove nearer to the group like a trophy in her hand.

"Warm your own food, peeps! I could only light it up for you all." Anna smiled coyly as she placed the little stone on the floor.

"Careful, though, the floor is wooden, and we wouldn't want this *wonderful* accommodation to burn down," Erik warned everyone as he unwrapped his protein-packed wheat roll from the cling wrap and found a sharp metal skewer near where the stove had been. He cleaned the skewer with tissue paper and pushed it into his protein roll to warm it up on the stove.

"Mine's done! Does anyone else wants to?" He asked as he moved back onto the mat and took a large bite of his meal.

The others also warmed their pre-packed meals turn by turn and ate hungrily.

"I never thought I could eat such a heavy protein sandwich and not feel sick," Jeromy said with his stomach full. He felt refreshed after a long time, as none of them had previously eaten that day.

As the five recruits explored the village further to find a place to stay for the night, they came across a small church and decided to go into it.

"Whoa! It looks like it was built a thousand years ago!" Anna exclaimed, gasping at the beauty of the architecture that was probably designed by hand.

"It looks like it could be a thousand years old. We're back in a timeless realm. Remember?" Dakota reminded his friends.

The gate to the church was already open when the group reached its entrance. They let themselves in and heard the echo of their footsteps and the beating of their hearts. This place was phenomenal.

"This is bigger than it looked from the outside, no?" Akwiraron pointed out as the five medallions walked into the church's corridor, gazing at its vastness.

"Looks magical!" Jeromy gasped.

"Magnificent!" Dakota and Erik exclaimed in unison as they looked around.

There was sycamore growing from the roof of the church, and yet, the place seemed almost royal in an antique, fantastical way.

"I have a strange feeling that this is where the second portal might be," Akwiraron thought aloud.

"Are your Earth instincts telling you that?" Erik asked, and everyone became attentive to the idea that his imposition might have some truth.

"Well, yes, there is the instinct – a powerful one, too, that this place is not just Earth. It is more than that. It has different energies in here," Akwiraron said.

"Okay, so that should mean something," Jeromy supported his proposition and continued, "and, well, other than our friend's instincts, there is also the fact that Chief Cayuga had met us when we were on our way to this village. So, that must mean that we were on the right path towards our destination. Correct?"

He shot a glance at the recruits gathered around him to see if they agreed, too.

"Yeah, I'd think so," Dakota interjected, "And the fact that Chief Cayuga told us about the second portal while we were on our way here should be a hint for us to find the portal here, too."

"Yep, otherwise, he would have given us some hint about where we are going to find the portal in this endless world in a timeless realm!" Erik added.

The idea of the second portal being in this church seemed realistic to all the five recruits. They quickly began assessing the place for anything or any place that could be a portal.

"Hey!" Jeromy called his fellows to a fountain that no longer had any water flowing in it.

"I am not sure, but I feel like this might be something." As the others ran over to him, he pointed at five circular gaps in the fountain's walls. Those were basically five roughly shaped circles that were embedded into the fountain's boundaries and looked like a puzzle.

"What could this be?" Anna asked, confused.

"Honestly, I am not sure, but my instinct tells me that these embeddings have something to do with a puzzle on how to open the portal," Jeromy explained.

"Hmm… let's see." Erik sat on the fountain's boundary that was about two feet high and touched the embedded gaps lightly with his fingers to investigate them. They were all looking around to see if anything else appealed to them, like a puzzle or a test, as Chief Cayuga had hinted when Jeromy suddenly noticed something that could help him solve it. He looked closely at one of the embeddings and quickly slipped his hand into his waist bag to take out his opal stone.

"Uhh…" Erik was beginning to see what Jeromy meant, and the other recruits looked at his opal stone as it fit perfectly into one of the five embedded gaps in the fountain's boundary.

Suddenly, the opal stone started to radiate a dim blue light, and a few white speckles appeared on its luminous surface like it was star dust.

Struck with awe, the recruits looked at the opal stone that looked like it always belonged here in this vast church's dried fountain's wall. Jeromy looked at the others as they all took out their stones.

Anna placed her diamond into the gap shaped like it. Akwiraron and Erik took out their emerald and amethyst to put into the respective embeddings. All the four stones had clicked to fit into the gap, but what about the fifth one? They looked at

Dakota and remembered that he was not given a birth stone by Chief Cayuga.

What now? They all wondered.

Chapter # 17:
The Escape from the Frontier

While Jeromy, Erik, Anna, Akwiraron, and Dakota were trying to figure out what should go in the fifth embedded gap, the moon had risen to the sky. Its lunar light sprinkled the church with a dreamy glow.

"Dakota, do you have anything that might match the shape of this carved gap? Anything? I suppose it does not necessarily need to be a birthstone...." Jeromy asked Dakota, who was now feeling strange and having second thoughts.

"Uh... what if I was supposed to get a birthstone but did something wrong? What if I was not there at the right time when the stones were handing these out?" Dakota questioned.

"Well, buddy, any one of us can make mistakes, but I am sure Chief Cayuga would have found a way to get you the stone if you were supposed to have it at this stage," Akwiraron responded. It made sense to the other recruits, including Dakota.

Dakota got closer to the fountain wall and studied its texture and shape. It felt smooth and shiny where it was carved, contrary to the rest of the wall's texture. The embedding appeared to be in a rough circle shape, but it did not match anything that Dakota had.

"Nope. Nothing in my waist bag or backpack matches this shape...." Dakota paused, and the look in his eyes changed as if he remembered something. "My grandfather... he used to wear a locket that I just remembered had this shape... Does this mean he..."

"Uh… Okay. That puts us in a pickle. We cannot possibly get to your departed grandfather to get that. Can we?" Erik assessed the situation.

"No, but we might go to my place and get the locket from there. He gave me a box of his most precious items before he passed away, and I have that box back at home."

Jeromy and the other recruits thought about what they should do. They could teleport to Dakota's house and come back with the locket that had the birthstone. But the teleportation spell was an extremely heavy spell that could drain their energies for a long time.

"The last time we teleported, we were all knocked out for God knows how long, remember?" Anna reminded her fellow recruits.

"Then, let's do this: Dakota, I figure that it is better if you and one other among us teleports to your house and get the locket and then come back here. The rest of us can wait right here for you guys. That way, at least some of us would be here to guard the situation if anything goes wrong." Jeromy voiced his plan, and the recruits agreed that it could be the solution.

"Anna, I believe that you perform the teleportation spell best besides me, so either you should go with Dakota, or I should." Jeromy turned to Anna.

"I should. You should stay here and guard the birthstones." She instantly volunteered, finalizing the plan they had decided to follow.

"Yeah, I agree. And we should go quick now because the night is approaching soon. We want to be back in time, too," Dakota pitched in.

"Celik Praraha"

Anna held Dakota's hand, and a huge blue flash of light engulfed the two recruits and then disappeared with them. They had teleported away, and Jeromy, Akwiraron, and Erik had decided to settle in this church until their return.

When Anna and Dakota woke up, they were lying on the kitchen floor of Dakota's house. It was a small house with nothing extraordinary except one large cabinet that could be seen in the lounge from the kitchen's floor.

Anna's eyes opened and darted towards that cabinet through her spinning vision. She was too weak to get up immediately, especially because she had never performed a teleportation spell this strong. They had literally traveled through places that were geographically exceptionally far from each other and through time itself. She had brought the two of them into their original present time instead of the time realm they were in for the recent part of their journey.

Dakota woke up with a groan and looked at Anna, who was lying still with her eyes open.

"Hey…" Dakota's voice was husky and tired. "Are you all okay?" He asked Anna.

"Uh… my head hurts. Everything… hurts," she grunted in pain.

Dakota found the strength to slowly get up and helped Anna up as well, supporting her steps until she could be seated at the dining table's chair.

"Water…" Anna yelped.

He quickly grabbed a glass from inside one of the top cabinets and filled it up with tap water to hand it over to Anna. "Here you go."

"Thanks," Anna said when she had drunk half of the water.

"So…" Dakota's head was hurting, too, but it was not too much. "I'll just go get the locket, yeah?"

He asked Anna before he could go look for it because he wanted to make sure that Anna was okay first.

"Great, I'll be here," she gestured and then put her head down on her folded arms on the table's surface to close her eyes and take a few deep breaths.

Dakota walked away into the lounge and opened the cabinet. A cloud of dust emerged into the air from inside the cabinet as it had been days or maybe even months since the house had been cleaned. As Dakota coughed and searched for the locket, Anna rested to restore her energy for the return journey.

She opened her eyes when she heard Dakota's footsteps approaching her in the kitchen. She saw him standing there with his eyebrows furrowed up in worry.

"Is something wrong?" Anna dreaded the question and the answer from the look on Dakota's face.

"It's not here. It was. I know that it was! Before I left from here, the locket was kept in a wooden box in that cabinet!" He pointed towards the cabinet that was left open and was all scattered now from Dakota's panicked search. "Everything else that was in the box is still there except for the locket! Oh, damn it!"

Dakota could not believe that their purpose could not be fulfilled even after such a draining teleportation journey.

"Shit… can it be anywhere else in the house?" Anna asked. "I can help you search for it if you want."

"No… The box was locked when I had left it, but someone opened it. The lock was broken when I checked upon our landing here, and I am sure that someone stole the locket." Dakota sighed and pulled out a seat for himself at the dining table.

"What did it look like?" Anna knew she had no more energy for teleportation to take them back to the church through the timeless realm anytime soon. Hence, their only option was to wait there and see if they could somehow retrieve the locket with the birthstone.

"Well, it was shaped the same as that rugged circular embedding in the fountain wall with all the other birthstone placements. It was jet black in color, though – like a splash of black water. Shiny and very reflective." Dakota explained.

"Do you think someone would have believed it to be something precious to sell, maybe like gold?" Anna inquired, trying to put together a hint to begin searching for the stolen locket.

"Probably… yes. Anyways, I don't want to go back to the church empty-handed, so how about we go out to the police station and see if something can be done?" He suggested, getting up from the table and opening one of the windows to see how the weather is outside.

"I agree. I mean – it's no use going back there until we find the stone."

Anna and Dakota gathered all the energy that they had and exited the house to walk towards the police station.

* * *

Blaine, the wicked son of Magua, looked at the shiny black piece of a birthstone in his hand. He smirked, knowing that his revenge was soon to be achieved through this locket.

He was in the dark Forest of Limbo accompanied by several of his companions, and they were all eager to see how the revenge plan was executed.

In the darkest area of the forest where light did not touch the ground in years, Blaine Keir stomped his gnarled foot in the wet soil and crushed a small brown plant under his heavy boot. Then he took a step back and started to murmur a spell under his breath.

"Njedhul saka lemah...."

The ground beneath his feet shook, and his companions suddenly became aware, but he gestured them to stay calm and stay in their places. The spot on the ground where Blaine had stomped had formed a luminous crack. Amazingly, a thick tree emerged from the ground and rocketed to the sky with a large hole in the trunk. Its branches expanded several feet away over the heads of all that stood beneath it, struck with awe.

"Behold!" Blaine Keir announced with an evil grin on his long, fissured, unappealing face. "Behold, my companions! We have completed one of the three steps to unleash the dark portal!" He announced his half-achieved victory proudly as he stood with his arms spread and the shiny black birthstone in his withered palm.

Next, the birthstone began to glow.

"Asmodeus, bring me the blood." He ordered.

His servant moved forward, quickly holding a small glass vial, and handed it to the Dark Lord. The latter held it in one hand and carefully poured one drop of the blood onto the stone in the palm of his other hand.

"Bertha Skahonhi, by your blood, I shall now become whole. *Gawe awakku wutuh.*"

Within seconds, the Dark Lord no longer appeared like the shriveled creature he was earlier, crippled on a chair, dependent on Asmodeus to feed him. He was now in his true, powerful form: He was gigantic as compared to other humans and had a strong exterior. He looked at his hands, arms, and body and let out an evil laugh.

The black birthstone was the key to unlocking the first of the three portals to unleash the evil spirits that Blaine Keir could form an army of. The three portals were going to be unlocked when the three invisible magical trees were all ungrounded by the Dark Lord.

"Now, for the sacrifice...." His voice became more serious and somber, and his tone was as determined as it could be. His army of French men, his mercenaries, looked up to him, and they were all dedicated to his victory.

"I have waited years and years for this day to come! Years..." He slowly shook his head from side to side to display his disappointment in what was done. "Years have passed, and now, I have achieved some of what I had wanted. I had plotted my revenge for ages, and with every passing day, my intent got only stronger, and so did my powers!"

His army of French men cheered for him, somewhat hypnotized by his evil magic.

"Now…" His evil grin returned, and his gaze had a thirst for blood. "I have been freed. I have broken my prison. I am now released!"

The first one was already ungrounded in the Forest of Limbo. Now, there were two more that were under the ground. These were invisible magical trees to be found by the Dark Lord and his French army in order to form the triangular portal between the three ungrounded trees. That triangular portal could open the pathway in the Earth to its very core, allowing for all the demons and evil forces to run free in the world, of course, under the Dark Lord's kingdom.

"I am thy Dark Lord!" Blaine Keir reinforced his powers on his awe-struck French army. "Do as I say, and you will never fail nor falter…." He paused in his speech to his men, and it was the pause that said that the actual news is yet to be heard now.

"Hail, the Dark Lord!" The French men said in unison as their chant echoed the dark forest of Limbo.

"Shh! Now… for the sacrifice…." He shushed them and emphasized his next action plan. "Cayuga's army is out there somewhere. He is recruiting and training, as I have heard. That means that he is not ready yet…." The pride of power further intensified in his gaze.

"Opening the dark portal requires a human sacrifice. This beautiful stone in my palm needs to be bathed in the blood of another human… and I want… the next blood sacrifice… to be of his most prized recruits!"

There was the thirst for revenge in his voice and the hunger for victory in his gaze as he continued his speech in the dark forest of limbo, "There are four or five recruits, I have been informed, who are being trained to lead their coteries...."

His men listened to him intently. Each word had a careful precision because this was the plan. This is what his French men were being ordered to do.

"Of them, one is the most precious. Now, I want the sacrifice of that one precious recruit of Cayuga to complete my revenge!"

He ordered his men and then said a spell: *Akuwutu Lituns!*

The trees around the opening made a rustling sound in the wind as something moved among them. Something significant. The wind started to blow faster, and a large black horse galloped in from behind the trees. It had jet black skin that shone like silk under the dimmest of the moonlight that fell on it. The French men gasped in amazement at its sight. It was not a usual horse, but the horse made for the Dark Lord to ride on, and its snake-like green eyes looked venomous, just as its rider's eyes. Its tail was long, green, and slimy.

Blaine Keir jumped up on his black horse and whipped it as it neighed and galloped away in the woods, disappearing into the darkness. His army was now ready to begin the journey under his instruction as they started the search for the dark forest to find the second tree to be unground. It would be another milestone completed in Blaine Keir's revenge plan.

Chapter # 18:
The Hidden Passage

Jeromy, Erik, and Akwiraron had been awake since early morning. There was still no sign of Anna and Dakota arriving anytime soon.

"I am worried now… I mean, they should have been back by now, right?" Erik broke the silence in the church.

"Yeah… But teleportation spells are never that easy, anyway. They might just need some more time to rest and gather enough energy to travel through such long distances in time and dimensions again." Jeromy explained optimistically.

"I agree, but I have this bad feeling that something is wrong," Akwiraron interjected.

The three men sat there and discussed different plans for what they could do to get out of this situation. On the one hand, they had to stay here and wait for their fellow recruits to show up because this was the plan, and they had to guard the birthstones on the fountain wall. But, on the other hand, they were not sure how much longer to wait for Anna and Dakota because they did feel like their fellows were in trouble and that they should go for their help.

"Uh… you guys, I think I know what we can do," Jeromy proposed. "We should wait until tonight to see if they come back, but if they still do not show up by midnight, we should pick off the birthstones from the fountain wall and go search for them. Okay?"

Erik hesitated. Akwiraron seemed fine with Jeromy's plan and decided to go with it. Jeromy stood up from the mat they had been sleeping on, on the church's marbled floor, and walked towards the fountain. He noticed the birthstones were no longer glowing as they had been last night.

"Well, that is strange...." He said to himself, but it was loud enough in the church's echoing environment that the other two recruits heard him.

"What is it?" Erik asked, immediately concerned that someone might have stolen their precious, precious birthstones while they were asleep.

"They… They are not glowing now. They were last night, weren't they?" Jeromy asked to confirm.

"Like stars! They were glowing like stars under the moonlight last night!" Erik answered and quickly ran over to the fountain wall where Jeromy was standing. Akwiraron accompanied his little run, too, to see what had changed.

"Uh… Yeah, something has definitely changed…." He confirmed, too.

Jeromy stared at the birthstones on the dried fountain's boundary and then looked up at the crack on the church's roof where the sycamore was growing. He noticed that the moonlight was falling on the birthstones last night when they were glowing. He tried to put together the pieces to explain the sudden change in the magical appearance of the stones set in the embeddings.

"Uh… what if… what if it has something to do with moonlight?" He worded his thoughts carefully, trying not to sound dumb to his fellow recruits, and then looked at their faces to see if his words made any sense to them.

Akwiraron looked at the roof, too, following Jeromy's words and gaze.

"Yeah… that might be it. We would find out about that tonight, then."

"Yeah, we're staying here till midnight anyway, so let's see." Erik agreed.

As the day passed, the sky became darker. The sun slowly set, and the moon started to rise. The three recruits were increasingly worried about Anna and Dakota's prolonged absence as the night approached.

Jeromy was pacing around the church when they heard footsteps nearby. He came to a halt and listened intently for the source of the sound. The other two men became attentive, too. There was a set of two different footsteps, which means there were two people nearby. Since the village was empty, any sound of existence in the nearby areas could be clearly heard.

Could it be Anna and Dakota? They wondered as they waited for the source of the footsteps to reveal themselves. The sound got louder, and soon, they could see four stripes of shadows under the church's large gate's moonlit gap – two pairs of feet it was.

The church's gate creaked open, and to the recruits' relief, it was Anna and Dakota, but they did not look so happy… or even healthy.

Jeromy quickly ran towards Anna, and she collapsed into his arms like she had no energy left to stay on her feet anymore. He held her in his firm grip and carefully lowered her to the ground so she could sit – propped up by the fountain.

Erik and Akwiraron rushed to the gate, too, and helped Dakota seat himself on the ground. There were fresh wounds on Dakota's arms, and his face looked like he had fallen face-first onto a rough surface.

"Wh – what happened to you, guys?!" Jeromy asked both of them.

Anna was too exhausted to answer and slightly injured, too. She opened her mouth to say something but could not get any words to escape her mouth. Of course, teleporting through time and a great distance twice in twenty-four hours was one of the hardest things they could do, and Anna had spent all her energy on it.

"The Dark Lord… Blaine Keir…" Dakota murmured as an answer to Jeromy's question. "He has escaped from the frontier… We met Ahiga from the Olta on our way back here…."

The other recruits were taken aback. They were not prepared for this; they were just getting closer to the second portal. Even that did not give them much power yet, because they did not know what the portal would unlock for their mission.

"He… His men attacked us. Anna torched several of them, but we were vastly outnumbered and were lucky to get out of there alive. He has the fifth birthstone… The one we had gone ahead in time to get." Dakota explained.

Jeromy, Erik, and Akwiraron were shocked. This was terrible news. The second portal could not be opened without the fifth birthstone, and that was with the Dark Lord, so it was almost impossible to open this portal here unless they could retrieve the stone from Blaine Keir. And, of course, there was no way that Keir would hand the stone over to them without a fight. But were they ready for a fight?

Jeromy looked at the bruise on Anna's arm and felt the worst anger rush through his veins. It reminded him of his mother and how she was discriminated against and tortured for being a Native American.

Their ancestors' history and suffering made these recruits the chosen ones among the many. They belonged to the tribes that had suffered cruelty, especially their women, and had been forced out of their homes and onto the streets. The fire in their hearts was wild and eruptious, and now, Jeromy could not watch Anna being subjected to such pain in this battle.

"Okay, that's it. We have to go deal with the Dark Lord before he causes any more destruction." Jeromy's speech was steady and confident. It was clear that his ambitions were stronger than ever, especially now the Dark Lord's men had hurt Anna.

"Yeah, but Anna can't… I mean, look at her and Dakota. They are in no condition to fight or even travel… at least not for now." Erik pointed out.

"Not now. No. They need to rest tonight. Then we can set off tomorrow morning." Jeromy laid out a quick plan.

"But the Dark Lord must have more powers than we do – We are not at full force yet. Right? Do you think that is a wise decision? To go fight him?" Akwiraron said in response.

"Chief Cayuga will come for us if we are not ready for a conflict. Otherwise, we're going. We cannot just sit back and watch the show." The recruits had never heard Jeromy being so serious, and even he felt a change in himself. For some reason, he knew he could achieve his goals with his intent and motivation.

"Obviously, we will work on our strategy before moving on." He clarified, and the rest of the recruits nodded in acceptance, convinced that this was the way to go.

The night passed slowly, with Anna hardly being able to speak and Jeromy running his fingers through her hair to help her relax and sleep as she laid her head in his lap. All the recruits slept with turns and tosses all night on the cold floor of the church. The thin mat they had laid on the floor was not of much help, either. Jeromy also fell into a dreamy sleep, just leaning against the wall with Anna's head laying across his lap.

His slumber was interrupted by the sun's rays falling on his face from the cracked roof of the church. He opened his eyes with a slight backache from sitting up all night and saw Anna was lying awake in his lap, too.

"Ann?" He whispered as he saw her eyes were open, and she seemed to be lost in thought. The light scrapes on the side of her face looked more prominent under the sunlight now, and it enraged Jeromy to even imagine that someone hurt her, just like it did when his mother had laid hurt and injured on the roadside after some policemen had pulled her car up and slammed her face down against the footpath. Back then, Jeromy was just a five-year-old boy sitting in his mother's car strapped by the seat belt, watching his mother plead against the injustice.

Injustice. It was a word well known by these recruits and many non-recruits who had seen their loved one's suffering the cruelty for simply being Native Americans.

"Hmm?" Anna let out only a little sound.

Jeromy put his hand on her forehead to relax her with his touch, but felt her head burning with a high temperature. She was sick. Indeed, Spirit Magic has a price, and the teleportation spells had drained her of all her energy. Of course, the last clash with the Dark Lord's men made it only worse for her.

"Ann, you are burning. You have a really high temperature!" Jeromy said as the other recruits woke up from their slumber, too.

"Mhmm. I'm hot. What can I say?" She chuckled weakly.

"Not the time for jokes, Ann." Jeromy held her hand and looked around to see his fellows awake. "Guys, is anyone's first aid kit still intact? Mine was all used up when I was on my way to find you in the dark forest. Several evil spirit animals and creatures had attacked me on my way."

Jeromy removed the medicine bag he had hanging around his neck.

"It's time to return this to you, Ann."

"I think I have my first aid kit," Dakota quickly searched his backpack among the five bags that were stacked up against a pillar in the church. He drew out a ziploc bag with a few first aid supplies, including some pills.

"Here, this should do for the temperature. It's paracetamol. It should help with any pain as well." Dakota handed out two white tablets to Jeromy. He had his water bottle ready in one of his hands and helped Anna sit up with the other hand supporting her back.

She swallowed the pills and said, "I don't think I am up for a war, guys. I can barely sit, let alone stand, walk, or fight."

She still looked utterly drained.

The men agreed. She had spent all her energy to teleport and was now too weak for at least a couple of days.

"Then we might need to prepare our strategy now," Erik said, unwrapping a granola bar from his bag to fuel him up for the day.

"Yeah, let's all have our meals and discuss what we can do. We obviously need the black birthstone from the Dark Lord because, without it, the second portal does not open." Akwiraron suggested.

"Mhmm. And, if the second portal does not open, I am sure the world will be in a lot of trouble. It was obvious through the urgency in Chief Cayuga's orders when he told us about this portal, right?" Jeromy stated.

The recruits agreed and had their breakfast sitting in a circle, discussing what strategies they could opt for to extract the birthstone without putting their own lives in danger.

"The year is still 1760, and the French and Indian War is still ongoing. On our way, we had heard of another battle starting. The unjust government has held Mohawks in the cruelest circumstances, and the evil is being fomented by the Dark Lord." Dakota explained.

"We need to fight against the injustice – that is what our mission is. That is what they recruited us to do." Erik stated the group's purpose in an attempt to keep them focused.

"So, it is decided, then…." Jeromy described the plan they had agreed on. "We are splitting up. Dakota, Erik, and I will embark on the journey to find the Dark Lord and extract the fifth birthstone from his grasp, okay? And… Anna and Akwiraron will stay here to guard this portal and our four birthstones."

The group agreed on this strategy, but Anna was worried. She did not want to let them go into a war zone without her, especially Jeromy, but of course, she understood that she would only slow them down if she went with them in such a weak state.

"You take care of yourself, Anna." Jeromy cupped her face with his palms and looked deep into her raven black eyes.

The look in Jeromy's eyes told Anna that he would be all right. He was confident and strong, both mentally and physically, and Anna felt comforted with that look.

"Don't worry about me. You… be careful, Jer. I want to see you again soon.…" She said through the pain that was wracking her body. She could literally feel each bone in her body aching as she moved her hand to hold Jeromy's forearm and kiss his palm gently to say goodbye.

Splitting was their only way – Anna could not move around too much and needed to rest here. Meanwhile, the birthstones must also be guarded because losing even one of them could send them backward in their journey and cause further obstacles in their goal to open the second portal.

Jeromy, Erik, and Dakota scavenged and then left the church with their backpacks and their waist bags refilled and checked for all essential resources. Obviously, they could not get any new supplies. Still, they had picked up whatever useful items they could find under the village's roofs. It was just after noon when the men had begun their journey, and while they currently had no clue about which way to head for, Dakota suggested they go North. They had to leave their birthstones behind with Anna and Akwiraron to guard until they returned with the fifth birthstone. So, now, using Jeromy's opal to show a map and guide them was impossible.

"We should have picked up the opal, though…." Jeromy said, thinking whether going back to take it would be wise.

"Let's just go for now… the birthstones are a risk to take further on this journey, you know, especially because we are going towards the Dark Lord himself." Dakota made sense.

"We had entered this village from the South of the Dark Forest, right? So, I don't know, but I suppose any way forward should be North?" He suggested.

Since the other two recruits had no clue about the way either, they agreed to walk towards the North and see where the path takes them. They exited the village, and the landscape became quite hilly, which took them over two days to cross halfway, and all they saw ahead were more hills with scattered piles of desert sand.

"It appears that there will be a desert ahead. These piles of sand don't belong here," Erik said, investigating some sand grains with his fingers.

The sun set, and it was twilight when the three recruits realized they saw a dim orange light somewhere in the distance. From what it seemed, it might be a fire. They figured that there might be other travelers having a bonfire in this hilly range and started towards that point.

As they walked nearer, the bright spot appeared lesser like fire and more like… a golden scroll levitating in midair! They ran towards the floating scroll, and Erik grabbed it. When he opened it, the scroll was blank, yet luminous. That was a good sign because it proved consistent with Chief Cayuga's previous golden scrolls. That meant that help was sent by him.

Erik saw the words appear on the scroll in his hand.

"Find the hidden passage. It will lead you to the key."

The three recruits looked at each other, appreciative that Chief Cayuga had left them a hint.

"The key... That must be the fifth birthstone, I am guessing." Jeromy concluded after he read the message on the scroll.

A bright luminous circle started to glow in the center of the scroll, and the words burnt off while the blank scroll remained in Erik's hand. Then, a map appeared on the golden scroll, which showed with a blue mark where the recruits were currently situated. As they moved a few steps ahead, the mark moved, too.

The recruits were delighted at the help they had received. This made things easier for them and gave them a clear direction towards the Dark Lord's location, as well as the passage that could be their safest route.

They were already on the right path, and they were right to assume that a desert was ahead, too. As they moved forward into the night and into the hilly range, colder breezes blew, but there was no stopping them anymore.

They followed their path to the desert and then worked their way through it, following the map. The map had a tunnel marked with a glowing outline.

"That must be the hidden passage that Chief Cayuga had hinted at." Jeromy pointed out as they walked ahead. Soon, as they reached a closer point to the glowing tunnel on the map, they could see a large boulder sitting in the desert with a man-sized hole in it. According to the map, this was where the hidden passage was.

"Should we go in? Inside the boulder?" Erik asked skeptically.

"We have to. I have no doubts about the accuracy of this map as it is a guide provided directly by Chief Cayuga." Jeromy reinforced.

"Then… let's step in!" Dakota and the other recruits stepped closer to the boulder, and under such a dim moonlight on a dark night, the tunnel – if there was any – looked like an endless fall into the Earth's core.

As Jeromy, Erik, and Dakota went into the tunnel one after the other, they stopped when they saw nothing but a stone wall as soon as the tunnel even began.

"That's strange…." Dakota said. "There is no way ahead."

The tunnel was dimly lit with two lanterns that had a purplish flame alight inside their glass exteriors. And, just a few feet ahead of those lanterns was the stone wall that was stopping them from going any further in this apparently hidden passage.

"Well… we are on the right spot as per the map," said Jeromy, rechecking the map under the lantern's light as he walked closer to it. "Hmm… the red mark of our location here shows that there is a path ahead of this wall…."

"Does that mean we break down the wall?" Erik asked, confused how they would do that without any wall-breaking tools.

"I don't think so… because then, the passage would not be so hidden anymore," Dakota made a fair point that both Erik and Jeromy agreed on.

"Then this has to be another one of the tests or riddles that Chief Cayuga said that we would be put through. Let's inspect if there is anything around here that may open the path for us," Jeromy stated. He walked closer to the purple lanterns to inspect if any of their elements could be a clue.

Erik noticed that one of those lanterns was burning brighter than the other, and when he looked closely at its bright purple flame, he saw that there was a small key at its center.

"What?!" He yelped, and his two fellows walked over to see what was so surprising. "Is that a key? How can a key open a wall of stones?!" He spoke.

Dakota stepped ahead and told his fellows to step back with a gesture of his hand. They observed him as he reached for the lantern with his hand and struck it with a quick, yet strong motion. The lantern fell off from the hook on the side wall and broke on the floor. Obviously, its bright purple flame died out, and the tunnel was darker than before now.

However, one lantern's light was enough to show them the key that was now outside of the broken lantern, among the shattered pieces of its glass. Dakota bent to pick up the key that was a burnt bronze in color.

"Looks antique," He pointed out as Erik and Jeromy had a closer look at it.

Jeromy took the key from Dakota's hand and walked closer to the wall of stone standing in their way. He mumbled a spell under his breath – a spell to show hidden paths nearby, and an ancient-looking wooden door suddenly appeared in the center of the stone wall.

"Of course! What's a hidden pathway without a hidden key?!" Erik joked as the boys cheered for themselves.

Jeromy put the key in the door's keyhole and turned it until it clicked. They opened the door slowly. Ahead, the three recruits could see a long tunnel dimly lit by warm candlelight along the way.

As the three recruits stepped through the door and went to the other side of the stone wall, they looked back to see nothing but the stone wall. The door had vanished as if it was never there.

"Well... the key better work when we need to leave from here. I don't want to live underground!" Erik exclaimed humorously, glad that they had made it so far.

They were all confident that this was the hidden path that would lead them to their purpose, and their goal was well-defined in each of their minds. Their mission was to get the fifth birthstone and be strong enough to fight off the Dark Lord and defeat the unjust government. They were fiercely passionate about achieving it.

They each had a goal because they each had a scar. They had all lost someone close, someone dear, someone who did not deserve to suffer at the hands of the government and its people. All these recruits were emotionally motivated to achieve justice for all the Native Americans who had suffered for no reason, so they were spiritually and physically soldiers who would fight until their last breaths to achieve this cause.

As they walked through the tunnel, they found it to be an adequately developed pathway that someone royal might have designed. It had lanterns that stayed lit for God knows how long.

It had stairs and variations in slopes. And, it even had carved designs into the walls and their boundaries at several points.

The recruits had been walking for quite a while and decided to rest at a point that they deemed fit.

"How long do you think we have been walking for?" Erik asked his fellows.

"Probably more than four hours. It must be morning by now." Dakota yawned as their footsteps slowed down from exhaustion.

"I think this might be a good spot to rest for a while. That little corner that looks like a room." Jeromy pointed towards a small cubicle made of sanded walls in a corner. The door was only four feet, so they had to bend to get inside it, but there was enough space for the three of them to spread their mats and sleep there.

"Boy, am I hungry!" Dakota exclaimed as soon as they sat down and took off their backpacks.

"Then, have something to eat. You do have your meals, right?" Erik confirmed. "I might have a sandwich, too."

Dakota and Erik opened their bags and had their meals. At the same time, Jeromy laid down with his eyes closed, wondering how Anna might be doing now.

"Nglacak lan maca sesanti."

He murmured under his breath to perform the telepathy spell. He had sent the message: "Are you better now, Ann?"

He kept his eyes closed and mind focused on the spell to work, but received no response from her. After a few seconds of trying harder, he did feel like he had received a message from her but could not read it in his mind. It was like receiving a letter but being unable to open it yet.

Regardless, he was tired from the journey and knew that greater adventures awaited him the next day, so he felt satisfied with the fact that he had at least received a response from Anna. Even if he could not read the message, the response at least ensured him that she was all right, and for now, that was all that mattered to him.

Erik and Dakota were done with their meals by now, and the three recruits slept soundly for a few hours before some loud footsteps awakened them.

They stayed quiet and did not make a sound – they definitely did not want any unwanted attention in this place that they knew nothing about.

"Personne n'est là!"

A man's voice echoed just outside the room that these recruits were in. He was talking in French, and naturally, Dakota assumed it must be one of the French men from the Dark Lord's army. He had encountered one of these army men when he was returning to the church with Anna, so he could tell it was his men just from their harsh, dead tone. Their voices were devoid of emotion and lacked any concern for anyone or anything.

After a few more dialogues in French that only Jeromy could understand, thanks to his knowledge of foreign languages, the voices faded away along, with their footsteps into the distance.

From what it seemed, they had walked in the direction that these recruits had entered this tunnel from, so now, they were concerned that the French men might see the lantern they had broken at the entrance of this passage and notice the missing key, which meant they had little time to get the black birthstone from the Dark Lord before his men were alerted.

"Psst!" Erik called for Jeromy's attention with a whisper, careful to make only as much sound to deliver his voice only to the other end of this small room.

"Yeah?" Jeromy looked at him.

"You know French, right?" Erik asked.

"Yeah, somewhat." He answered.

"Well, then, what were they saying?" Erik questioned.

"They were looking for us, probably… I mean, they had a doubt that someone had entered the tunnel, and they were just looking around but had not found any evidence yet. One of them was saying that it might be a false alarm."

Jeromy explained as Dakota and Erik listened to him carefully.

"So, should we get out of here or what?" Dakota asked his fellow recruits.

"We should. We have very little time because Blaine Keir's men have gone towards the wall of stone that we have surpassed, so if they see the broken lantern, then they would obviously know what's going on." Jeromy warned his recruits.

The three recruits packed up their mats, and Erik peeked out of the room to see if the path was clear.

He gestured his friends to come out after him as he stepped out of the sandy room with his backpack. The path was clear for their safe movement. Jeromy and Dakota followed him out and took a breath of relief – the little room they had slept in was not too spacious, so being out in the open space again felt more comfortable.

"Shall we?" Erik asked Jeromy, pointing at the direction they were originally going in – opposite where the French men had walked off to.

Jeromy nodded, and the three recruits walked ahead towards their destination. Their footsteps, despite being careful, were lightly echoing in the hidden underground tunnel, so they were cautious to not make any sounds. There were only whispers and footsteps throughout their journey.

"It has been two days since we have been traveling in this passage… right?" Dakota asked in a quiet whisper.

"I suppose, yes. Are you tired?" Jeromy asked him.

"I most definitely am! I wouldn't mind resting a bit." He responded as they slowed down to catch their breaths.

"Well, I don't think we can rest now, Dakota," Erik said.

"Yeah, I agree – not now. We do not have much time anymore. Those men may come back looking for us anytime now, and they obviously outnumbered us, so we would be in a lot of trouble then," Jeromy explained.

After taking a sip of water from his bottle, Dakota sighed and continued ahead behind Erik and Jeromy. After a few more hours of walking, they saw a brick-layered well at the end of the tunnel. The well was lined with red bricks and had a purplish tarry liquid that was sticking around its corners.

"Whoa… what's that sticky, glowy substance?" Erik pointed out towards the well.

The three recruits stepped closer to the well and looked curiously at the luminous purple liquid to inspect what it was. Since spirit magic was nothing new in their dictionary, they knew that this could be both a hint or a trap, and that is why they had to be careful.

"Just don't tell me we have to go down this well. Don't tell me this well is the hidden passage because I am not too fond of…." Dakota's words faded off mid-sentence as he turned his head towards his right to see Erik standing there and smiled as if he found an answer, and then said through his smile, "Water!"

Erik shrugged, knowing that this was his area of expertise. Water was his powerful element, and he had the ability to travel through it along with his fellows.

"But wait, don't get too excited too soon. Let me check if it's safe first." Jeromy held up his hand to signal the other two recruits to step away from the well. He did not want them to touch the mysterious liquid without knowing its effects.

He picked up a few stones from the side of the tunnel's wall and threw one of them into the well to check its depth. After a few seconds, they heard a thud. A solid thud. That indicated that there was not really water in the well, and even if there was, it was too shallow to make much difference.

"That's not good. The well is apparently too deep for us to just jump into it." Erik concluded.

"Sure sounds like it...." Jeromy agreed, but then he stepped closer and, just out of curiosity, tossed another stone, aiming it at the border of the well. The stone was comparatively bigger than the previous one, and it landed right onto some of the sticky purple substance.

At first, nothing happened. Jeromy looked at Erik and Dakota, and they were all confused about whether or not this was the safe way to go.

"Well, I don't see another way to go forward from here, so this might be it." Erik expressed his opinion on the matter.

"And Chief Cayuga would not send us down here on such a long path if it did not lead to the fifth birthstone, so this has to be it. The well is the way." Jeromy said and stepped forward, but then suddenly stopped.

"Wait… where did that stone go?" He asked, confused.

"The icky purple goo ate it?" Dakota joked, but was genuinely curious to find out if there had been any reaction by the sticky liquid while they had their eyes off of the stone.

Erik bent and picked up one of the other pebbles lying on the ground beside his feet and tossed it onto the well's boundary, just like Jeromy had.

"Umm, okay, let's just focus on that now." He said to his fellows. And, as they observed, the pebble slowly disappeared!

"Whoa! What?!" Dakota exclaimed. His mouth was wide open in surprise. "Did that rock just become invisible?!"

The guys were very confused but amazed at what they could see as the potential of this magical liquid surrounding the well.

"Does that mean…?" Erik's eyes were wide as he awaited confirmation of his assumption.

"Probably," Jeromy smiled with determination. He moved forward and extended his hand to touch the purple liquid, and gradually, his hand started to fade out. Starting from the tip of his fingers and moving up towards his arms, his hands were now disappearing from the effect of the purple liquid.

They looked in wonder as they realized just how powerful this liquid tool could be for them. When Jeromy had disappeared entirely, he called out to Erik and Dakota to ask them if they could see him.

"We can only hear you! Where are you?" Erik answered.

"Right here by the well! Touch the magic slime, you two. Maybe this is the most important power to help us reach the fifth birthstone without being caught!" Jeromy told them, and they did the same. Within a few seconds, all three of them were invisible to the naked eye… but visible once more to each other.

"Erik, even if there is a little water down there, do you think you can use your powers to bring up that water and help us travel down into the well?" Jeromy asked.

"I suppose so." He said and then peeked into the well that looked endless in depth.

"*Akuwutu mepwoku,*" Erik said the spell out loud. Then the recruits could hear the splashes of water growing louder as a flat platform of water emerged from inside the well and landed at the well's top.

"Hop on, guys!" Erik said, stepping onto the platform along with the other two recruits.

Erik placed his hands in the air in a manner to gesture the platform to push it downwards. As he did, the platform made of water that was levitating on the well's top surface started to lower steadily like an elevator, and landed on a watery surface. The platform disappeared in a flash on the ground, and the three recruits walked ahead with their feet ankle-deep in water. The tunnel that they were now walking through was dimly lit and did not look too long to reach the end of the straight path.

A wide staircase led up to a narrow corridor right in front of them. From what they perceived, this might mark the end of the hidden passage to their destination – that meant that they would soon need to get into action.

Jeromy, Erik, and Dakota were still invisible to others. Still, they could hear and see each other in about thirty seconds. They did feel a strange nausea creeping up on them ever since they had touched the purple invisibility liquid, but this was needed right now. Their invisibility was a blessing for them.

The recruits walked up the stairs and saw no way out other than one wooden door to their right, and suddenly, they just knew what was on the other end of the door.

"The Dark Lord is there…." Dakota confirmed the other two recruits' presumption. "Don't ask me how, but I just know it…."

"Yeah, me too." Replied Jeromy.

Before deciding to step across the door and face the Dark Lord, Jeromy could not help but think about Anna and wonder if she was okay.

"Let's go," he said in a strong, determined whisper to his fellows before attempting to open the wooden door leading into the Dark Lord's room. But, as he put his hand on the door's handle, his hand went right through it. He was not sure whether the door was designed to let people through like this or whether the invisibility had given them this ability. Still, it was of great help to simply slide through the door's surface without having to open the door as it avoided attracting unnecessary attention.

The three men slid through the door and entered an enormous royal hall. They saw a large bed on which a tall, ruthless-looking man was sleeping. Three French men were fast asleep on mats near the door that exited from the hall, and one man stood by that door to guard it. The huge man sleeping on the bed was wearing a locket around his neck, and it held the black birthstone that Dakota had kept since his grandfather's death.

"That must be the Dark Lord," Erik whispered to warn his fellows, but Jeromy held a finger to his lips, signaling him to stay quiet. The recruits could see each other and hear each other, and while the others around them could not see them, they could definitely listen to them. So, whispering was off the table, especially when they were in such a risky situation.

Jeromy stepped forward and looked at the beautiful black birthstone embedded in a golden frame under Blaine Keir's neck with a rusty chain. Of course, the chain was a common element attached to an extraordinary and antique gift.

Jeromy waved at Dakota to catch his attention, pointed at the black birthstone, and gave him a thumbs-up sign with a questioning facial expression to ask if this was the birthstone they were here for.

Dakota nodded confidently in affirmation. This was the time that Jeromy had come so far for, and for him, it was not just about the heroic mission anymore, but for personal vengeance, too. Blaine Keir was responsible for the worst of what the native American people went through, especially through his whispering into the minds of the Colonial and US rulers, and he was the reason Anna was in such a painful state.

Jeromy was outraged just thinking about the pain that this being had caused in alliance with the government and taking the birthstone away from him would only be the first step towards getting his revenge by making him powerless.

As the Dark Lord snored, Jeromy stepped closer to him and put his hand in the air, palm facing down, just above the locket in his neck. He closed his eyes and said a spell before the black birthstone disappeared from its place in the locket and reappeared in Jeromy's hand. It was a teleportation spell to get the birthstone without manually dismantling it.

Erik and Dakota watched the action with the utmost feeling of respect and victory and then followed Jeromy out of the hall from the exit door. There was a large corridor with pillars and sculptures across a long way. From what the boys knew, the architecture of this place seemed like a royal castle made by Egyptian and Greek architects.

After going through a couple more hallways and rooms, they finally found a large gate that would lead out of the castle-like building that they were in. It was a good thing, too, as they had begun to become visible again.

As they exited through the main gate, they emerged on an undeveloped, rough road. Jeromy took out the map from his pocket that they had followed to get to the secret tunnel in the first place. The map showed they were currently one forest away from the church in the village they were walking towards now.

"That was cool, wasn't it?" Jeromy snickered, happy to be on his way to see Anna again and having fulfilled his purpose of this journey.

"So cool! I didn't know you could do that!" Erik patted Jeromy on his back and laughed.

Jeromy held out his hand with his palm facing the ground as they walked, and used the same spell to teleport a twig into his hand.

"Okay, stop showing off!" Dakota teased him. It was around midnight, and walking through the forest did not seem like a great idea at this time, especially when they had not eaten all day and had little energy left.

According to the map, the three recruits walked closer to the forest and observed how long it might take for them to cross the forest based on how huge it appeared on the map.

"This looks half as long as the tunnel, and it took us around two days to get through the tunnel…." Erik pointed out his observations.

"Hmm… That should mean that we will cross the forest in two days?" Dakota asked.

"No. Probably lesser than that. Maybe just two minutes." Jeromy smirked. He could not find a better time to use the teleportation spell. "We need to teleport back to the church as soon as we can to open the portal before the Dark Lord realizes that the black birthstone has been taken away from him."

Chapter # 19:
Rise of Rebellion

Jeromy looked at the black birthstone shining under the moonlight in his palm and slipped it into his waist bag before zipping the bag close.

"Yeah… That would create a whole lot of unneeded drama," Erik agreed.

"Celik Praraha"

Jeromy said the Wektu spell, and under the moonlit sky, in front of the dense forest, a whitish blue dome emerged to cover the three recruits as they stood together. The glowing dome quickly shrank, and with its disappearance, the recruits disappeared, too.

When Jeromy opened his eyes, he felt like he had awakened from a bad hangover. It was expected, really, after the teleportation spell that he had read to get here. When he looked around, he saw a blurry room. His two fellow recruits, Erik and Dakota, were lying on the floor and just beginning to sit up. But one thing was for sure: This was not the church that they had intended to teleport to.

"Ugh…" Erik sat up with one hand on his head and squinted his eyes from the headache. He looked around and shook his head. "This is definitely not where we wanted to be."

"Gah! I've got to get used to these teleportation headaches, man!" Dakota shook his head, as if shaking away the pain and trying to come to his senses.

Jeromy was still weak because he had performed the spell, but was still in good condition to get up and get going. His hands quickly found their way down to his waist bag to confirm that the birthstone was there, and thankfully, it was. Dakota had asked Jeromy to keep his birthstone with him because he was the leader of the medallion recruits, and Dakota trusted his guardianship more than his own.

"We are not too far away from the church, though. It is nearby." Jeromy stated to his friends.

"Yeah, when I last teleported with Anna, we landed in a similar place, too, but we had to face Blaine Keir's men on our way out." Dakota reminded them.

Jeromy sighed and stood up, which was more difficult at this moment than it usually was after such a spell. He had woken up fine, but the pain had just found him within seconds. His entire body, especially his spine, felt like it had been lined with acid that was burning him up.

"Well, let's just hope we do not run into those French men this time before reaching the church."

Jeromy walked to a small window covered by a curtain in this little room that they were in. When he pulled it aside, he could see that they were in the same village as the church that was their current destination.

He gestured at his friends to follow him out of the room. "Let's go. Anna and Akwiraron must waiting for us."

He opened the creaky wooden door and stepped out into the village's undeveloped roads. The sun was intense, and its rays had made the ground hotter than the last time these recruits were walking on it. As they walked in the scorching heat, they saw the church they were looking for on their right.

"We're here, finally," Erik took a sigh of relief.

Jeromy stepped forward and opened the church's gate. It was large and dusty, and the rust on its sides prevented it from opening quickly. It made a screeching sound when it opened, and Jeromy's eyes wandered to detect Anna in the hall, but she was not there. He saw Akwiraron sitting in one corner, and he painfully stood up when he saw the recruits. There were also dead bodies and several piles of smoldering bones and ash scattered across the floor – evidence of a recent fight.

There was blood on Akwiraron's forehead, and the look on his face did not show that he was happy to see his fellow recruits. His face was sending a clear message that something was wrong… Something was *very* wrong…

"Wh – Where is Anna?!" Jeromy stuttered, not sure if he was ready to hear the answer.

Dakota and Erik were equally confused. Akwiraron's injuries and Anna's absence were troubling enough to demonstrate that something terrible had happened while they were away. Dakota's gaze fell upon the fountain's wall where the other four birthstones were before they left for the fifth one. To his utter surprise, none of the birthstones were there anymore.

"She… She got taken away. They… They took her captive," Akwiraron said with his heart heavy and his voice swollen with defeat. He felt like he had failed his team.

"No!..." Jeromy looked at him, disappointed. He grabbed Akwiraron by the collar of his shirt and yelled at him. "No! That cannot be! You!! You did not guard her! I left *you* with her to protect her! Damn it!"

Jeromy's voice cracked as tears welled up in his eyes. He knew what it meant to be taken captive. He had heard enough stories to know that they drain the life out of their captives by torturing them in every way possible, both psychologically and physically.

"I – I'm sorry, man. I tried! I tried to keep her safe, but she had become weaker and used the last of her energy trying to fight with me against the evil army. Then… she fell unconscious. It was too much for her after the earlier spell and the later attacks! I did everything in my power to keep her safe, but in the end, I was fighting alone against too many of the Dark Lord's men! But… I was knocked out myself." Akwiraron apologized, knowing well that Jeromy was deeply hurt by the incident. Anna being away was bad news.

Jeromy backed away from him. He knew it was not Akwiraron's fault and that he was wrong to yell at him, but what could he do?

He felt helpless at this time and questioned his own decision to leave Anna here at the church. Aggressively walking over to a wall, he punched his fist into it.

"Akwiraron, I'm sorry, man. I'm sure you did everything you could. I'm really sorry. Dammit!"

Erik put his hand on Jeromy's shoulder in an attempt to comfort him and asked him, "Jeromy, I know this is not a good time to keep going, but we need to. If Blaine Keir's men found their way here earlier, they can come for us – for the black birthstone – again, too."

Jeromy knew he made sense and that he needed to keep this mission going for even more personal reasons now than before. He wiped away his tears on his sleeve and turned to face the other three recruits.

"Okay, we need to do things faster now." He said in a low, husky voice that declared his determination loud and clear.

"The birthstones… The other four birthstones are not here…" Dakota pointed out hesitantly. He was unsure if this was the right time to bring that up.

"I have them. I had hidden the birthstones as soon as you guys had left." Akwiraron answered, limping as he walked towards a corner of the church. He bent down and removed a large piece of rock that revealed a small dug hole in the ground under it. Akwiraron reached into the hole and pulled out a little pouch from it.

"These are the four birthstones." He handed them over to Jeromy. "Were you successful in getting the fifth stone?"

"Yeah, luckily," Jeromy said briefly and reached into his waist bag to pull out the black birthstone and showed it to Akwiraron. He admired its beauty before they placed the five birthstones in their respective embedded placements.

One by one, each birthstone clicked in its place. The opal, emerald, diamond, and amethyst. All perfectly set into the boundary of the dried fountain and started to glow. As soon as the last birthstone, the black onyx, was put into its place, all the other birthstones glowed more intensely. A whooshing wind began to surround the recruits as they stood around the dried fountain.

The glow intensified further as the moonlight fell onto the birthstones, and the three recruits stepped back in awe as a giant blue portal opened in the air, levitating just above the fountain. While this was happening, the recruits heard the church's door being opened with its creaky screechy sound. When they turned around, they saw Chief Cayuga walking towards them, wearing a proud smile on his face.

"You did it, my medallion recruits!" His voice echoed outside his magical appearance in the abandoned church. The four recruits were impressed with themselves. They had opened the second portal, and now Chief Cayuga was here to congratulate them.

"Please step outside with me." The proud Cayuga commanded.

All this time, their success was tinged with the fact that Anna, one of their strongest members, was not here to witness this achievement of an important milestone. Still, they knew that their next mission would be to get her and the other captives freed from the unjust rule.

When they arrived outside, the recruits were very pleased to see that Chief Cayuga had already brought several hundred native warriors who stood ready to fight. All were wearing red buckskin uniforms.

When they were a short distance away, Chief Cayuga turned toward back toward the church, raised his palms skyward and pronounced, *"Li Kunsu Hinwali!"*

At first, the church appeared to vibrate or shake, and the recruits could feel the ground shaking beneath their feet. Then the holy edifice began to shimmer. Within seconds, small bursts of bright blue-white light began bursting through at dozens of points across the church's slowly vanishing surface.

Less than 20 seconds of transformation elapsed when the church was completely gone and was replaced by a gigantic blue-white portal which continued to expand in length and width. Brilliant light burst forth in all directions, along with a tsunami wave of sweet, electrified air.

The veil between the spirit and living worlds was now open.

The blazing portal lets out an entire army of spirit legendary beings and spirit human warriors dressed in a red uniforms.

Recruits watched in wonder as the armies arrived. Both the human warriors and creatures from native legends were chanting mottos and roaring with fury and enthusiasm as they marched out in their glowing glory. Some of the magical spirit creatures emerging from the portal had wings, including several winged thunderbirds with flesh-shredding, razor-sharp talons – and they breathed fire and spewed ball lightning. Some were fierce, flesh-eating Wendigos.

They were extraordinarily grizzly and emaciated, with sunken eyes, gray skin, and shredded bloody lips. Enemies unlucky enough to be within a few feet of the Algonquian legendary monsters would likely pass out in a pool of their own vomit just from the deadly odor they emitted.

Where the church once stood was now a vast, open field being filled with all kinds of beings that looked straight out of a movie. They quickly spread out to the open grounds nearby.

"Jeromy, this is your coterie. They have been waiting for you to lead them in this war, and they will fight under your command." Chief Cayuga instructed Jeromy, who was smiling proudly upon welcoming his army. Chief Cayuga clapped his hands, and with sparks flying everywhere, Chingacgook's weapon appeared. He handed it to Jeromy. "This is your special weapon gifted to you by my father. Your reward for taking on this mission so honorably." Cayuga's words touched Jeromy's heart. For some reason, at this time of such emotion, he could not help but miss his sister, Issabelle.

"You will do wonders, mouse," she used to call him by this nickname to tease him. Jeromy's heart welled up on this memory of hers, and he was even more motivated to win this battle and make the world a better place for her and all others.

"BattleBlade!" Jeromy exclaimed, looking at the beautiful weapon he held.

"Show them!" Cayuga commanded Jeromy.

With that command, Jeromy fiercely demonstrated his skill to the roaring delight of the other recruits and the assembling army. In a fearsome demonstration, he spun, thrust, kicked, flipped, and spun the BattleBlade.

"Jesus, Jeromy!" the three recruits watching jinxed.

Everyone was awestruck… and then the cry went out: "White Feather, White Feather, White Feather!"

One by one, three more armies of men, women, and magical beings walked out of the large portal. Each of the recruits spread out and were followed by an army onto the same field as Jeromy's. Without having to be told what to do, the medallion recruits began shouting orders, forming columns, and assembling their armies.

Chief Cayuga walked over to what would have been Anna's army.

"They have taken your leader captive. She had sacrificed her health and power constantly for the achievement of her and our goal." Chief Cayuga made a speech addressing Anna's army, but everyone else listened carefully. After all, they were all on the same team.

"Jeromy," Chief Cayuga called him to stand by his side. "You have stood out in your powers, abilities, and leadership qualities. Hence, until Anna is freed and brought back safely, I believe you would be fit to lead her army alongside yours."

Jeromy was sad at the thought of Anna being away. Still, he felt responsible for taking care of her army during her absence and instantly agreed, "I'd be honored, but I believe Dakota has earned the place to lead until we find Anna."

Cayuga smiled. "I agree."

The coteries included Native Americans in red buckskin uniforms. Each one of them had suffered the worst forms of injustice, either directly or indirectly. Each coterie also had a large horse-like creature that had a horn on his head like a unicorn, and the horn was made of fire. The creature was powered with two large wings on each side, allowing it to make higher jumps or gallops than regular ones, but it could not fly. The exception was Jeromy's coterie. To his delight, Cayuga thunder-clapped his hands again, and instantly, Jeromy's horse Red Thunder appeared spectacularly. Jeromy ran to him and stroked his glowing red coat, and welcomed him to his side.

By this time, the brewing war was now becoming more evident. The medallion recruits were ready with their armies. When Chief Cayuga left the village, he left each of the four recruits with valuable information and essential resources, including spells, weapons, and maps. They each had unique powers that could work independently or complement each other's actions.

On the other hand, the Dark Lord had awakened and found out that the black birthstone was missing from his locket. He was furious. And, after capturing Anna, he knew very well who had taken the black onyx, and he immediately signaled his legions of French mercenaries and demons to prepare for war.

"We will take all that is ours and all that is not!" Blaine Keir announced with venom dawning from his face.

But just as the Dark Lord's fury was fueled by the black onyx being taken away, thus forming an obstacle in his plan of revenge, the medallion recruits were increasingly motivated to defeat the unjust forces that have made their people suffer for ages and have taken one of their most valued members as captive.

* * *

Jeromy and the other recruits led their coteries to Stanwix, where they saw the French army already gathered. The towering Dark Lord stood nearby with a dominating, robust exterior and gruesome dark and gleaming weapons slung across himself.

On their way from the village to this battleground, the recruits received much appraisal for their purpose by the ordinary people they had met in the neighboring outskirts of the abandoned village. Many of them even joined the armies voluntarily.

The battleground was now full of fierce, frustrated, angry people who each had a purpose of being there. Under Erik's army, there was one creature, a crystalline blue giant, who had lost its offspring because of the Dark Lord's heartlessness. It was in excruciating pain and had returned for its revenge.

When the recruits reached there, they were prepared for a full-fledged war. Jeromy trotted Red Thunder forward to the front of all their armies combined against the Dark Lord's legions and announced: "You have ruled and lost, and we have loved and lost. We are not here for bloodshed if you surrender to our conditions and release our captives!"

The Dark Lord laughed an evil laugh before responding, "But I am here for bloodshed. I am thirsty for your blood, and with your blood, I will make the human sacrifice to open the third portal! Where is your Chief... that *LORD* Cayuga now? Hiding somewhere behind his little army like a coward?!" He spat out the word *Lord* as if it was abuse.

"I hope you have heard the common saying that when the white man dies, he thinks he is at peace, but when the red man dies, he knows how to torture even the souls of their enemies!" Erik stepped forward and announced, further aggravating the Dark Lord and his French men.

Blaine Keir was on a large black horse, the same one he had been riding on in the dark forests. He stepped down from the horse and stood with his nose high and arms folded across his chest.

"Return the black onyx, son, and I will let your woman go." The Dark Lord addressed Jeromy as two French men stepped forward and stood by him, with Anna between them. She was chained, swollen, and badly bruised, and her eyes welled up at the first glance at Jeromy. Her mouth was stuffed with a cloth that prevented her from speaking. Still, Jeromy could read her eyes and tell that she had suffered enough under this captivity.

Jeromy felt a pang of pain as he watched Anna in this position. She looked hurt, yet her eyes had the fierce look of strength in them as always, and that was the strength that Jeromy had fallen for. He knew that this was the time, the war, the sacrifice that Chief Cayuga had been preparing them for all this time, and now was the execution of all that they had learned on this journey.

"Ann… Stay strong. I'm here for you." He said to her and then averted his gaze towards the Dark Lord, who stood tall with a smirk on his face. He was vastly taller than most humans and had a broad physical build, but his face was marked by dark fissures and an ugly scar on his right cheek.

"Cayuga… He is my enemy, my eternal enemy," The Dark Lord said in a husky voice as the fire of revenge flamed in his icy gaze. "When that Mohican named Chingachgook killed my father, Cayuga returned and took away my father's throne… *MY* father! Magua! He banished us into a life of a prisoner!" He spat out the words angrily as the opposing army and the recruit leaders listened to his side of the story.

They knew that Blaine Keir was set on regaining the kingdom of the darkness, and more than that, he wanted to have his revenge. He wanted to have blood on his hands of all those who got in the way of his father's unjust kingdom. Now, following in his father's footsteps even after his death, Blaine Keir had already established himself as the Dark Lord and taken control of the government's actions, making them do his dirty work.

The government was corrupted anyway, so its members – at least, most of them – complied to his evil strategies without a crease on their foreheads. But, the Dark Lord did not understand that he had made the government brutally unjust towards the Indians, towards the Natives, all for his revenge. Of course, they were not going to sit back and watch with their lips sealed forever. There had to be a war. There had to be rebellion. There had to be a rise of power against discrimination.

"You… Bloody traitors! You turned your backs on my father, Magua. You gave Cayuga the power he has! You made that insignificant ant think of himself as someone big enough to fight the Dark Lord?! *You*!" Blaine Keir was clearly expressing his anger that had built up over his years of imprisonment in the frontier under the ground, and now that Jeromy had taken away the black birthstone, he was even more helpless as he could not open the third portal to fulfill his evil desires.

"Well, we don't have the black birthstone anymore, and we definitely don't want any bloodshed. We're here to take back what is rightfully ours. Our place in this country with dignity and respect. This is our home, and you or your government cannot just push us around like we are nothing!" Jeromy announced.

"That black birthstone is what is rightfully mine! And so is the government and the next government to come! If you don't return it to me, you will see her dead face!" The Dark Lord was fierce, and he held up a sword in front of Anna's neck.

Jeromy's heart skipped a beat inside his chest. He could not just stand and watch this anymore. He lashed out at the Dark Lord, "If… you… make even ONE move to hurt her; I swear that I will rip your heart out and feed it to your own damn demons!"

The words coming out of his mouth surprised him. He did not even know who he had become because the previous Doctor Whitefeather would never raise a voice, let alone threaten a lord of dark forces! He had grown so much on this journey, and the events that had led him here had only sparked his motive for justice for his people, even more like the other medallion recruits.

In response to Jeromy, the Dark Lord intentionally slid the sharp edge of his sword along Anna's neck at an angle and drew a drop of blood. She flinched in pain as the little cut started to swell and as a few more drops of blood emerged from it.

Jeromy had had enough, and so had the other recruits.

"Jeromy, wait no longer! We can't let him get away with all of what he has done and what he intends to do!" Erik said out loud to him, and before he could await a response, Jeromy had already started acting on his advice.

Erik saw Jeromy kick Red Thunder, who exploded forward at lightning speed - powered by spirit magic. It was then that Jeromy pulled BattleBlade from his back and began swinging it fiercely.

The Dark Lord saw the weapon and instantly let out a howl.

"Whaaat?! You dare to come at me with the weapon that killed my father!?"

Jeromy didn't break a stride and kept charging towards the Dark Lord, yelling. His army and the others charged forward, too, following his move and leadership. In the meantime, the two French soldiers who were holding Anna quickly moved to a side, dragging her with them and shut her in a large wooden box. The Dark Lord moved back onto his gigantic black horse and said a spell that made a cloud of black speckled dust emerge around him. When the dust settled, he could not be seen anymore, and neither was his horse there.

Yet, Jeromy did not stop moving towards the opponent's army for an attack, and his army followed him. The Dark Lord's army was larger in number than Chief Cayuga's recruits and their troops. Now, as soon as the Dark Lord cast a spell to hide himself on the battleground, his army of French mercenaries and hellish demons also moved towards the recruits with full power and speed.

Chapter # 20:
The Battle of Stanwix

Erik, Dakota, and Akwiraron ordered their armies to charge after Jeromy's, and a full-fledged war began. The human warriors under the medallion recruits' command fought the French human soldiers. In contrast, the magical creatures in their armies fought the demons. Of course, that was the only fair way to fight this battle.

Swords were clinking, blood spilling, people yelling in pain and anger. Spells flew back and forth, causing the air to fill with ozone from all the shocks and electricity. Weapons clashed and sparked everywhere. Sons cried for their mothers and wives, and curses filled the air. The battlefield became covered with blood, ooze, and gore. Fires ignited, and the confrontation quickly became conflagration across the smoke-filled field of death.

At one end, the medallion recruits were fighting for their people's right to live without the fear of injustice and to avenge the suffering that they had seen their loved ones endure. While on the other hand, the Dark Lord's army was fighting to retrieve the black birthstone to open the third portal that would release all the evil forces from the nine circles of hell and to rule the world with the evil powers that the third portal can gift them. Of course, behind all of this was the Dark Lord's intention to avenge his father's death by Chingachgook and his own imprisonment that Chief Cayuga had caused while trying to save people from his wrath.

While Jeromy was ferociously fighting off the French with his BattleBlade from horseback, he was looking for a chance to get to the wooden box in which Anna was locked up. He knew she was in no state to be out in the open battleground right now, and it had been days since she had eaten anything, so she could not fight anyway. So, he decided to get over with the war first and then release her from the imprisonment.

It was a large wooden crate, and from what the recruits could tell, the other captives taken by the Dark Lord were also in it. As Jeromy made his way fighting through the tenacious and vicious enemies, slicing, piercing, cutting off the arm of one and penetrating his blade through another's chest, he saw the Dark Lord standing beside the wooden container. Everyone around him was fighting, but he stood there, glaring and drooling, watching Jeromy, as if waiting for his attention.

Then, he pulled out Anna from the box and threw her on the ground. She fell at his feet, and Jeromy pulled at Red Thunder's lead rope and made a sharp turn to gallop in Anna's direction. She was trying to sit back up and even tried to say a spell. A small ball of fire began forming in midair, but the Dark Lord delivered a fierce kick to her side, and it vanished as she gasped and tried to cry out.

Extremely weak, she tried to crawl on her elbows to get away from the Dark Lord, and he let her go a few feet away before pulling out his sword and placing it vertically above her upper back, all while maintaining sinister eye contact with Jeromy as he made his way through the thick crowd of men fighting each other.

While Jeromy was still pushing people out of his way and riding towards Anna, the Dark Lord lowered the tip of his sword until it was touching Anna's back.

"Ceraha Pelik!" Anna slurred the spell to teleport to a nearby site away from the battleground, but it did not work. The

Dark Lord laughed out loud with a menacing comfort apparent on his face, as he could see his revenge plan in action.

Using the last of her strength, Anna turned around and tried to grab Blaine Keir's hand in which he was holding the sword to snatch it away from him. Still, her sudden movement took him by surprise, and he slashed his sword right across her abdomen. Anna struggled to her knees.

Jeromy's eyes flung open in horror, and he cried, "NO! Anna!"

Erik, Dakota, and Akwiraron suddenly turned their attention towards this scene. In utter shock, they began running towards the Dark Lord while fighting away anyone who got in their way. They could not believe that one of them was gone, and they could see Jeromy's heart being shattered into a million pieces as Anna clutched her bloody abdomen and fell flat on the ground with a thump, motionless. She laid there with her blood pooling around her, and the Dark Lord said his spell and disappeared in black speckles of dust again.

When Jeromy reached Anna, her voice was a diminished sound that he could not comprehend, and her eyes were half-closed. A painful knot formed in Jeromy's stomach as he realized he might lose her. He jumped off from the horse and kneeled down beside her, temporarily unaware and broken away from the war that was going on around them. He held her hand in his. And, with tears falling from both their eyes, he gently leaned in and kissed her. It was her last breath, and she then fell silent with a lost gaze and an open mouth.

While Jeromy closed her eyes with his fingers, Akwiraron said a spell to form a protective dome around him so that he does not get attacked while he is mourning. But, while he was focusing

entirely on Jeromy and Anna, he was still out in the open on the battlefield and felt someone standing close behind him. Akwiraron paused the spell and quickly ducked and rolled to a side. But before he could get back up, Blaine Keir, the Dark Lord, was standing there looking down at him and had kicked him down.

The Dark Lord placed his booted foot on Akwiraron's chest and formed a magical black ball levitating above his palm. It was called the black ball of hell: a brutal magical weapon that tortured the victim psychologically before poisoning their blood and giving them a slow death. As the ball grew in his hand, within a matter of seconds, Dakota saw an advantage and swung his sword across the Dark Lord's back, opening a bloody gash.

The attack also hid the blistering sprint by Jeromy, who screamed a war cry, leaped into the air in a spinning motion and delivered one of BattleBlade's deadly razor-sharp ends into the evil flesh. The attack cut through armor, bone, and sinew in a wound a foot wide across the Dark Lord's own abdomen.

They had taken him by surprise and pushed him down to the ground.

He fought back futilely with his swords and his forearm, thus receiving more injuries from the spinning, kicking, and lightning-fast Jeromy who blocked every single attack, and in the meantime, Akwiraron had also gotten up, and he had cast the spell to send the Dark Lord back into the imprisonment in Hell as Chief Cayuga had taught them.

"Awirya hetop nuisica!" He proclaimed and then chanted several more parts of the spell to complete the procedure. At the same time, Dakota and Jeromy kept striking him to keep him on the ground. Shockingly, the weakened Dark Lord, who was now spitting, cursing, and sputtering all manner of evil, kept fighting

back and shouting spells, one of which started to call a storm of black, red-eyed bats in the battle zone.

Dakota quickly formed a protective dome around themselves with a spell to avoid any disruption in the process. Within a few more seconds, the ground beneath the Dark Lord opened up and crept onto him with dark, earthy hands, pulling his rapidly withering body into the ground and sewing back up on the surface. His screams could still be heard as he was taken into the Earth's core for the imprisonment that he deserved.

The three men fell on their backs on the ground in relief and exhaustion.

"We did it!" Akwiraron said, rejoiced, looking around him to see the demons fading away in the form of black smoke and the few remaining French mercenaries falling to the ground. The armies of the medallion recruits were not completely wiped out, but many had lost their lives or returned to the spirit world in poofs of blue smoke. Yet, more than half of their entire army remained, which was much needed for the next stage of the war.

"Not yet done... We still have to fight the US government...." Jeromy said sadly.

He knew that this mission would change his life forever, but he did not think that it would leave him so empty inside. Anna's loss hit him profoundly. His pain and grief were excruciating – but he needed to be the leader – he needed to hold it in for the benefit of all.

"We're sorry...." Dakota put his hand on Jeromy's shoulder to comfort him. "She deserved to live. But she made a sacrifice. For us. For you. For her people...."

Jeromy wiped away his tears with his sleeve and looked around.

"Where's Erik?" Jeromy realized that another one of them was missing.

Dakota and Akwiraron looked at each other for an answer, but neither knew.

"The last I saw him was when he was fighting a tall black figure, when Blaine Keir had cast the bats' spell," Dakota remembered.

The three men got up to find their fellow recruit, especially as this battle of Stanwix was over for now, but did not see him around. They started to walk a little farther and saw Erik lying semi-conscious on the ground.

A group of his armed men was gathered around him, and a magical creature that looked somewhat like a human giant with wings was also kneeling at his side. When Erik's army and the creature saw Jeromy, Dakota, and Akwiraron walking towards them, they all stood back in a line in respect. Erik was struggling. He had become pale and was coughing blood. He turned his head towards his fellow recruits in a painful movement, and they saw the mark on his face that had knocked him down. There was a deeply scarring, three-lined wound on Erik's face that had partially damaged one of his eyes. Fresh blood glistened across his face in the sunlight.

The medallion recruits could not keep facing death one after another. They were heroes, and while it was their mission to serve justice and eliminate the evils that were making their people suffer, each sacrifice of their lives was a heavy burden on the others to walk with. Each departed soul left the recruits and their armies with all the more reason to rip the enemies' hearts out, and there was no way that the sacrifices of two of the medallion recruits could be forgotten.

Dakota sat down beside Erik and looked into his eyes. He looked like he had died a long while ago, yet there was still some slight movement in his body.

Jeromy screamed at the sky and fell to his knees in agony. He had watched the love of his life die in thirst, hunger, and pain, and now, when he had not even finished mourning Anna's death, one of his closest companions of this long, long journey was dying, too. He closed his fists and punched into the sandy ground until his knuckles turned red, and tiny speckles of blood appeared on them.

Erik's body was now completely drained of life. The slight movements he was making earlier were no more there. When Akwiraron tried to examine his wounds, finding it strange for him to die of a deep scratch on the face, he realized that the scratch was not from a human nor a human weapon.

"He was attacked by a demon...." The bald-headed giant explained, reading the look on Akwiraron's face.

Jeromy looked up with fierce, reddened eyes. It was a shock to everyone that a demon had attacked a human warrior, which was not allowed. It was a breach of the rules of the battle zone, and despite the Dark Lord's mischievous tactics, they all believed him to be a warrior who fought fairly.

"It's not right... We kept following the rules, and we lost two of our most precious leaders!" A middle-aged man from Erik's army said, infuriated at his leader's unjust death.

"What could we expect? Those who don't live fairly… I don't know how we expected them to fight fairly." Dakota shook his head from side to side in disappointment.

"Where are the rest of our armies?" Jeromy asked the few people of Erik's army that were standing there.

"They were ordered by Chief Cayuga to return to the camp nearby. We are supposed to join them there and then, as Chief Cayuga said, one of you, the chosen recruits, will lead us towards our final destination: The White House," a woman from the army members responded. She was a human warrior, but had magical commands like the other recruits.

Jeromy nodded. All the emotions visible on his face during the last phase of the battle of Stanwix were comparatively gone. He looked numb, as if someone had emptied him out, and now, he had nothing to lose and nothing to fear. He took in a deep breath.

"We need to get going."

Dakota and Akwiraron looked at Jeromy. They had just lost two fellow recruits – their friends.

"First, we will honor our fallen friends and comrades."

Jeromy walked across the field, lovingly picked up Anna's lifeless body, and gently laid her down next to Erik. Taking a few steps back, he extended his arms, held his palms upward, and looked toward the heavens.

"Great Spirit - these children of men have lived and fought bravely. They came into life just as your sun rises. Now they leave this life just as your sun sets. No more will they know pain, loss, or sadness. We ask that you bring new life to their brave warrior spirits and guide them into the light of the eternities. Please carry them home."

There wasn't a sound. Nothing stirred. As they looked on, a figure materialized before them. It was Jeromy's grandmother, who was glowing brilliantly white. She smiled and briefly exchanged loving looks with her grandson, and then, in the blink of an eye, she and the two bodies were gone.

Jeromy wiped a tear, took a deep breath, and simply said, "Let's go."

"Follow me. We have no time to waste," Jeromy ordered, and kept walking towards the camp that the armies had rested in before setting out for the battle with the Dark Lord's army.

The other two medallion recruits, and the armed soldiers followed them.

"We have won the battle but lost our dearest people in this war...." Akwiraron sighed. "God knows how many sacrifices it will take for the US government to leave their unjust rule in the future battle."

Dakota sighed, too, as he walked with his hands in his pockets and looked at the ground beneath his feet. Somewhere far below it was Hell, he thought. Far below their sad yet determined footsteps was the Dark Lord imprisoned, but it was not over yet. Of course, it was a more extended battle than just that, and the bloodstains on the sand underneath their feet were proof of that.

When they reached the camp, it was full of their remaining army men and women, and, of course, creatures. Jeromy walked into the base and announced for attention.

"People!" He said as everyone turned their faces to face him. "We are the representatives, the warriors for justice for our people! We have loved, we have lost, and we have won! But now, even tougher times lay ahead. The final battle will take place in the year 1830 but it isn't happening years from now for us. We will be traveling to 1830 to begin the battle – a battle against injustice. A battle for our liberty! A battle for humanity! And it may take everything that we have. We have to be ready to sacrifice our lives! Are you ready for that sacrifice?"

Akwiraron and Dakota came forward to stand beside him, and the air in the camp became dense. *Were they ready for a bigger sacrifice?*

"We know we're ready!" Dakota announced, hoping to create a response from the army.

"The war is not over! It is yet to come, and we need you, each one of you, to build back the nation that we deserve!" Akwiraron added as everyone listened intently.

Many people in the army were injured. Some were dying, some had died, and some were watching their friends whimper in pain as the after-effects of the Battle of Stanwix.

Jeromy could tell that these people were determined, patriotic, and strong enough to fight the second war against the US government. Still, he also understood the trauma of watching people die left and right around you. The magical creatures were already on board and ready for the second war, but the human warriors were struggling for now. Of course, they had just come back from a fight and faced a near-death experience.

"Chief Cayuga brought you all together as an army for us, and he trained us through tough experiences and tests to make us eligible leaders for you. We just lost two of our most precious warriors and leaders back on the battlefield of Stanwix, and trust me, I know the fear and pain in your hearts. I am just like you, and one of you." Jeromy's speech was now attracting the attention of all the army men and women that remained in the camp, alive.

"We did not come this far and make this many sacrifices to give up! You all did marvelously and fought fiercely in the battle against the Dark Lord and his army, and you all have the potential and the motive to make a bigger change!" Jeromy looked at Dakota and Akwiraron at his sides and felt stronger standing there.

"I lost Anna to this mission...." His speech was loud enough for everyone to hear, but his tone was now lighter. "But my pain made me strong enough to fight off the Dark Lord, and with the help of my fellow leaders, we successfully sent him into the imprisonment of Hellfire again, just as he deserved...."

When Jeromy announced this, a wave of murmur and surprised gasps took across the armies. They were not aware of this until now, and it considerably lightened their hearts.

"But, even though the Dark Lord himself is gone, for now, his work as the Whisperer has left his evil plans still in action through his agents in the coming US government and even among the nation. If we don't step up against those who are working for the Whisperer, then what is the use of putting him away into imprisonment?" Jeromy could feel that the many hundreds of living people in front of him were becoming more convinced and motivated.

"In the near future, in the White House, there are agents of the Dark Lord that must be ridden of their power," Dakota added into the speech.

"So, the Cherokee, the Apache, the Mohawk, the Arapaho, the Sioux, the Pawnee, the Blackfeet… all Indians know their value and the power they are entitled to…."

Jeromy added, "We also know of the millions who have perished, and millions more who will suffer and perish. Are you ready to serve the purpose of your existence and wage the war that will make the most difference for our people and us?"

Several groups of voices emerged from the crowd of people that said "Yes" and "We are!".

Jeromy inhaled deeply and ordered, "Then let's begin preparations for the march to the future White House."

Chapter # 21:
The Fall of the White House

The three remaining recruits assembled their coteries and then met to devise a new strategy because their numbers had decreased, and Jeromy was anxious to move on to the White House while they still had their remaining forces.

Dakota was concerned about him.

"Buddy… take some time off. This can wait for a week or two. Relax, mourn, and then when you're ready, we can begin planning our next move," Dakota advised him, but Jeromy shook his head.

"I will not rest… and I will ensure that the enemies don't get the time to rest either. Guys, we don't have time. We have lost too many precious people over hundreds of years, and it is up to us to save millions more in the coming centuries. We have made big sacrifices. More are to follow." He insisted.

"You know what? Our wounds are fresh from our loved ones dying in front of us. That pain is a motivator at this point. Avenging their unfair deaths is all the more reason to wage war and overturn the unjust throne," Akwiraron sided with what Jeromy proposed.

"All right, then. If you're ready, I am ready," Dakota patted Jeromy's back. "Uh… There was something I wanted to tell you. A few of my coterie's men informed me that some of the other men in the coteries were seen with the enemy troops recently…."

"That is a challenge to overcome, so we will need to strategize accordingly," Jeromy replied. Then he looked up from the ground and stared at Dakota. "Spiritual beings or humans"

"Humans…"

"So… are you saying they are betraying us and our mission?" He asked, surprised.

"Well, I don't know who to trust, but I have indeed found some men in our armies trying to disrupt the coteries' peace and discipline," Dakota explained.

"Just before she died, a mortally wounded woman in the camp claimed that she was killed by her own people," Akwiraron added. "I was not sure what she meant back then when her dying words were something along the lines of 'beware of the traitors,' but I think it makes sense now."

This was new information. They could not wage war if the enemies were among their own. The three recruits began to think long and hard, trying to figure out a way to find the traitors and eliminate them. They hoped that Chief Cayuga would come to their help, too, but for a long time, there was no sign of him.

The three men brainstormed together and tried coming up with an intelligent strategy to knock the enemies out, but one thing was for sure, before the battle of Stanwix, the enemy troops did outnumber them. Did they know what was coming at them at Stanwix?

"What about Anna and Erik's coteries now? Do we divide them among our armies or what?" Akwiraron asked.

"No. I have a better idea." Jeromy stated. "How about we unite all the armies? Instead of leading three separate coteries, we can build one enormous army and then go on a hunt for more warriors who could join our cause and train them?"

His idea appealed to the other two recruits, and they silently thought about it for a moment before going on to nod and agree with it.

"I think that would really help us. If we all follow one strategy, one plan in the battle zone, we will be more coordinated than before." Dakota agreed.

"I remember that we were somewhat uncoordinated in the Battle of Stanwix, so centralization of the command chain should help...." Akwiraron added to their discussion, "But do we have enough time to go on a hunt for more warriors and train them?"

"We are short on time... but we will make the best use of it and do what we can. Even if we train about two hundred more warriors, I think we would have enough armed soldiers to take down the White House in the year 1830. Besides, if things start to go badly. I do have a backup plan," Jeromy responded hopefully.

Dakota and Akwiraron stared at each other but did not question.

They completely trusted Jeromy and were 100% on board with him leading the army as the leading commander. Dakota would oversee training and recruiting more members. Akwiraron was in charge of finding and eliminating the traitors in the group. Their roles were set, and their work had begun at full capacity.

Chief Cayuga would manage the time jump to 1830. Everything else was up to them.

Within a few hours and drawing from his knowledge of history, Jeromy had brainstormed several aspects of the war, including where enemy troops are most likely to be in 1830 around the White House, where the attack can be most impactful, and how the armies are going to be positioned. He was forming strategies to begin training the army accordingly with Dakota.

Meanwhile, Dakota had left the camp in the search of more people to join the army. The other two recruits advised him to stay nearby to avoid any mishaps, so his primary focus was the surrounding villages, and his main target was the young blood in these areas. He wanted youth - young men and women who knew what loss was and who had the strength to make a difference for their people.

On the other hand, Akwiraron had very smartly blended in among the army's men and women. He talked with them, sympathized with their experiences, and learned about their fears. He had the spell activated to read minds so each person he would meet in the camp would read their primary motives for being there. Some soldiers were fearless and entirely devoted to their purpose in this mission, and there were some who were fearful but strong despite their doubts. But then Akwiraron was able to detect some men and women who were just there because they were Natives and had no motive of fighting for the more significant cause.

Those – the latter – were the people that were most likely to be the traitors because they were not motivated to risk their lives and were playing only *smartly* to stay on the winning side.

It had been three days since Dakota had left the camp, and despite the trust in his capabilities, Jeromy and Akwiraron were worried for him. They had already lost two strongest companions and did not want to risk losing another one. But, on the third day, Dakota arrived after twilight with a group of 92 young men and women following him into the camp.

"Welcome on board, my warriors!" He introduced them to the army and showed them around the camp.

"They are all mostly Natives, but twelve of them are not. Some are black slaves who also want freedom for their own people. They want to fight for liberty and justice," Dakota informed Jeromy in privacy.

"Yes... liberty and justice for all. Has their training begun?" He asked.

"We trained along the way. They will be ready in two or three days." Dakota responded, and Jeromy smiled.

"Good work." Jeromy appreciated how quickly he had arranged and begun working with the new recruits.

Meanwhile, Akwiraron had eliminated 10 people who could be traitors. It was impossible to make them confess or study their cases in depth in such a short time, so whoever appeared to be an ethically or morally weak person, Akwiraron cast him out of the camp and ensured that no one left the camp other than those that were eliminated. This step was taken to avoid the exchange of information unnecessarily about their war strategies and other plans that could help the enemies predict and prepare against them.

"We have been doing very well," Akwiraron appreciated their work as a team. "What's the next step?"

"Now... we take them down," Jeromy smiled, but behind his smile was sorrow. He wished Anna could be there to witness this – the execution of their mission, but she had gone too soon. During their most struggling phase, she had gone, and he wished she could have seen their victorious accomplishments.

After a few more days of full-fledge training of the army, the recruits tested their soldiers for strength, spiritual alignment, and knowledge of essential spirit magic as a weapon. According to Jeromy's strategy for the war, they had taught some of the more spiritually capable and taught them a few simple spirit magic skills that could help them in the battle zone.

"You!" He pointed at one soldier who he had trained himself. "Perform the multiply spell!" Jeromy ordered him. The other soldiers, all humans and spiritual beings, had gathered around in a circle to watch the testing phase of their fellow soldiers and learn what they could.

"Miktuha lituns!" The soldier yelled, and within a second, there were about ten more versions of that same soldier around him.

"Excellent!" Dakota clapped, impressed by his performance.

"If the spell is done right and is applied to the entire army, we would appear ten times bigger in number than we are," Jeromy explained.

"So that is a fear tactic? The enemy would perceive us to be greater in number and might avoid attacking us first, right?" Akwiraron confirmed and smiled at the strategy. This was good.

Then, Dakota and Akwiraron were put in charge of the spiritual beings. They had decided that half of all the spiritual creatures would march in the front line when they go into the battle zone, and half of them would march at the back of the human army. This way, most of the human soldiers would be protected. The spiritual characters naturally had more strength and capabilities, so they were not at immediate risk unless their plan had been discovered and they came under attack by the Dark Lord's demons.

"Are we all set?" Jeromy shouted to ask everyone.

"YES!" A loud, enthusiastic roar filled up the camp, and it was an incredible sight for the three medallion recruits to see the product of their long, exhaustive journey. It was time, and they were just waiting for Chief Cayuga's instruction and assistance now.

They were ready, and nothing could hold them back anymore. They were fiercer, stronger, and angrier than before. And although their total numbers were less than 600, including humans and legendary spirit beings, they believed a surprise attack should easily overwhelm the primitive defenses of the White House.

Not much time had passed when Akwiraron called out his fellow recruits towards a camp.

"Jeromy! Dakota! There is a golden scroll here!" He came running to them, and they all hurried in the scroll's direction.

It had been quite a while since they had seen one of these, so when Jeromy held the levitating golden scroll in his hand, he felt a wave of nostalgia overwhelm him. The last time he opened a scroll, Anna and Erik were right there with them. His heart filled up, but his mind was focused. They were on a mission, and their emotions for the departed souls were only fuel to the fire in them.

"You are ready. March back into the portal on the church grounds." The message on the scroll said before it disappeared, like always. The glow of the scroll died out eventually, and the three recruits looked at each other, wondering what might be coming their way now.

"The portal, eh?" Dakota said after a long thought.

"Yeah… so, where exactly are we going to? Downtown Washington DC?" Akwiraron asked.

Jeromy chuckled. "Well, downtown DC in 1830 had cows and pastures, along with wagons and scattered houses. It is mostly wide-open space. No… we will arrive a little distance away just to be safe. We will land in Arlington, Virginia."

"When exactly?" asked Dakota.

"Generals, no one else but Chief Cayuga himself knows the exact time and place. Keep this quiet. We are about to leave the 18th century, the abandoned villages, and the retreating French and move forward 70 years into the 19th century. The date will be May 29th of 1830, the day after the United States Congress passed the Indian Removal Act to become law. One of the evilest presidents will have recently taken office and cause the persecution, suffering, and death of countless native men, women, and children. He will literally culminate the American Holocaust."

Dakota and Akwiraron stared at Jeromy with great anticipation.

"Brothers… we are about to unseat President Andrew Jackson and take over the White House."

The proposition made total sense. Of course, they could not wage war against the White House unless they went a few decades ahead. All these army men, women, and spirit creatures would move to take their knowledge about the White House and the mission with them, further protecting the plan from discovery.

So many of them had lost their kids, partners, parents, and friends to the torturing schemes put forward by the Dark Lord's agents both before and after the Revolutionary War. When the American lawyer and soldier, Andrew Jackson, took the seat as the seventh President of the United States, he crossed all limits of discrimination. When he signed the Act to forcibly remove the Natives from their homes and push them out of their lands, he tore loose their roots and changed the entitlement of the First Peoples forever.

Jackson normalized harassment, persecution, attacks, and killing to bring fruition to his heinous grand plan. Countless indigent peoples from hundreds of tribes would be killed brutally under his rule and numerous decades after.

There had to be an end to the pain and the torment. There had to be a better and brighter future.

"Let's go, then," Jeromy nodded. They understood the plan and trusted Chief Cayuga's wise advice. They knew his scrolls had always shown them the right direction, and now, it was time for the show.

The army was assembled on the grounds, and the three recruits led them towards the abandoned village where they had come from. They passed through the most isolated path to avoid drawing any attention from nearby villagers and marched uphill to reach their destination directly.

Once again, they were in the abandoned village, and the three recruits could not help but miss their departed comrades. This was also the place where Anna was last seen happy and healthy.

When they reached the place where the giant portal had replaced the church, the church was there once again. Jeromy told his army and his fellow recruits to wait while he went into the church and assessed the situation to be clear of any enemies or dangers.

"Don't go alone. I'll come with you." Dakota said, as he stepped forward with him.

The large gate of the church was mostly closed. Dakota and Jeromy opened it with a loud screech and entered the church. It was almost twilight. The dimmest light was entering the church from the crack in the roof where the sycamore had grown. Below it, there was the dried fountain. Jeromy walked forward to see if the birthstones were still there, and fortunately, they were. They were locked into their embeddings, and no power except Chief Cayuga could pick them out now. But the large blue portal that they had last seen here was not there anymore.

"Where's the portal?" Dakota looked around for any signs or switches to bring back the portal.

"I believe we have to wait for the moonlight to hit the birthstones. That is what happened the last time, right?" Jeromy explained, and Dakota nodded, remembering the past events.

Akwiraron peeked into the church and asked what was going on. Jeromy told him to keep the armies assembled outside the church's gate.

"When the moonlight hits the birthstones, I expect the portal will open. Then, we can all move forward as instructed by Chief Cayuga. Okay?" He replied.

"Got it!" Akwiraron nodded and went back out.

As an hour passed and the moon rose in the sky, the dimly lit church hall began to light up a little brighter with the lunar light. Eventually, the five birthstones on the fountain's boundary wall started to glow like they had previously. The recruits were expecting the portal to open up then, but there was no sign of a portal so far.

But then, the other gate of the church opened, and Chief Cayuga emerged from it.

"My medallion recruits!" He said, smiling. "Let's step outside."

Dakota and Jeromy followed through the doors into the church's courtyard, joined Akwiraron, and then the three stood attentively in front of him.

"You have made me proud. All have sacrificed enough to be called heroes in this journey, but you have more to fight for now. You have even more reason to initiate the war that achieves the goal of this mission. Your journey will then be complete." He announced.

"White Feather, please come forward." He ordered.

Jeromy stepped forward and stood within feet of Chief Cayuga.

"White Feather, the spirits and heaven are watching. You have been proclaimed Chief of this magnificent army of rebellion and restoration."

Both Dakota and Akwiraron stood nearby and nodded their agreement.

Chief Cayuga then produced a long, glowing White Feather with a leather band, and motioning Jeromy to turn around, he tied it to his head. And then, announcing loudly so that the assembled army could hear, he proclaimed, "I present you – Chief White Feather."

Roars of applause and huzzahs went up through the ranks of both humans and spirit beings alike.

Then Cayuga produced three beautiful beige cotton shirts that had raven, owl, and eagle feathers sewn around the necks. They looked as old as time itself… and they were shimmering light.

"Generals, these are your ghost shirts. They will protect you from most small weapons, but don't let a big one in, or you will join your ancestors."

Although it sounded funny, Cayuga said the words with great caution. The three leaders dressed themselves and announced that they were ready.

"Now, I will open the portal up for you. Follow your heart, strengthen your mind, and travel to your destination." Chief Cayuga said before saying the spell that could open the portal for them.

"Li Kunsu Hinwali!"

A thin luminous blue line formed in mid-air just above the courtyard's center, and then it expanded into a large circular portal that glowed at the edges and was pitch black in the center. Strong winds were blowing from it, and even though the recruits had seen it's like before, it was vastly larger this time, and they looked at it in amazement.

In the next few seconds, they realized that Chief Cayuga was no more there, and that was their cue to take the course of action as planned.

"Akwiraron!" Jeromy shouted, and Akwiraron stepped forward. "Are we ready?" He asked, looking at the portal in awe.

"Yes, Chief White Feather!"

"Dakota, are we ready?"

"Yes, Chief White Feather, we are ready."

The portal was quite large now.

Let's move the army forward." Jeromy commanded.

Akwiraron shouted, "People! Gather as you were taught! Wendigos to form the front line! Thunderbirds gather behind them, followed by humans! Rest of the creatures, hold your positions at the rear!"

With a low murmur of all sorts of languages and rustling sounds, the army took its position as it was told. Jeromy stood up on a nearby stool.

"You have prepared for this moment! When we go through this portal, we will land within direct sight of the battlefield and the enemy! Keep your weapons ready, and your minds focused! We must not fall back! We must regain our kingdom, our lands, our lives!" Jeromy announced enthusiastically to motivate the army before they proceeded.

Then, the three recruits lined up at the front of the army on their steeds, and the march began. They moved forward into the large blue portal first, followed by the wendigos, followed by the thunderbirds and the rest of the army, including humans and other spiritual beings.

It felt like they had stepped through a door. The world around them had changed drastically within seconds, and they were marching in daylight - moving steadily on the smooth road beneath their feet. The blue portal zapped into a strip and then disappeared behind them as the army stepped out.

Explosions!

They had poured out of the portal precisely as planned. They were in Arlington, Virginia, within 500 feet of the Chain Bridge, which would take them across the Potomac River and into Washington, DC. However, the United States army was ready for them.

Dozens of canons with a range of up to a mile fired in unison as soon as they saw the Army of the Rebellion come into sight. There were also mortars and howitzers as well, and foot-soldiers with muskets were firing in volleys.

There would be no surprise attack. Somehow, the agents of the Dark Lord had passed along the word of the coming battle forward into the future and done so long enough ahead of time to plan the defense of the White House.

As their army continued to move forward on Virginia soil, Jeromy, Dakota, and Akwiraron began shouting orders for everyone to take cover.

Explosions continued. Trees cracked and flew into pieces. Smoke and dust rolled across the ground. Wounded humans cried out. Legendaries shrieked in anger.

"We have to move back at least 1000 yards!" shouted Jeromy.

Staring angrily at the river before him, he crouched slightly and lowered his hands down almost to the ground. Then, springing upward, he brought both hands overhead and shouted, *"tembok banyu!"*

A wall of water rose up from the river to a height of nearly 50 feet. It obscured them from the enemy, and then the first movement of their arriving army was one of retreat.

Within 5 minutes, Jeromy and their forces were out of range; however, it was apparent that they had already taken losses. At least a quarter of their numbers had either fallen dead or poofed into blue smoke. Many dozens of others were wounded.

"What the hell happened?!" shouted Dakota.

"Betrayal," replied Akwiraron.

"Jeromy, what are we going to do? Do we have the numbers? Looking across that river, it looked like the US Army had thousands of troops – all with muskets firing away at us. And… those damn canons!"

Fortunately, Jeromy, Akwiraron, and Dakota had removed themselves with their troops intact. Miraculously, none of them were wounded. Jeromy pulled his two other recruits into a tight huddle. They were gasping for breath after their rapid backward dash.

"Guys, I will need to leave for about 10 minutes or so."

"What!?" Dakota and Akwiraron jinxed in shock.

"You need to trust me. Remember, I said I had a backup plan? Well, I think we are going to need Plan B right away."

"Hold everyone here just out of range. The US Army, on the other side of the river, is having a party over there whooping and hollering at what they perceive as our destruction and defeat.

"Do *not* advance until the time is right."

"Ah… How will we know that time is right, Jeromy?" asked Dakota.

"Believe me, you will know… And when it all starts happening, advance full force right across that damn bridge. Got it?"

"Yes, sir!" Dakota replied.

"You got it, Jer," answered Akwiraron.

"Trust me, guys. It will be okay. Just keep everyone together and hold their spirits up!"

Then Jeromy extended his left arm in front of him and held the palm of his hand facing upward. He placed his right hand over the White Feather dangling from the leather band on his head, closed his eyes, took a deep breath, and shouted, "*Jagad Roh!*"

In a poof of flames and blue smoke, he was gone.

"Holy spirits!" shouted Akwiraron.

As soon as he left, clouds began to gather overhead. With Jeromy gone, many of the humans started murmuring in the ranks. Still, Dakota and Akwiraron moved quickly to scuttle any thought that their leader had abandoned them. And it worked partly due to the fact that the sky and weather were changing in relation to Jeromy's sudden unworldly departure.

For ten precious minutes, they cared for the wounded and then reformed their ranks as the clouds darkened and gathered. Although no one knew how on earth they were going to attack, they prepared themselves to charge into the lethal weapons trained on their side of the river. They lifted each other up, preparing to mount their assault.

A chilly breeze swept across them, and a light, misty rain began falling. Rolling clouds obscured the sky, and everything became darker.

Akwiraron turned to Dakota. "Is Jeromy doing this?"

"I think so, brother. But I also think there is more to come. I don't think he left us just to water the grass."

Boom! *Flash*! Everyone grabbed their ears to protect them from the deafening explosions.

Thunderous lightning began striking everywhere on the Washington side of the river. Electric fingers danced, striking and zapping wildly. The air filled with the smell of ozone, and every single creature, human and otherwise, felt and saw the hair stand up on their bodies. The cacophony of explosive strikes was deafening, and just as noticeable, the huzzahs and rejoicing on the DC side of the river had come to a complete stop. Thousands of US Army troops suddenly found themselves without cover – out in the open, with all hell falling down upon them.

Soldiers shrieked and yelled. Many started falling to the ground as the blinding bolts burst upon their targets. Officers yelled at their troops to hold the line. Still, some began fleeing for any available tree, wagon, or other shelters.

More fell. Many were burnt black, and their bodies lay on the ground in the smoking stench, but some also held their lines.

After nearly several minutes of the supernatural assault, the order was given, and US troops began falling back to join demons and others behind anything defensible, including barns, wagons, and water troughs. Many simply dashed to join the other defenses around the White House.

"Is it time?" Akwiraron shouted.

"I don't know!" Dakota replied. "Jeromy said we would know, but I'm not sure yet!"

From their position in Arlington on the southwest of Washington, DC, they could see that the storm's fury held to the other side of the river. No lightning or heavy rain fell on them — only the same light droplets lightly pelting them by icy gusts of wind. All the human and legendary warriors exclaimed it to be a miracle.

An earthquake began rumbling throughout the Washington, DC area. Dakota and Akwiraron stared at each other with a combination of awe, wonder, and fear.

With the ground shaking, they noticed that the wall of water running along the Potomac had slowly collapsed. So, once again, they focused their gaze across the river at the retreating enemy, but they also began hearing shouting within their own ranks.

"White Feather is coming! White Feather is coming!"

A massive swirling cloud of dust had formed at their rear, but they could clearly see Jeromy riding in front of an enormous cavalry. Adorned in full red and black war paint and now wearing a full war bonnet upon his head, Chief White Feather was equipped with his BattleBlade and was flanked on each side by two of history's famous war chiefs – Red Cloud and Crazy Horse.

Behind them came a fully painted 50,000 strong Sioux Warrior cavalry with weapons and a war cry never heard before among the living.

"Form ranks!" shouted Dakota.

"Prepare to move out!" called Akwiraron.

The Spirit World had arrived, and they prepared to join them.

The waters of the Potomac began roiling and splashing onto the banks. The river looked turbid and angry as far as the eye could see.

As Jeromy and the chiefs approached Chain Bridge, a watery explosion occurred on the left side of the bridge.

Launched with a massive water column, famous warriors Geronimo, Cochise, and Victorio rose up, leading their legion of 10,000 Apache warriors right behind them. Their war cries pierced the air, blossoms flew off trees, and their shouts could be heard for a mile. They were dry as a bone when the horses' hooves made it to the slick, emerald DC grass, and they were off in a flash - racing with the Sioux to the White House. Cheers went up from Dakota, Akwiraron, and many others.

On the right side of the bridge, Sitting Bull and Rain-In-The-Face erupted with 10,000 Hunkpapa Lakota, with many more shouts and cheers.

Hundreds of yards up the left side, Cornstalk and Tecumseh blew out of the wild river with 10,000 Shawnee. The few remaining US Army troops trying to retreat from the river screamed.

Further downriver on the right, Black Hawk and his legion of 10,000 Sauk warriors slowly rose up out of the bubbling cauldron. Once on the surface, they started running on top of the water across the embankment. The few wounded that remained on the side of the capital simply sat or stood watching to their horror, with their mouths dropped open. Many were babbling and ranting frantically, *"Indians! Indians in the river!"*

The thunder kept cracking everywhere, and just before Standing Turkey, Two Moons and Dragging Canoe emerged with their 10,000 Cherokee, a giant bolt of lightning struck the White House.

The legion of Navajo led by Manuelito was vomited out of the Potomac. When they made it to the streets, panicked onlookers were already running crazily to get out of the way.

The Nez Perce Riders, led by Joseph, flew out of the water, followed by the Comanche cavalry led by Quanah Parker. They were followed by the Kiowa warriors, led by Sitting Bear and White Bear.

"Aye, Aye, Aye, Aye!" was their resounding war cry.

Hiawatha and Joseph Brant led the Mohawks. Red Jacket led the Seneca legion, and the Shoshone riders were led by Washakie and Pocatello. They joined the native stampede of fury behind Jeromy and the others.

The Choctaw, led by Tuskaloosa and Pushmataha, rode with fury. Hole-In-The-Day and Curly Head arrived adorned in full war paint on themselves and their horses and rode out in front of all the Chippewa Warriors. Jiconella Elk Mountain and Pope rode fast in front of the Pueblo riders. The Creek warriors led by Menawa rode next to the Seminole Warriors led by Micanopy.

Not far away, Ooray led the legion of Utes out of the adjoining Anacostia River, and Wahunsunacawh led the Powhatan riders out of the river as well. All began their massive dash to the White House as well.

By the time the Spirit World Warriors were all on the field, nearly a quarter-million glowing, armed and screaming Native American Spirit Warriors on horseback were riding with passion and fury to the White House.

The enemy had been confident of their plan and victory, so only a few cannons had been placed around the White House. Soldiers scrambled to load and begin firing them; however, there was little time for the accuracy or to form precise firing lines to handle the wave of Indian fury that was about to crash upon them. So, they simply loaded their muskets as rapidly as they could and began firing randomly… but the effect was too little, too late.

The doors of an old barn burst open, and dozens of demons rushed out to counterattack.

"Remember Erik!" Jeromy called out, knowing that the demons would not limit their attacks to their legendaries and would be content to kill humans.

The ferocity of the demon's vicious attack was surprising in the face of the numbers being so much against them. Nevertheless, they began shredding through anyone and anything they could get to.

Jeromy was still in the lead, and seeing the audacity of the fanatical demons, he first began throwing fireballs at them and then took the next step.

"*Malih dadi asu ajag!*" he shouted.

First, there was a flash. Then there was an enormous white wolf with fire red eyes the size of their most enormous horses leaping skyward to arc, landing him on top of the enemy. It took the demons by such surprise that he was able to shred the last of them before they could figure out what to do.

As soon as they were dispatched, he flashed back to human, jumped back onto Red Thunder and rode on toward the White House.

During Andrew Jackson's rule, the good energies had left the leadership of the United States. Goodness is born out of goodness, and the chain reaction of its energy lasts. Similarly, dark energies can last for centuries too. Energies pass on from generation to generation, from person to person, and place to place.

The White House was one of those places where the dark energies had been brewing for decades. The Dark Lord's agents were appointed during his reign, and his whisperings from decades ago were passed on from those agents to newer ones… to current ones in the White House.

The exhausted US troops were quickly overcome, and a few spirit warriors vanquished in puffs of blue smoke. Those soldiers who were left standing threw down their arms and held their hands high. They were ordered to lie down prostrate on the ground, and they complied.

The quarter-million spirit warriors surrounded the White House.

Before they could begin their walk towards the White House, the doors opened and let out a new band of people and demons led by an old, familiar face - Asmodeus. It was the dark army remnant, and they had prepared their last, ignoble stand to the memory of their Dark Lord.

Jeromy stood in the front center position with Dakota and Akwiraron at his sides. Right behind them and surrounding the White House were all the chiefs and warriors.

The enemy rushed out and stopped just 50 feet away from the recruits, screaming, drooling, and ready for a final conflict. To intimidate them, Asmodeus morphed into a giant 20-foot serpent. He flicked his long red tongue toward Jeromy's direction – itching for battle.

Jeromy pulled his BattleBlade but whispered to Dakota and Akwiraron, who quickly dashed back into the ranks. A few moments later, he made a gesture of his hands that was perceived as the signal to prepare a new attack. However, as he had communicated to his fellow recruits, he and the Chiefs along with the Indian warriors stayed their ground and made no more advancement.

Instead, the fire-breathing thunderbirds took wing and moved forward from above and took a position over the army of people and demons, flapping their large flaming wings, just at enough height to attack as well as protect against any oncoming attackers. Belching flames and ball lightning, they methodically began turning the screaming enemy into smoke and ash. The air was filled with their putrid, evil stench. Asmodeus looked shocked, and to his surprise, never saw Jeromy coming. In a moment, it was over.

When the remaining evil ones saw what was happening, dozens of them began advancing toward Jeromy and the Indian army. But then a new threat emerged – the wendigos. Jeromy and the living had taken a deep breath, and they held hands over their

mouths and faces as the ravenous, carnivorous creatures rushed forward and began shredding and devouring the remaining enemies. When it was done, they spared only those who had surrendered, given that they remained lying on the ground. A frightened few had stood up during the spectacle only to perish as well.

All the demons were vanquished.

There was no exchange of words during the final conflict. It was simple execution.

The word of the Dark Lord's imprisonment had come with news that his agents should prepare for a future fight against Chief Cayuga's recruits and their army. For 70 years, they waited but never expected to be so convincingly overwhelmed.

Dakota and Akwiraron took a dozen warriors with them to scout the White House for further enemy resistance. While inside, Jeromy and the chiefs ordered all their warriors to form ranks. Everyone was awaiting an arrival.

Nearly ten minutes later, Dakota and Akwiraron emerged from the White House doors onto the front steps, dragging an angry President Andrew Jackson, cabinet officials, and two generals. All were bound and gagged.

Jeromy stepped forward just feet away from the President.

"Mister President. My name is Doctor Jeromy White Feather. I am a professor of Native American studies, and I have come here from the 21st century."

President Andrew Jackson looked shocked and confused.

"In my time, our peoples have suffered and died for 500 years since the first white men came to this continent. The members of my own tribe are the poorest citizens of the entire country, and what remains of us are living on a reservation as a result of the theft of Indian lands, forced relocation, suffering, neglect, and death. However, a new future will now be written."

Jeromy stepped closer to the President and stared at him with lethal sincerity.

"I need you to understand that nothing will ever be the same again. We will remain here as an occupying force until discussions about the future of this country and these lands are concluded. If it takes a month – so be it. If it takes a 100-year occupation, we are fine with that, too. The country will still be the United States of America. However, there will be a place at the table for us from now on and forevermore. There will be liberty and justice for all. Effective immediately."

Jeromy turned to Dakota and Akwiraron, "Please untie them."

The other two recruits untied the President and other officials. President Jackson adjusted his clothes and cleared his throat.

"This is an outrage!" He roared.

Jeromy responded by placing the tip of his BattleBlade at the president's mid-chest.

"We will tell you when you can speak. Until then, you will listen."

Jackson appeared further flustered but remained silent.

"The Declaration of Independence states the following: *'We hold these truths to be self-evident, that all men are created equal, that they are endowed by their Creator with certain unalienable Rights, that among these are Life, Liberty and the pursuit of Happiness.'*

"Without our intervention, your presidency will lead to mass suffering, persecution, and permanent poverty for the natives of this country. You broke nine treaties before you even took office."

Jackson stared at Jeromy and rolled his eyes.

"During your years of presidency, you would sign another 70 treaties with Indians – and then they will all be broken."

"Mister President, this makes the words of the country's founding fathers a lie... unless you believe the words apply to white men only."

One of the generals started shouting.

"Of course, it applies to white men. White men founded this country!"

Dakota stepped over to the general and cold-cocked him with a war hammer. He fell limp onto the ground. Jeromy continued without pause.

"The leaders of our country have lied and deceived... have stolen lands and broken treaties. They have also brought black slaves thousands of miles from their homes of origin. And you treat women like cattle. The only way for Native Americans, black Americans, women, and all humans to be treated as if they are created equal is for everything to change.

The discussions will begin with an amendment of emancipation acknowledging that all humans are created equal and must be treated equally. There will be no theft of lands or forced relocation. Slavery will be no more – it is over! And, beginning with the next election, every man and woman over the age of 18 will vote. Everyone!"

"To assist with the drafting of the new amendments and laws, we have sent for a young man on a homestead 10 miles west of Decatur in central Illinois. His name is Abraham Lincoln. He will serve as a permanent Presidential Chief of Staff until 1860. You will also assist him in his law studies."

President Jackson looked mortified.

"Further amendments will provide for a permanent Supreme Court number of justices. Mister Lincoln has a sharp mind and will be invaluable in this. There will continue to be 7 permanent justice positions as there are now in 1830, and among them will always be women, Indian, black, and Hispanic judges. The reason for the last one will become apparent in time. Mister Lincoln will help us sort out the language; however, of the 7 justices, there can never be less than 3 women – 4 or 5 would be best but never less than 3."

Jackson could remain silent no longer.

"Jesus Christ! The congress will never allow such a crazy idea!"

Jeromy adjusted his blade a little to just break the skin. The President let out a groan and winced.

"This is a roadmap for future peace in the country, and as I said, we will not be leaving until the work has been done. This is the best deal you will get. And, if there is any trouble or disagreement, we will disband the Congress and place our own congress in place. And if there is resistance, I will bring 5 million spirit warriors next time, not just 250,000."

Jeromy briefly turned to the assembled army and shouted.

"Miktuha lituns!"

Within seconds, all the forces began repeating the phrase, and one by one, each warrior multiplied into ten warriors.

Over 2 million warriors now filled the fields around the White House.

"Jesus Christ!" the President replied in horror. "I - I understand!"

Jeromy raised his right hand into the air, made a fist, and then pulled the fist downward quickly.

"Lumrah!" he shouted, and all the multiplied forces were gone in a flash.

"So, for 500 years, we have called out to our ancestors for help. Today you are witness that the call was answered. As we move forward, everything must change. We will be working with you and the Congress to institute significant revisions to the lives of Native Americans and everyone else. You can call this reparations or restoration or whatever you want. If you cannot live with that concept, we will simply call it equality and justice. But make no mistake, from today forward, the Indian will no longer be neglected and will no longer live as a ghost or guest in their own lands."

Roars of *whoops* and *hollers* went up from the quarter-million assembled spirit warriors.

"I promise you that we will be far more generous, charitable, and understanding than the white man has ever been to us. But, everything is about to change in this country.

"And now, we have important guests that I will introduce."

A few feet away, a small vortex appeared. Grass and leaves spun in a circle, and then, with a flash of light, three individuals stood before them dressed in full native regalia from head to toe.

"Chief Cayuga!" Dakota declared.

"Welcome, Chief," Akwiraron joined in.

Jeromy went over to the three men. One by one, they embraced. Then they turned to President Jackson.

"President Andrew Jackson, I present the Great Chief and his sons Chief Cayuga and Uncas. They are from the Mohican Tribe that was almost completely eliminated."

Chingachgook stepped forward, carrying his impressive staff. He looked around, surveying the grounds of the White House. All the spirit warriors bowed their heads in respect as he did so. Then he turned to President Jackson.

"You have heard the words of Chief White Feather." He resumed. "He is as wise as he is brave. Listen to his counsel."

"I am Chingachgook. They thought me to be the last of the Mohican peoples." He gestured with both hands to the spirit tribe surrounding them. "A brave and wise civilization that nearly ceased to exist due to the white Europeans' advance and the brutality by you and your forefathers. We almost became extinct. Other tribes have become extinct.

"In the last of my days, I said that the palefaces were masters of the earth, and the time of the red men had not yet come again. Because you have never evolved, and because you have killed, persecuted, and forsaken the Indian upon these lands, and because you have even forsaken the very land itself, we have come back."

"I will be leaving you today, but, make no mistake, I will be watching. The time of persecution and neglect has ended. If it returns… so will I. And, next time, we will not be so compassionate. Instead, we will meet you with what you have done to us for over 500 years. We may even send you back to Europe, or at least what is left of you."

He paused for effect, looking dead serious and directly into the President's eyes.

"The native peoples of this land are mostly loving and compassionate and want the very best for their families, just like all of you do. They also want the very best for the land itself. That is our nature.

"We are also one with nature. I look around and see that shortly, the majesty of this magnificent land lies nearly in ruin because of your abuse and your waste. If you need us to help you make everything right, our people will help you. However, if you do not make everything right, I will be watching that, too. These are my words. I have spoken."

Chingachgook stared hard at the President and gave him a look that said, *'I will be watching.'*

Then, he let out a fierce war cry to the heavens that shook windows and seemed to last forever, and he started rising off the ground. He began radiating light when he was about 100 feet in the air. It became brighter and brighter, and then, without warning, he simply burst into a million flower petals that floated down among the congregation. The Great Chief was gone.

Next, Cayuga and his older brother, Uncas, stepped forward to speak with Jeromy.

"You performed brilliantly, White Feather," Chief Cayuga appreciated his victory. "You have been a strong leader, and the Great Spirit is proud of you. I am also proud of you." And then he stepped closer to Jeromy and whispered, "Your grandma Blossom is proud of you, too."

Jeromy whispered back, "Thank you, Chief. How is the family?"

"They are well. My children and their children will live better now thanks to you, the recruits, and our peoples."

They both smiled at each other. After half a minute, the silence felt a little awkward to Jeromy, so he spoke.

"Chief Cayuga, you are still smiling. Is there something else you want to say?"

"No, White Feather, but there is someone that wants to speak with you."

Puzzled, Jeromy looked around. Most of the quarter-million spirit warriors were smiling, too.

"Ah… what is going on, Chief?" he asked inquisitively.

It was then that he heard a dear, familiar voice.

"Hey Jer, you didn't think you were going to take down the White House without me, did you?"

Jeromy turned, and his heart nearly stopped beating as he saw Anna emerging from the ranks. A glowing Erik ran forward too and was greeted by Dakota and Akwiraron.

"Anna!" Jeromy cried.

The two of them rushed together and embraced. Anna was wearing the spirit warrior uniform of her tribe, and she glowed brilliantly. Everyone except the President and other officials laughed and applauded.

Chief Cayuga stepped forward toward Dakota and Akwiraron. "Medallion recruits, you have also performed bravely, and you will help with the reorganization of the government. If you need me…" He paused and looked over at President Jackson. "… *or millions of warriors*, simply call to me. I will come."

Then he turned to Jeromy, Anna, and Erik.

"And now it is time to go."

Akwiraron and Dakota looked surprised.

"Brothers," Jeromy began. "The two of you will also be supervising the occupying forces. We will leave 100,000 spirit warriors and legendaries with you until the amendments and changes are in place. Use your spirit magic as you need to. Enforce the changes. If you need help, we will come."

The medallion recruits all exchanged well wishes, hugs, and handshakes. Then, still holding hands, Jeromy and Anna went with Erik and stood beside Chief Cayuga and Uncas. The five of them waved goodbye and then stood in a small circle. Looking upward, Jeromy declared, "*Menyang Jagad Roh!*" and all of them were gone in a flash of light.

Epilogue

In natural time, Jeromy arrived by train in the quiet of early dawn. It was 6:00 AM. A sole individual waited for him at the station.

As the puffing iron horse came to a stop, Jeromy descended the steps to the platform. He was immediately hugged by his excited and smiling sister, Issabelle.

"I missed you, Jer!" she cried.

"I missed you too, Izzy." He lovingly replied.

Then, feeling his shoulders and upper arms, she remarks, "Woah! You got really buff, mouse. Look at you! And hey! Where are your glasses?"

"Everything changed, Izzy."

"You can say that again."

Jeromy looked around and could tell that things had changed at the station.

"Did they upgrade the Rapid City station, Izzy?"

"You could say that." She smiled a reply.

As they drove to their grandma's home, Jeromy looked out the window and began making comments such as:

"What are all of these lights? When did that school get built? Where did those tall buildings come from?"

Issabelle would chuckle and laugh, but refused to say anything.

"Hey, Izzy… What is going on?"

"Don't be dumb, Jeromy. Think about it all for a moment, and while you are thinking, a little surprise is waiting for you. So, I will ask a huge favor: Please close your eyes and take a nap for the rest of the trip. Okay?"

A while later, Jeromy awoke to a loud band playing and cheers from thousands of natives, blacks, whites, and many others. They held signs of welcome, and everyone was shouting. "Welcome, White Feather! Welcome, White Feather!"

Izzy parked the jeep and ran around the other side to be with her brother. Jeromy slowly stepped out of the jeep – his jaw dropped wide open.

"Welcome to Pine Ridge City, Jeromy."

"Pine Ridge *City*? Is this the Rez, Izzy?"

"There is no '*Rez*!'" she replied excitedly. "Reservations never happened."

Jeromy began smiling ear to ear with delight.

"Jer, Pine Ridge City is a modern city with over 400,000 people. There are many natives, but we all live here in harmony. Heck, there are over 40 million Native Americans in the country now!"

Jeromy saw beauty everywhere, and amazing architecture that reflected his native heritage. There were wide, well-paved streets with intersections and traffic lights. Everything was clean,

well-lit, and there was an actual marching band playing in the middle of downtown Pine Ridge City at 7:30 in the morning. The drums had Pine Ridge City Eagles imprinted on them.

A stage had been set up off to one side, and Issabelle informed Jeromy that the Pine Ridge City Council was waiting for him.

"At 7:30 in the morning?" Jeromy replied with surprise.

"Yes! At 7:30 in the morning. After all, our brothers and sisters have been waiting nearly 200 years for your return, White Feather."

Jeromy remained delighted and confused. He was walked to the stage by adoring welcomers who wanted to shake his hand, hug him, or pat him on the back. Some he knew, most he did not.

They seated him in a place of honor. Issabelle sat next to him.

Mayor Russell Tall Elk and several members of the city council gave speeches, including Councilwoman Issabelle Two Bears - his sister, who had married a local doctor 10 years earlier. Jeromy would later get to know his nephews and nieces.

At the end of the ceremony, a tall, 25-foot statue was unveiled in the town square. It depicted five brave recruits who, nearly 200 years earlier had changed the course and history of human rights and the nation.

When it was over, Jeromy still couldn't wrap his mind around how Izzy could still know him and yet also know everything from 200 years ago. How could knowledge of both timelines coexist? He looked at his sister with amazement and wonder.

"Izzy?"

"Everything has changed, brother."

"But… Izzy?"

"Thank the Spirits, Jer… thank the Spirits."